Praise for Pamela Crane's award-winning psychological thrillers:

"Her writing is dark, intriguing and she is a master of the unexpected twist. Ms. Crane cleverly blends a series of plots and subplots together to produce a satisfactory ending. Not all questions are answered and I'm looking forward to the next book in the series." – Peter Ralph, white-collar crime fiction writer, author of *Blood Gold in the Congo,* #1 Amazon best-selling author

"Pamela Crane introduces a mind-twist that takes everything you love about thrillers, pushes it outside the box, and electrifies you with clever prose and a plot that will terrify you. A must-read thriller...an instant best seller!" – Southern Editor Reviews

"A captivating mystery with prose that fans will devour." – Literary Lover Reviews

"If *Dexter* and *Gone Girl* had a love child, this would be it!" – reader review

"An author to watch, Pamela Crane packs a punch to her prose and will keep you on your toes with her twisted plots. Let your mind be blown—I guarantee you'll savor every moment. *The Art of Fear* is psychological thriller fiction at its best." – Thriller Fan Reviews

"I'm a die-hard thriller fan. But Crane duped me! Just when I thought I had figured it out I was thrown for another loop...and loved it. Kudos to mastering the mystery genre!" – reader review

THE
ART
OF
FEAR

Thank you for your support,
and I hope you enjoy the book.
Hugs!

Pamela Crane

THE
ART
OF
FEAR

PAMELA CRANE

Tabella House
Raleigh, North Carolina

ISBN: 978-1-940662-114 (hardcover)
ISBN: 978-1-940662-084 (paperback)
ISBN: 978-1-940662-091 (eBook)

Library of Congress Control Number: 2017941917

Thank you for supporting authors and literacy by purchasing this book. Want to add more gripping reads to your library? As the author of more than a dozen award-winning and best-selling books, you can find all of Pamela Crane's works on her website at www.pamelacrane.com.

This book is dedicated to you.
May fear never hold you back. May it never change you
from who you're meant to be.

The stroke of death is as a lover's pinch, which hurts and is desired.
— William Shakespeare

Do the thing you fear most and the death of fear is certain.
— Mark Twain

Prologue

Durham, North Carolina
April 2016

D eath is a beautiful thing, if you think about it. Elegant, even. That moment when every touch, every taste, every teardrop electrifies each cell. Imagine it—delicate crimson droplets and bruised hues of purple and yellow all creating a palette of color on an endless hide canvas. Then there's the sweet smell of sweat as panic sets in and the pungent coppery tang that accompanies that first slice of flesh. The soothing sound of a blade working its way through a crackle of skin, then sinking dully through fatty tissue, at last finding its resting place in the slosh of blood.

Mere minutes after the penetration is the calming realization that the end is near. A peaceful cocktail of reflection and fear.

Then serenity.

The ultimate freedom from the taut restraints of life. The bindings that hold one back from experiencing true sovereignty. You become the master of your own fate through death. There is nothing more comforting than that.

How is that not eminently exquisite?

And more to the point, will you not find it equally magnificent when I intimately introduce you to it—death?

Even years after I first laid eyes on you, I still find you

captivating. Your high cheekbones and contemplative eyes like shiny pennies drew me into the artful composition that was your face. Your features promised a hopeful future of attraction and self-worth. It was my appreciation for beauty and art that slaughtered my resolve to kill you back then.

Words like *slaughtered* make me tingle. Not in the sense of a sociopath hungry for blood. I'm no sociopath. In fact, I love what I do. I feel joy in opening these gifts given to me—gifts that keep on giving as they free me to free *them.* It's all about *them,* really.

These pretty creatures turned ugly by life. Disfigured by pain.

Now, however, no amount of outward loveliness can save you, for I know your blemished heart. Only I can save you now.

I close my eyes, letting the visions engulf me. I imagine every heated moment as I first slip into your home. It's dark and empty, but I smell you. Not the vanilla lotion you lather all over your skin, but an intoxicating earthy scent of grit and determination. I snake around your sparse living room furniture, padding across the dull carpet, heading into your bedroom. There I open your closet door, my fingers frisking the mixture of cotton and polyester clothing hanging from a metal bar, all cheaply made garments that scratch my fingertips.

Pushing the hangers aside, I slither against the wall, adjusting the fabric to hide me. I gingerly close the bifold door behind me, peeking through the slats into the gaping darkness as evening falls heavily. There I wait, my breaths shallow and calm, belying the anticipation that sets my heart pumping excitedly.

When I hear the click of the front door, I know the time has come. First the pale light that reaches across the hallway, narrowly slicing through the bedroom. Then keys clattering against the throwback periwinkle countertop. The thump of your kitchen-sink-sized hobo bag beside them. The soft steps across the trampled carpet as you head toward me.

A moment later a blast of light brightens the bedroom, but I'm hidden in shadows. I must practice patience, waiting for just the right moment.

Then it arrives. Through a crack I watch your silhouette slide past me and hear your footsteps on the bathroom linoleum. I am officially between you and the only means of escape, and that is my cue.

Soundless, I push the closet door fully open, careful to keep my attention on the corner of the bedroom where the bathroom door hangs ajar. Your figure creates dark waves against the bathroom light, the back-and-forth movement following along the carpet. I watch as it disappears further into the bathroom. The toilet flushes, and I pace forward. A rush of water from the sink, and I know your back is toward me.

I must move quickly, keeping to the side to avoid being seen too easily in the mirror. But by the time you do see me, I'll already have overpowered you.

Softly I step into a puddle of light that drenches me. Yet you do not notice my movement behind you. Within two steps I'm directly behind you, a hot wet breath away, and you see my reflection smiling back at you and you yelp. As you turn, one hand presses to your mouth, the other plunges a knife into your abdomen—knowing I hit the inferior vena cava, something *CSI: Miami* taught me—and you slink to the floor in a heap of gasping pain and fingers clutching my arm as your cries dwindle to whimpers.

Vivid red blossoms into the threads of your shirt, and your trill of fear gives me goose bumps. I kneel beside you, still holding my palm to your face. I'm numb to your watery eyes hovering over mine, pleading but unable to focus, like two egg yolks. All I see is fading fear and encroaching peace take over you—tranquility for us both.

As I relish the euphoria, a jerking sensation overtakes me, waking me to a reality where you are a parking lot away. I open my eyes, but I don't let it spoil the moment.

I glance down at my wandering hand, my dull nails biting and scraping across my flesh, but it's not your skin I'm tearing at. I'm disappointed at the reality.

Sitting in my car quivering after the finale, the distance between me and you saddens me. These are the moments I live for but rarely get to enjoy. It's a recurring dream that is usually out of reach, but I find peace in the knowledge it will soon be in my grasp.

While some may accidentally stumble into my radar, you are special. You're chosen. Predestined. There's a point of no return in life, when you've stomped too hard on someone else's territory and smashed too many hopes. Take most families—masters at the art of loss. Negligently losing their children for the sake of their own selfish wants. Rather than sacrifice, they toss their children to the wolves.

They're filled with fear. Fear of too little money. Fear of change. Fear of loss.

It all boils down to fear.

That's the problem.

Luckily for you, I'm a master at the art of fear.

I've been watching, waiting patiently for my turn to move. For days I plotted and planned, a farmer tending his crop until the harvest. With my scythe in hand, I'm ready to reap a grim yield.

At last your turn has arrived. Let the countdown wind down until your death.

I relish the anticipation.

Perhaps you will be the final masterpiece I create. Or

THE ART OF FEAR

perhaps you're only the beginning.

Chapter 1
Rosalita

San Luis, Mexico
1976

As the baby snuggled up against her milk-swelled breast, Rosalita Alvarez knew—they say a mother's instinct can defy logic—there was something evil about him. Something broken. Something sinful behind those coal-black eyes.

Four tiny teeth peeked out from unyielding pink gums slathered in spittle and breast milk. The emerging white tips were crooked yet sharp, pinchers that could draw blood if clamped hard enough. Although he was her first, Rosalita innately understood it was the way of a baby— always testing the limits of a mama's endurance. The opener being the labor pains as her body nearly split in half at the baby's arrival. Then months of sleeplessness at the cries of hunger or need for comforting. And one mustn't forget the excruciating tenderness during breastfeeding, coupled with the dwindling stores of energy the baby stole during these round-the-clock feedings.

Indeed, motherhood shook and rattled a mama's previous life until she shattered into unrecognizable bits of her former self, then pieced herself back together into a shape-shifting puzzle of worries and what-ifs, memories and meaningful firsts. At the first strangled cry a mama dutifully retreated into nonexistence while the baby became all that she was, is, and ever would be. It was both beautiful and horrifying how a squirming little creature with dimpled fingers and a ridiculous round ball of a head could overpower one's self-will so easily, inspiring both heartbreak and adoration with a sharp cry or playful chuckle.

Yes, motherhood shook Rosalita awake from a sleep she never realized was her former life. Such extremes of joy and ache, all at the hands of the baby boy she now cradled in her weary arms. Her eyelids weighted down with exhaustion as her surroundings faded to black, then sprung back alive at the baby's squiggling arms and legs.

Rosalita sat with her child in the living room of the concrete block bungalow. On the outside the blocks were unpainted and mildewed; inside, they had been a vibrant burgundy once upon a time, when her father had first painted them when she was a little girl, but they had faded over time to the color of a fresh bruise. The blocks met the soot-stained plaster ceiling, cracked and buckling from a leaky tin roof, in jagged lines. The beige floor tiles, freshly mopped, were cool beneath Rosalita's bare feet as she attempted to rock the baby to sleep, but the worn sofa offered precious little give to the gentle back and forth.

The wooden front door hung open, its orange paint brightened by a feverish sun sweeping across it, but the warm air was breezeless and suffocating today. An old rattletrap, belching great plumes of smoke, bumped along the dirt road, its grinding gears and blaring mariachi music momentarily drowning out the calls of the children at play. From the sofa Rosalita had a ringside seat of the doings in her humble San Luis, Mexico, *barrio*—the porch sitters pecking for gossip, the raggedy *culo* rummaging through trashcans and dumpsters, the sweat-drenched men replacing a rusty tin roof, the teen lovers exploring

7

each other's charms in shadowy alleyways. Beating the dry heat of the listless summer afternoon required cleverness. A resourceful youth had figured out how to open a fire hydrant, attracting a throng of kids and even some free-spirited adults to splash in the cool torrent.

Dust from her shared front yard billowed around the scurrying feet of children playing Red Rover, an American game in which a team of children, clutching hands, invites a child from the opposing team to hurl him or herself against their chain with the intention of breaking through—until, as was the case today, the children inevitably collapsed in a heap of wriggling legs and arms. Even after years of watching the game unfold, Rosalita had yet to figure out the rules or logic behind such a violent premise. What ever happened to the simple, diplomatic games like *el patio de mi casa*—or as the Americans called it, Ring Around the Rosie—that she had grown up enjoying?

A squeal. Then a gurgling coo.

Gazing down at her son, Rosalita swaddled him as he restlessly squirmed, his fussing rising to an ear-splitting squall. His cheeks reddened with fury; he balled his chubby hands into fists and kicked angrily. Closing her eyes against this fitful backdrop, the words came out in a whisper, then hung over his unfurling screams as the Spanish lullaby her mother once sang to her cast its spell:

"A la nanita nana nanita ella, nanita ella. Mi niño tiene sueño bendito sea, bendito sea.
My boy is sleepy, blessed be, blessed be.
Little fountain running clearly and profoundly.
Nightingale that in the jungle sings sadly,
hush while the cradle rocks."

The mellow tune eventually soothed him, her voice

sweet and pure like the molasses her *abuela* spoon-fed her as a child. Though his cries ceased, Rosalita's eyes remained shut, for she couldn't muster the courage to watch her monstrous creation as his mouth sought her brown nipple for nourishment.

By all appearances he was a normal child. Deeply olive-skinned like his father, coarse black ringlets like his mother. Cheeks thick with baby fat, legs wobbly with uncertainty.

Always probing, always watching ... but not in the curious way that infants do. There was a knowing behind his piercing black eyes. An eerie darkness. Rosalita first noticed it when he was about six months old.

"He's evil, I tell you," she had once confided in her husband, Eduardo.

"How can you say such things of our *mijo*?" Eduardo demanded. "Your lack of sleep makes you *loco* like your mama," he added with a stern glare, then a warning that no such nonsense should be spoken of again.

While those dark thoughts remained buried in her nightmares from that day onward, the intimate fear of its truth never abated. Day after day Rosalita looked upon her son with a foreboding knowledge that something wasn't right ... *El diablo*, perhaps, clung to him, devouring his infantile virtue.

A gentle tug on her deflated breast forced her awareness downward, where her gaze met her son's. Though a baby, he was no longer a newborn. He had already cultivated his own cruel brand of humor. Crawling gave him independence, clearly savored as he destroyed every object within reach.

With her flesh firmly tucked between his taut lips, his raven eyes met hers—soulless orbs in which she saw twin reflections of her haggard face. A chilly smile played upon the little brown face.

"Okay, Josef, time to let go," she urged, pressing her pinkie between his jaws to unlock his grip.

But he only became more resolute.

She probed again, firmer still.

Again he resisted with a sly grin, then he looked at her, his eyes alien and spiteful.

It happened so swiftly that the details rolled over each other like angry waves. A screech, a sharp flick, a wailing sob, a rivulet of blood trickling down her flushed skin, soaking into the folds of fabric at her waist. Amid the pain she nearly tossed Josef to the floor ... nearly, but caught herself. Roughly dropping him down beside her on the cushion, Rosalita gripped her chest, examining the injury through the fresh blood oozing out. The wound had disfigured her nipple as he ripped at it with his teeth, leaving a vulnerable gash upon the callused peak. Cursing him, she pressed a soiled burp cloth to her chest, soaking up the oozing blood.

From his upright pose beside her, the baby giggled with fascination at her wound-tending antics. Bits of flesh showed between his teeth in a crimson smirk. Warily fishing through his mouth with her index finger, his jaw clamped down. She cried out and tugged the finger free with a smart pop.

"You evil creature!" she spat through hot tears. "You bit me, and you liked it."

Josef chuckled with glee, and at that moment she knew it wasn't superstition, or postpartum depression, or first-time motherhood that besieged her with these haunting thoughts. Indeed, she had birthed evil incarnate ... and nothing could be done about it.

Or was there something? Something drastic ... but necessary.

Decades of superstitions trickled down the lines of her family—fabricated stories of punishments for sins woven into the folds of time. Sins of lust, theft, lies … murder. Rosalita was only privy to a handful of those secrets, each passed down from mother to daughter, generation after generation. Whether truth or fiction, Rosalita didn't know. But she did know one thing. Josef was the culmination of God's retribution for her own sin, a sin only she knew about. A sin she kept hidden in her bosom, tucked away until her last breath.

The only way to stop this curse that she knew would forever revisit her family was to kill baby Josef Alvarez.

End the cycle.

She rested on the corner of the sofa cushion, dirty white stuffing spilling out of the ripped seams. Gazing at her son, she pondered the finality of what she was about to do. Yet sadness—there was none. Fear—aborted. Only hope for a better tomorrow.

A dull gray pillow was crushed between her back and the sofa. She pried it loose, held it.

Breathe, she commanded herself. *You must do this. It's the only way.*

She placed the drab pillow on her lap and ran the pad of her index finger along its frayed seam.

"Do it!" The words slipped out unbidden, giving voice to her thoughts.

She grabbed the pillow firmly with both hands, lowering it with infinitesimal slowness. If her hands trembled, she didn't notice.

She rested it on his plump face at first, gently, almost motherly. She leaned forward, giving weight behind it. The little sausage fingers clawed the air, legs kicked in protest. She increased her mild pressure. The squirming came in spasms now.

1 … 2 … 3 … The seconds passed. *4 … 5 … 6 …*

Then a muffled sob shattered the deviant silence—but not an infant's wail.

Startled, Rosalita looked up to find little Juanita Juarez, a neighborhood kid, standing in the doorway, struck dumb from shock. Her big doe-eyes, wide with fear, filled with tears.

As terror sent Juanita running in a panic, Rosalita's mind cleared, jolted to sudden awareness of the lifeless silence. Had she actually killed her own child? Tossing the pillow aside, she pulled the baby to her chest, but he hung limply in her arms.

"Please, Josef ..." she pleaded to his pale blue form. Pressing her mouth to his, she forced air into his tiny lungs.

Nothing. Deadness.

Another breath.

Then cries shook the little bungalow—from Josef's blue face, and from Rosalita as she wept for forgiveness in a crumpled heap on the floor.

"What the hell is wrong with me?" she yelled, stomping the tile. When her fury exhausted itself, she hung her head in shame. "For my sins I must pay."

Although her punishment was yet to be revealed, Josef's piercing gaze caught hers, as if he knew something she didn't. As if he sensed the darkness clouding her, or had created it.

Perhaps Josef Alvarez would be that retribution after all.

Chapter 2

Ari

Durham, North Carolina
April 8, 2016

I dipped tentacled fingers into my soul, searching for my humanity, but nothing was there. A hollow had swept clean the place where my heart should have been. I didn't mind the vacancy. Nothingness is freedom. The heart-shaped void is liberation. The weightiness of pain just wasn't worth *feeling* anymore. Most normal people would disagree—the whole "better to have loved and lost than to never have loved at all" syndrome people were too attached to. But I was being logical. Grief hurts, period. Why not escape if you can?

Anniversaries always brought out the raging cynic in me. Wedded bliss—screw you, because single life is the only life. Twenty years on the job—why celebrate a daily grind that gets you nothing but a corny watch? But the death of my sister ... that was an anniversary I couldn't escape. It blindsided me year after year, its arrival disentombing the old anguish from the day she died. *Died.* The word was too prosaic. I always preferred the term *murder*, but that was the sadomasochist in me talking. After all, since I was the one who killed her, didn't that earn me the right to name it?

Mottled sunlight dappled the acres upon acres of

tombstones jutting up from the earth around me. But I was only here for one.

My eyes glazed over as I read the words at my feet for easily the hundredth time:

Carli Lily Wilburn
February 21, 1994 – April 8, 2002
Beautiful daughter, beloved friend of all who knew her,
now God's angel

Her headstone sat aged and naked before me, littered with grass trimmings from a recent mow. Somehow I never made it into the inscription; nothing to acknowledge our sisterly bond. But I suppose I lost that right when I snuffed her too-young life from this earth exactly fourteen years ago today.

Sunlight fingered the edges of the marker, slick from the morning's dew, spattering pinpricks of light across the marbled hues of crimson and gray. While my sister lay buried beneath tons of wet earth, my own soul lay buried beneath swells of guilt. Session after session, therapists had tried to excavate my id, but it remained as lifeless as Carli's crumbling bones.

An icy dawn breeze aroused an eruption of goose bumps on my bare arms, a stark reminder that I'd overstayed my graveyard visit. Mom and Dad would soon arrive, and it was best they not see me. Our last interaction a couple years ago only resulted in a terse exchange of non-pleasantries:

Ari, what are you doing here? Mom in her hushed-yet-stern voice, like she was reprimanding a child while pressing her palm over a phone receiver.

I'm visiting my sister's grave. What does it look like I'm doing? My defiant reply that sounded more argumentative than I had intended.

THE ART OF FEAR

You shouldn't be here. She acted as if I had never been a part of the family. As if I hadn't spent my life loving Carli, adoring Daddy, obliging Mommy.

I need to be here, Mom. I loved her too.

But one thing I realized hadn't changed about Mom—her superhuman ability to be unreasonably unyielding. *Please, I'm asking nicely, Ari, for you to leave. Don't disgrace your sister by being here.* Mom's insistent urging rose with her tone. Her voice reached a dog whistle pitch when she was upset.

You're not the only one who misses her.

Oh, that's rich, coming from the one who killed her!

Screw you! I have just as much right to visit her as you do.

Mom gave an embittered *haha* intended to wound. *Oh really? A loving sister wouldn't have done what you did, Ari.* Then she turned to Dad for support in sledgehammering my will. *Burt, do something! She shouldn't be here. Make her leave,* Mom's plea, to which Dad contemplatively stroked his mustache, then shook his head at me in apology. I muttered cuss words at their backs as he firmly guided Mom away by her shoulders, whispering consoling words in her ear.

I wasn't ready for round two and stalked away in the opposite direction.

I had just hit my twenties at the time, and I hadn't seen them since.

Good riddance to bad rubbish. We weren't a family anymore, just surly acquaintances bound together by tragedy.

Pushing the sour memory aside, I gently placed a thick cluster of summer-sun-yellow dandelions on Carli's grave. As kids, the eye-catching weeds had grown in abundance in our yard and became our favorite flower, dotting our hair, peeking from our pockets, and enchanting our

15

bedroom décor. Grownups considered it the peskiest of weeds, the bane of the suburbanite's perfect lawn, but we adored them unconditionally. I knew that wherever Carli was watching me from right now, she laughed at the irony. Always laughing ... up until her very last breath.

It was a moment I would never—*could* never—forget.

While the before and after evaporated into a foggy haze, a memory slipping away like sand through my fingers, our final moments together burned like a brand.

Blood pooling in the grass, trickling between the blades like a tiny red snake in flight. Carli sprawled out, spread eagle, unblinkingly staring up at me, a subtle smile lingering on her lips. *Now you can have your own room, Sissy.* A sardonic laugh later she was gone. Eyes an empty pond of algae-green, glassy and still. Sunlight kissing her pale face goodbye as her life drained into earth's carpet beneath. And me, ever watching from above, frozen stiff with shock as she left me—her killer.

It was that horrific moment that would turn me against myself. Little by little my self-loathing stripped me down to nothing. No one was laughing now. No one would ever laugh again in my little world.

Staring blindly at Carli's gravestone never got any easier over the years. As my eyes glazed over with salty tears, I could feel my heart quickening as the angst—not that third cup of coffee—fermented in my gut. Cheeks and neck flushing, palms sweating. The air swirled around me, threatening to hurl me onto the ground face-first.

I recognized the face of this monster inside me clawing to get out. Anxiety—a constant companion that, over the years, had made my life a living hell.

Breathe, I reminded myself. *Slow breaths. In. Out. In. Out.* I'd eventually get through this one, but I'd never shed this prickly skin altogether. It was Death's brand on me. Killing had a way of scarring you permanently. Old wounds heal slowly, but the most scab-resistant are the ones we inflict on ourselves and pick at until the blood flows freely.

Chapter 3
Josef

April 7, 2016
One day earlier

A picture-snap moment back to childhood flung Josef Alvarez into the nether regions of his subconscious where the serrated blade of the cheap steak knife no longer ripped apart his vulnerable flesh. While the pulsing jab to his abdomen leaked lifeblood, his eyes fluttered closed ... allowing ancient history to whisk him away.

A hazy summer afternoon. A seesaw of gigglers creaking up and down. A screaming knot of daredevils trying to stay aboard the merry-go-round before centrifugal force flung them off like rag dolls. Here Josef was, just a kid on his neighborhood playground, jostling the girl ahead of him to be first on the slide. It was a day of reclaimed innocence.

Dust shrouded Josef as he clambered up the rungs and whizzed down with a *wheeee*, the breeze rippling his black hair, the hot metal scorching the naked thighs in his cut-off jean shorts.

A momentary peace ... before the torment of impending death.

As his scruffy Chuck Taylor sneakers slammed against the packed dirt at the foot of the slide, Josef was jarred back to reality, the reality where his assailant was prepping for the kill. Bleeding away his awareness, Josef backed up against the sofa behind him for support. His attacker stood before him, eyes squinting with hot anger, kitchen steak knife in hand, lunging at him, but Josef held up his hands, pushing the knife aside before it rounded back at him.

But his drugged state turned his world into a dizzying amusement park ride, twisting the double images into a helter-skelter reality his mind and body couldn't track. A hand gripped his wrist, yet his resolve to fight surrendered. A knife slid through the air, caught his arm, then chewed its way down the skin toward his hand before releasing him. The jagged slice was an act of vengeance for Josef's sins—and there were many—a final accounting, and Josef rang up short.

With his unscathed hand Josef gripped his stomach, attempting to herd the gore back inside him but instead only sopping his shirt with the blood. Wooziness swept over him again, consciousness wobbling unsteadily, until a tidal wave of nausea fetched the bile to his throat. His legs quivered like two sticks of string cheese, his palm gripped the arm of the sofa, but slipped—a buttery sensation that sent him crumbling into the cushion. The fall gave him a temporary distance from his killer, a moment to whimper for mercy.

"Please, please ..." he wept. "Please don't kill me. I'll do anything. Please."

His heart beat a voodoo drum tattoo, and his head was filled with a strange whooshing sound, like when he'd held a conch shell to his ear as a kid. Blood seeping—his— drowning out his words. But his attacker heard. Josef could see it in the unclenching jaw, the sympathetic stare, the lax arm still holding the knife.

"Forgive me, please. Let me live. Let me make it up to

you."

But it was too late for *I'm sorry*. Too much blood. Darkness was already settling in.

His tangle of limbs drooped lazily from the cream pleather sofa that over the years had flaked plastic peelings all over the ragged beige carpet. A lake of metallic red pooled in the gauzy fabric, staining it with his essence.

Heavy eyelids drooped up and down, Josef fighting the urge for sleep. Feeling an obscure cool emptiness around him, he pried his eyes open, searching the living room. No one. He was alone ... for now. Possibly forever. His vision lurched in and out of focus. An outdated plasma TV sat nobly on a card table he had borrowed from a cousin several Super Bowl parties ago but never returned. A mismatched La-Z-Boy sat permanently open next to him, the wreckage of a drunken-stupor temper and misguided kick. Other than the sepia-striped wallpaper, the two-bedroom house was a shithole even worse than the ones in the *barrio*. He fled Mexico hoping for a second chance here in Dunn, North Carolina—a colorless Podunk of pig farmers and tobacco cultivators. But the past that he ran from had eventually caught up to him. And here he was, playing tug-o-war with death, with no apology sufficient to turn back time.

Wondering where his visitor was, he listened. Past the sound of his ragged wheezing. Past the adrenalin forcing him to cling stubbornly to life. Water rushing. The bathtub?

Light footsteps approached. His last sight, through the narrowing slits of his eyes, was two near-drained *el caballito* shot glasses of Jose Cuervo Clasico Silver tequila, neat. The drink of champions. And then it made sense— the why. He should have seen it coming.

As his slumped body exhaled its last, panicked thoughts seized him. *What will happen to my corpse? Will anyone care that I'm gone? Can I reach that last sip of tequila? I hope they bury me in my good suit ...* Odd, random thoughts for a dying man. And then somewhere in the void between living and dead he felt it ...

Fingers probing.

A tender pat on his cheek, then a quick slap. Almost a love tap, but it stung.

A killer's final good-bye. A nonverbal *I'm sorry for taking your life this way, but it had to be done.*

Is this forgiveness? he wondered. For Josef Alvarez, absolution didn't come cheap.

Chapter 4
Ari

Fifteen days until dead

A warped circle of foggy faces searched me—each yearning for something different, like children startled from nightmares and seeking tender hugs. I didn't know them, their needs. Only that they all came here for a reason. Help. Advice. Freedom. I didn't have all the answers, but I hoped I could at least offer a fresh start for the downtrodden and beaten, the victims and sufferers. For broken people like me.

Welcome to the Triad Suicide Support Group.

I had regretted the name after I already printed dozens of flyers. Coming up with a clever name without sounding positively Kevorkian was impossible, so in a hazy midnight oil moment, the group made its informal debut, artless *Snakes on a Plane*-type title and all.

We were a group of misfits, executives, druggies, model citizens—a mishmash of success and failure, sweet and salty. While our stories diverged into crooked highways and byways of suffering, we all shared one thing in common. We had all at one time faced suicide—either an attempt of our own, or of one we loved.

That's us, flaws and blemishes bared, but still walking among the living. The little things of life hadn't killed us yet.

THE ART OF FEAR

I exhaled, stood up, and faced my audience, pivoting in a crescent so that I could meet each attendee's eyes. They were a kaleidoscope of shapes and colors, some sitting stiffly, others stretched as comfortably as one could on a cold metal folding chair. The table of Kroger brand glazed donuts and lukewarm coffee rested against one wall, untouched. On the other wall was a row of windows overlooking faded concrete parking spots sprinkled with a dozen cars. I wondered if I should have invited everyone to help themselves to the food before we began.

Christian Assembly Church, hugging the outskirts of Durham, North Carolina, was an elegant church in the modern style, with a simple cross on the broad triangular frontispiece in lieu of a steeple. The pastor had granted me the use of their fellowship hall.

A demure cough drew my gaze. A woman of unguessable age with alligator skin and long, honey-blond hair that may or may not have been a wig smiled from her seat, warmly handing me the courage to begin.

"Thanks for coming, everyone," I began, doing my best to stifle the pulsating anxiety that followed me daily, hourly, sickening me with its grip. It was my cruel companion, my shadow. Anxiety was the puppeteer and I was its puppet. But living by it meant not living at all. So here I was, facing it, feeling it quicken my pulse and delivering a punch to the gut that tasted sour in the back of my throat.

"I'm new at this, so bear with me. My name is Ari, and I'm a suicide survivor. I started this group so that those of us who have attempted suicide, experience suicidal thoughts, or know someone who committed suicide can share our stories and our pain, shouldering the burden together. I hope y'all benefit from our group." Despite my best efforts, the Southern drawl dribbled out at the end.

Mom and Dad hailed from Pittsburgh, Pennsylvania,

but me having grown up in the culturally diverse town of Durham—not the Deep South, but proudly and colorfully Southern just the same—it wasn't without its influence on my dialect. Though my western Pennsylvania roots slipped out on occasion, such as when I drank a *pop* instead of a Coke, or ate an Italian *hoagie* rather than a sub sandwich.

My interlocking fingers wriggled around one another, as if scurrying to find safety within my damp palm. Suddenly aware of my fidgeting, I wiped them on my ripped skinny jeans and pocketed them. With my thoughts adrift, I fought to reel them in.

"You don't have to share anything you're not comfortable with, but I've had enough secrets in my life, so it's full disclosure for me. Anything you wanna know, I'm an open book."

Not that there was much to tell about me, the life of Ari Wilburn. The perpetually-single, apartment-dwelling, retail girl. Folding, hanging, hanging, folding. My life consisted of break room bitching over crumpled shirts fusty with old lady stink and heaps of fitting room clothes left behind by lazy shoppers who couldn't give two shits about the boring work they created for me. And then the registers. Don't get me started on registers.

Checking out line upon line of customers with coupons—I referred to them as Coupon Queens—then customers without coupons who wanted coupons, expired coupons, coupons from other stores. I even had one customer try to pass off a handwritten coupon, I shit you not. Then there's customers who swear the price was marked differently than what rang up. And the damn lookyloos who bring one of everything in the store to the register to price check, hoping they'd ring up cheaper than marked. Of course they'd leave their heaping piles of stuff on the register for me to return—God forbid they clean up after their damn selves. And the barterers—do they really think I have a say over the price of an item? This is a friggin' store, not a bazaar in Chiang Mai ... And on and on it went, day after day, an endlessly bland existence. My sole purpose in life was to fold clothes and clean up after slobs. I wondered if mothers felt the same way.

They say idle hands are the devil's workshop. It was only a matter of time before I'd join a cult just to get out of retail.

A cough like a duck getting sucked into an airplane turbine brought me back to the room. The same gorgon-faced woman smiled encouragingly at me.

"How about we take time to introduce ourselves?" I belatedly added, scanning the group.

To my right, a woman with *Friends*-era Jennifer Aniston hair turned to glance up at me with doe-wide hazel eyes like tarnished bronze.

"Share your name, why you're here ... whatever you feel compelled to say. And take whatever time you need," I said with a self-conscious simper. I had no clue if I was doing this right, but did it really matter? I was here to help others like me, etiquette be damned. Then I sat—the universal *thank-God-go-ahead-I'm-done* signal.

The woman stood, said "Hi" in a theatre voice, too loud for the occasion, then recalibrated to a lower volume. "Uh, hi. I'm Mia Germaine. I recently lost someone I cared about to suicide, which is why I'm here. Lately death seems like it's been following me. It feels like—I'm sure you all heard about the Triangle Terror?"

A murmur of acknowledgment ran through the audience. The only serial killer that had made it into our local news during my adult life. A horrifying tale of woe, and too many young lives lost—not much younger than me. Apparently he targeted girls—"set them free," according to his twisted logic. Mia Germaine, I remembered reading somewhere, caught the killer that no one else could. One more reason to hate cops for letting him slip through their fingers for too damn long. I didn't follow the news much, but that story was unavoidable if you were living and breathing in Durham. I was sure Mia's story was a book by now.

"Well," Mia continued, "I knew some of the victims and needed a place to unleash the pent-up emotions and thoughts after everything. To find healing, I guess is what I'm here for. And to connect with others who may be going through the same pain I'm going through, and learn from others how to work through those dark nights of remembering. Thanks." She plopped heavily into her chair, squeakily skidding a few inches back.

Dark nights—those I was familiar with.

"Thanks, Mia, for joining us. I hope you find what you need here. Next?"

My eyes shifted to Mia's right, inviting a lanky hipster to rise. A fedora leaned jauntily on a thick swath of hair swept stiffly across his brow, and despite the eighty-degree temperatures that Mother Nature visited upon North Carolina in April, a patterned scarf snaked around his neck. The requisite beard, fastidiously trimmed, traced his rugged jaw. He took his time standing up because hipsters—being, well, hipper than thou—take their sweet time about everything.

A creaking sound caused all heads to crane around toward the back of the room, where a petite little thing crept through one of the swinging doors, peering hesitantly around its thick edge.

A blast of silence. Then her tiny voice pushed a speedy sentence out:

"Is this the support group for … uh … suicide?" Her cheeks flushed blotchy pink.

"Yep, sure is. Come on in and take a seat." I pointed toward an empty chair.

"Sorry I'm late," she said without further excuse. As she neared, I noticed her red-rimmed eyes, wet like chocolate pudding. The poor girl had been crying.

Her olive skin was as smooth and shiny as a Red Delicious. I guessed she was in her late teens, early twenties. Spikes rose in sharp towers from her scalp, the tips a platinum blond contrast her to black roots. Her lips were a shade of villainous red I only wished I could pull off. Trendy armbands clinked as she made her way into the circle, finally settling the tap of her high-heeled ankle boots as she sat.

"Should I go?" The question tugged my attention back to the hipster-in-waiting. I watched as he looked around him, his eyes a penetrating topaz, then he settled his sights on me. Either his lashes were incredibly thick and dark, or he was sporting guyliner. Either way, it worked for him. Tight leather pants hugged every curve, and a deep v-neck T-shirt crawling with dragons previewed his smooth chest. Despite the neatly studded eyebrow—I hated needles and everything that went with them—I was oddly attracted ... in a Gavin Rossdale circa Bush kind of way. Those rock god pants left little to the imagination about his impressive package. I couldn't stop my gaze from going there and staring just a little too long. *Bad girl, Ari, bad girl.*

"Oh, yes, I'm sorry. Go ahead."

His hand came up in a genteel wave, a red bandana cuffing his wrist. "'Sup. I'm Tristan Cox. I've been struggling with depression and suicidal thoughts for a long time. Since I was a teen, at least. I can't say I've tangled with any serial killers or survived anything horrific"—he nodded in Mia's direction—"so there's not much to say other than I guess I'm here to try to learn to battle my personal demons—tamer ones than most of you guys are used to. Uh, I guess that's it. Thanks." Another wave, then he poured himself back into his seat with a wan smile.

Brief. Succinct. And I wanted to know so much more.

The simplicity of his plea—and that boyish grin!—snatched my breath away. Until I felt a roomful of focus on me, an unspoken request to move things along.

Several more names, several more heartbreaking stories.

Destiny Childs, who recently found—then lost—a daughter she'd given up years ago. The aftermath sucked her into a depressive vortex. Her striking blue eyes moistened as she relived the tale.

Gypsy, she called herself, who found her husband of thirty years dead, swinging from a backyard tree.

Ryder, whose mystery lingered after a cursory nod and vague introduction.

All in due time I'd hear their stories and hoped to relieve a portion of their burden.

Over the hour it became a how-to manual of survival, a list of suicide do's and don'ts. Those who had attempted suicide shared what had driven them to that brink, and what made death so morbidly appealing. Those who lost loved ones advocated for those left behind here on Earth. It was a babel of voices, all suffering but all still standing. We were heroes in my book. We faced death and told it to back the hell up off us.

We won.

The last to stand was the late arrival—Crying Girl. By now her tears had dried up, and the red shame of her tardiness faded into her naturally bronzed skin. She stood in a jangle of metal as her jewelry chimed with each movement, first a nervous scratching of her neck, then the wringing of hands.

The horror that brought such a young girl here prickled my skin.

"Hi, everyone." She lifted her chin, trying to be brave. "I'm Tina Alvarez. I'm here because I found out …" Her voice shook, then stilled. Her eyes watered, and a hand swiped too late as tears trickled down her face. "I'm sorry. It's been a difficult couple days. I just lost the only family I had here and I have nowhere to turn. I'm sorry," she said through emerging sobs, shoulders shuddering.

In sorrowful heaves and raspy breaths, Tina wordlessly laid bare her pain for the roomful of strangers to watch, like a gruesome accident we couldn't pull our eyes away from.

I stood and moved slowly to her, unsure if I should make contact. Should I soothe her? Let her be? Comfort seemed appropriate for a crying girl—for she was merely a girl, wasn't she?—but years of incarceration had calcified my heart to such emotional nakedness. So I found the middle ground and rested my palm on her back, delivering tight circles of reassurance that everything would be okay.

But would it? I had no idea.

The round face of the wall clock ticked away the last couple of minutes, so I adjourned the meeting, inviting everyone to return to learn some coping skills for those days when dark thoughts catch up to us.

Still Tina stood in the center of a stage of pallid linoleum and gray aluminum chairs, weeping into her hands, me awkwardly by her side, as the swinging door *whooshed* behind the last of the trailing group. Eventually the minutes did what they always did—took the sorrow and tossed it behind, leaving the apex of the pain in the past. It was only then that Tina looked up at me.

"You okay?" I asked, my voice soft like talking to a child.

"Yeah, I'm sorry I lost it," she replied, rubbing her fingertips under her eyes to catch the running mascara, and only succeeding in turning them into Rorschach inkblots.

"It's okay. You wanna talk about it?" I offered.

"I guess I probably should."

I cupped her elbow and guided her to two chairs, since I had no idea how long we would be standing. If she was a talker like Chelsea from my former group home, we could be here all day. We sat in clumsy silence for several beats, then she spoke, her gaze fixated on her knees, mine on a black skid mark along the floor from the sole of a shoe. My fingers toyed with loose strands of blond hair that had escaped my ponytail—a nervous tic, my coping mechanism. Somehow the stimulation collected my racing thoughts.

"Yesterday I found out my father killed himself."

And that was it—all she said. So matter-of-fact. The blow of her loss—only *yesterday*—caught me off-guard, and I looked at her, examined her. How could she possibly be holding up so well, so soon after?

"Oh my God. Yesterday? I'm so sorry, Tina. I don't even know what to say ..."

Followed by a lull. I hadn't been prepared for this ... not *this*.

Then she chuckled softly, an inside joke with herself. "Yeah, I'm kinda in shock too. Not that my father didn't deserve to die, but still ... I never got a chance to confront him before he died. To tell him how he hurt me."

"He hurt you?" I asked. I was tentative about probing for more, unsure I wanted to loosen her burden and heft it on my own shoulders. But after years of friendships—if one could call delinquent housemates *friends*—based solely on shared resentment, it became habit.

"I don't wanna go into a bunch of detail, but yeah, he basically kicked me out when I was a kid and I never looked back. I hate him, y'know? But he's the only family I had left, as crappy as he was. And now he's gone ... by his own hand. How is that even fair?"

"I'm so sorry, Tina. I understand ... shitty parents seem to grow on trees around here. I'm here for you, whatever you need." It was all the comfort I could muster with a girl I just met, though I sensed she wanted more. Maybe in time I could scratch open my wounds and let Tina watch them bleed, but right now wasn't that time.

"You know, I just can't accept it," she said irritably, drastically shifting her mood with a hurricane's force.

"What do you mean?" I probed.

"It's not like him—suicide. He's not the selfless type. Killing himself would be too noble for him."

"You think suicide is noble?" I asked gently, not wanting to start a debate, but I couldn't help but wonder how anyone could see dignity behind it. "Most people call it selfish—to end things without consideration for others. Leaving all the pain behind you for others to deal with while you get to escape."

She glared at me, eyes burrowing, searching.

"I'm not judging, Tina," I blustered. "I attempted it more than once, so I'm talking from experience. I'm just saying it's not exactly selfless."

She shrugged noncommittally. "I guess so ... Regardless, I don't think my father would've had the guts to carry it out. He cared too much about his boozing and gambling and whoring to off himself."

"Are you suggesting that he didn't kill himself?"

"That's exactly what I think. I think someone murdered him."

"What did the police say?" I understood it intimately— the stage of denial. It was well-trodden territory for me. But there was a point where we could easily get ungrounded, and I hoped to help gently bring Tina back to Earth. "I'm sure they considered that but ruled it out."

"They said it looked like suicide because of his blood

alcohol levels and how he was holding the knife when they found him. Plus a note was left behind. But they have no idea how Josef Alvarez could hold his liquor. He didn't get all weepy and self-loathing. He got angry. Angry people don't kill themselves. They kill other people."

"He killed other people?"

"Not that I know of, but he could've."

We were swiftly heading into the realm of conspiracy theory here, and it was in Tina's best interest that I reel that in. "Regardless of what happened, Tina, don't you think you should let it go? Maybe he finally hit his breaking point."

"And if he was murdered?" she challenged me.

"Then I'd stay as far away as possible from the mofo who did it."

"Easy for you to say. But what if whoever killed him comes after me next?"

And cue paranoia.

Maybe she wasn't following the standard grieving script—denial, bargaining, depression, anger, acceptance. We were going off-book here, adding suspicion to the list. But clearly she didn't want to be reasoned out of it, so I'd have to work with what I got.

"Do you feel like you should look into it more? Maybe talk to the cops about your concerns?"

Tina exhaled, a breath weighted with burdens no daughter should bear. "Part of me wants to, but part of me is afraid to. Any chance you want to come with me?" She snorted a laugh, and I joined in, but when she grew silent and fixed a wondering look on me, I realized she was serious.

"Oh, you're for real," I declared, a little shocked at her ballsy request. But then again, Millennials were often blunt—and that included me. "Well, I guess it wouldn't hurt to go to the station together and see what they say

...” I regretted it the moment I spoke, but when her eyes misted in gratitude, I knew I had done the right thing.

She mumbled thanks, then dropped her guard and hugged me. My instinct was to push away, fall back, resist—the robotic methods I had conformed to for so long. But instead I drew her in, let my body do what bodies are meant to do: connect.

“Do you need help planning the funeral?” I offered, wishing at that moment I could retract it. Funerals were not my thing. Never would be ... since Carli. Maybe since ever. I’d never been the best emotional crutch.

“Nope. Not doing one. Not my problem. Let the morgue figure out what to do with him.”

“Really? You don’t want closure?”

“He’s dead. What more closure could I get?”

I did the math: Her father was possibly murdered. Unworthy of a funeral. Apparently he was really unpopular.

I’d help her figure out who killed him—if he was in fact murdered—and not out of obligation. Not out of making amends for my own sins. But because my decayed muscle of a heart had survived my life, and for once I cared about something. Someone.

Maybe I needed Tina because she reminded me of the little sister I’d lost.

Maybe this was my chance at finding purpose.

Perhaps I was human after all.

Chapter 5

Ari

Dunn, North Carolina
Fourteen days until dead

One long car ride and two summaries of our lives later, we arrived in the town of Dunn—home of rock-n-roller Link Wray, whoever the hell that was.

We had been standing outside the red brick Dunn Police Station on East Broad Street for over five minutes—I attentively, or what Tina called *impatiently*, counted each minute away on my cell phone—while Tina, now three smokes in, paced the stamped concrete walkway. With the cigarette perched tensely between her lips, her steps formed an indecisive waltz.

"We gonna do this?" I prodded. But my biggest concern wasn't making it home in time for a Netflix *American Horror Story* binge watch before bed. It was the fact that I *hated* cops. I'd spent enough time with them as a kid to fill two lifetimes, so seeking them out voluntarily went against my grain. All I knew was that I earned a friend of the year award for this, and I better damn well get it.

As Tina puffed obliviously to my question, my good graces were melting. I hadn't anticipated it to be an all-day project on my only day off work this week. As luck would have it, Tina's father was from Dunn, about an hour south of Durham. So the trek there and back was a long one,

34

especially with the construction on I-95 and all the pricks on the road. I needed to watch my potty mouth. Put me behind the wheel and road rage made me swear like a sailor.

I could feel my impatience boiling, but I reeled my frustration in with a mental reminder that she had been through enough. Harping wouldn't help.

But still ...

"I'm starting to get sunburn we've been standing out here so long," I whined. "I'm leaving if we don't head in now." Tough love it was.

"Yeah, yeah. I'm finished, let's go," she said, tossing the orange butt on the sidewalk and snuffing it out with a twist of her foot.

We headed up a sidewalk with a berth between us two cars wide, circling around an American flag flapping wildly in the brisk spring breeze. Tina expertly reapplied her cherry lipstick while maneuvering up the walkway, and I couldn't help but be jealous. I couldn't remember the last time I wore lipstick—or any makeup, for that matter. I had always been a plain canvas, but Tina—she was art. It was no wonder I was still single when unconventional beauties like Tina, comfortable in their own skin and blessed with *je ne sais quoi*, trolled the streets. I had no idea who Tina really was, what she was really like. I only knew that she had youth and vivacity going for her, and I envied the stable of studly friends with benefits presumably at her disposal. For those reasons, not to mention her perky rack and a fetching ass that was a perfect apple, she was altogether hate-worthy. Maybe she'd grow on me, but right now all I felt was a burning jealousy.

Oh God. I wanted to be pretty.

What was happening to me?

Two steps led up to the portico, then inside the double glass doors we went.

Sweat beaded on my forehead and each quickened breath grew a little more strained. Anxiety was poking me, toying with me, and I was losing it. *Get a hold of your shit, Ari!* It took me a few moments to regain my composure as I watched the parade of cops going about their daily grind in a sea of blue. Wiping at my face, I closed my eyes and counted to five, feeling the pressure slip away, then I stepped up to the front desk.

Before us sat a tuft of black-rooted blond curls with a plump woman underneath. Her fat jaws were busy smacking on a gray piece of gum that made a disgusting cameo appearance between her teeth when she mumbled a curt greeting, never once looking up. After asking her who we could talk to about a death investigation, she made a call—not once missing a beat with that incessant cud-chewing—and with a nod, directed us to Investigator Jordan Moody, whose messy office we finally found after navigating through a maze of look-alike blue cubicles.

A broad-shouldered man easily six-foot-two stomped toward us, his white mustache outlining a firm jaw. His buttoned suit and tie were stiff and no-nonsense, a good sign of good hands to be in. As he neared, his gait never slowing, I stepped forward to introduce myself ... until he gruffly stalked past, oblivious to me. What the hell? Following his retreating form with my gaze, I didn't notice the young gun behind me.

I felt a knobby bump at my side. "Ari," Tina whispered.

I pivoted back to her and came face-first with a lanky, fresh-faced guy wearing a wrinkled button-down shirt untucked over jeans and a blue tie for good measure. At less than a buck fifty soaking wet, he barely filled out his clothes. I wondered if his mama tied his necktie for him.

He held his hand out, and as I shook it, it felt oddly feminine in mine. Like we could share gloves.

Surely this *kid* wasn't who we were referred to?

36

"I'm Investigator Jordan Moody. I was told you wanted to speak to someone about a death?"

Tina looked at me, tossing the torch my way.

"Um, yeah," I began, a little disappointed that, sure enough, we were at the right desk. "Mister—"

"Detective Moody," he corrected pleasantly, as if he was used to people calling him the first generic title they could think of.

"*Detective Moody,* we wanted someone to look into her father's death." I placed my hand on Tina's shoulder. "We suspect it wasn't the suicide that police ruled it."

He nodded, sat down in a cushioned beige swivel chair behind his stark metal desk, then gestured for us to do the same in the mismatched visitors' chairs, apparently uncomfortable by design. "So I'll need you to fill me in on the details and I'll pull the report on file."

Tina stared blankly, until I turned to her, nudging her along with my raised brow.

"Oh, sorry. Um, my father, Josef Alvarez, was found dead from a knife wound two days ago. But when I found him like that, it didn't look like a suicide at all. I think he was murdered."

"One sec," he stopped her, raising his palm, then dashing his fingers along the keyboard. "So you're the one who found him dead, and I can assume you're also the one who reported it?"

"Yeah."

"What?" I hadn't meant to say it out loud—and with such force.

"I'm sorry I didn't tell you, Ari, but it was just so horrible ... I really couldn't stomach talking about it. But I went to visit him—first time seeing him in years—and when I got there, the door was unlocked. I went in and found him on his sofa covered in blood with a knife in his hands. But I knew something about the scene wasn't right. I just couldn't figure out what."

Suddenly I felt a connection surge through me, a sisterly bond through loss. We had both witnessed firsthand the gruesome face of death taking a loved one. "Tina, I'm so sorry you had to see that."

In this moment of weakness my eyes watered for her, for the ever-punishing anguish she must be feeling. If ever I was determined to help someone get answers, it was her—now.

With an interruptive cough, Moody brusquely reentered the conversation, but his words showed a touch of empathy. "I'm sorry for your loss, Ms. Alvarez, but we'll do what we can to get answers for you."

"Thank you. I appreciate it," she replied.

"What I have here," he said, eyeballs darting down his computer screen while his thoughts caught up, "is that Mr. Josef Alvarez suffered from two wounds—a puncture to his abdomen and a cut down his wrist. Generally a cut straight down the wrist is more in line with a suicide attempt, not a defensive wound. As for the abdominal wound, well, he might have done it to himself to bleed out faster, end it quicker." He looked back and forth at Tina and me and sheepishly added, "Sorry, didn't mean that to sound so callous."

Bleed out faster, end it quicker.

That did it.

My phobia of cops and cop stations hit me like a sock in the gut. I stared blankly at a cubicle where one cop was bent over the desk of his partner. They were looking at a report, grim-faced. Suddenly they started braying like jackasses. A gallows humor thing, I guessed—their coping mechanism for dealing with lurid crimes. They looked my way; our eyes locked. They seemed to rush toward me while everything in the background receded, like that scene in *Jaws* when Roy Scheider is sitting on the beach and witnesses the shark attack, and the camera warps his perspective. I screamed a silent scream just as I felt something grabbing my arm.

"Earth to Ari. *Earth to Ari.*"

It was Tina. I looked at her, tugging on my elbow, and blinked myself back to reality.

"Uh, is that a normal way people kill themselves?" I asked, composing myself. "Jabbing themselves in the gut? Seems, uh, unusual."

"People attempt suicide more ways than you can imagine. And there's something else. There was a suicide note at the scene."

As much as I relished belittling conspiracy theorists, I had to agree with Tina. Something about it sounded too neat and tidy to be legit. There had to be more to this.

"Hm," Tina uttered pensively. "It just doesn't ... *feel* right."

Teen Cop leaned forward, elbows supporting him, and picked up a pen and tablet. His chicken scratch on the canary paper looked like hieroglyphics. "What exactly doesn't feel right? Any details you can provide helps."

"Well, for starters he was always drunk but never depressed. At least not that he ever showed. The only reason I could see my dad killing himself was to deny the pleasure from someone else, and even then only as a last resort. But a knife to the gut ... it just seems too ... simple. Too easy."

"Well, you just stated that you hadn't seen him in years. So how certain are you that he wasn't depressed?"

Interesting catch. Maybe Teen Cop wasn't as clueless as I thought.

"Because I know him. Some people don't change. He was one of those people."

"Assuming you're right, do you know anyone who might have been after him? And what about the suicide note?"

"That could have been forged," Tina said, shrugging off its pertinence. "Did you make sure it was his handwriting?"

The detective rolled his eyes. "Have you seen the size of our town? We don't have handwriting analysts at our beck and call."

"Well, anyways," Tina continued, "I know he gambled a lot. Could be related to that."

Moody sighed heavily and leaned back, his tie flopping to the side. "Look, it sounds like you're fishing. I know you don't want to believe your father would take his own life, and maybe he didn't, but without more to go on than his gambling debt, I don't know if we can reopen an investigation into this. I want to help you, Tina, I really do. But right now you're telling me to use our sparse resources to look for a murderer where there might be none."

So easily shot down and defeated, Tina huffed and bolted from her chair. "Fine, let's go, Ari."

"Wait," I said, an idea brewing. "Mister—?"

"Detective Moody," he corrected not quite so pleasantly. Clearly it was a point of pride for him. My bad.

I never could remember names.

"*Detective Moody*," I emphasized, "could we get a copy of the case file? Like, the police report and stuff?"

"Sure, I just need Tina to fill out this form, since I can only provide the redacted document."

"Huh?"

"Redacted—where we remove any confidential personal information. Though, Tina's the only witness, and her father is the victim, so this should be easy. You are an adult, correct, Tina?"

"Uh, yeah," Tina huffed. "Just turned eighteen."

"Sorry. Had to ask."

After opening a screechy metal drawer, he laid a paper in front of Tina. It only took her a handful of minutes to fill out the single page of basic personal info while he retrieved the file.

"I've made photocopies of everything for you. If you think of anything else, my card's in there."

"Thanks," we chorused.

"And Ms. Alvarez—" he added as we turned to leave, "I hope you find peace." Sincerity warmed his words.

As we left the precinct, I exhaled relief that it was over. I couldn't have stood another five minutes of the suffocating atmosphere.

"You okay?" Tina asked. "You scared the shit out of me when you zoned out."

I should have been the one asking her, not the other way around.

"Yep," I chirped. Maybe she wouldn't notice I was lying.

"Not buying it. What's wrong?"

I hadn't realized how readable I was. I had unknowingly tipped my hand. For the first time I felt like maybe with her my secrets weren't meant to stay hidden.

"The whole police scene reminds me of losing my sister. I had been interrogated and still today remember the room, the smell, the feeling like it was yesterday. Hard to stomach the memories sometimes. But it's nothing some fresh air can't cure."

"Or maybe you need to stop blaming yourself."

"Who says I'm blaming myself?"

Clearly I was an open book that Tina was flipping through.

"I can just tell."

"Can't really put the blame on anyone else but me. I'm the one who was responsible."

"No, the driver of the car that hit her was responsible.

A ten-year-old kid can't be responsible for anything, especially another person. Kids that age can't even take care of themselves. So get comfortable with your past, because you can't let it haunt you, torturing you like this, or it'll strip away any life left in you."

From the mouth of babes ... Yet her words were impassioned, wise beyond her years. And they came from a fluency in painful living. She now knew me, for I had shared my darkest secret with her, and she had shared at least part of hers; I couldn't put my finger on it, but something told me she hadn't given me the whole truth about her father kicking her out. Our mutual agonies trekked along a parallel path as our youths were corrupted, two lives forever tarnished. And yet somehow Tina had been able to overcome hers and move on, be normal, feel ordinary. So why couldn't I? Why did my pulse still race and my stomach clench when I entered the police station? Why couldn't I get *comfortable* with my past, as she put it?

Because the reality was that there was nothing comfortable about being a murderer in a den of cops.

That's what I was—no matter how much Tina came to my defense.

Chapter 6
Ari

April 8, 2002

I don't know how to save a life, only lose one. I'm only ten. But as my little sister lies motionless in the grass, curls splayed around her like she's under water, red tendrils darkening as they soak in a spreading pool of blood that the earth just as quickly drinks up, I know I'm as helpless as she is.

Tires squalling, the car speeds away, leaving a smoke cloud stinking of roasted engine oil in its wake. Before me, paralyzed in the vibrant spring-green grass, is my sister. Eight years young with a kid's built-in invincibility against childhood traumas, but as her eyes remain closed far too long now, I realize this may have broken her.

I hadn't meant to get angry with her, but it's too late. It was just a stupid game.

"Carli?" I ask, sprinting with wide strides to where she lay. "You okay?" I ask it with a motherly tone, as if she just scraped her knee and needs a kiss on her boo-boo.

No response. No movement.

It's serious, I know.

I shriek with an eagle's intensity. "Mom! Dad! Help!" The words come out broken amid my sobs of panic. Below me there's a flutter of eyelids at the sound of my voice, but she's not fully awake. Again I scream for my parents, this time with more urgency.

43

I'm at Carli's side now, holding her hand in an unspoken plea not to leave me. I'm afraid to touch her for fear of making it worse.

"Carli, you're gonna be okay," I promise emptily. I don't know that. I only know I'm supposed to say it. But I can only assume it's true because scary things like death don't happen to kids. Again I yell, turning my voice toward the house to avoid startling my sister. "Mom, Dad, help! Carli's hurt!"

"Ari?" Her voice is weak but at least she's alive—barely. As she speaks, her assortment of baby and adult teeth are tinged with Radio Flyer wagon red. Is that ... blood?

My stomach churns a warning that I'm about to lose my breakfast.

Her eyelids drift shut, hiding flecks of yellow and green, then they slide open drunkenly. A smile lifts her lips. "Sorry I cut your Barbie's hair," she says. "You can't be mad at me for it anymore, promise?" She laughs like her death is a joke, and all I can do is laugh with her, like we're playing doctor. I can't let on that I know something she doesn't—that she might not make it.

"Promise." Hooking my pinkie in hers, I make the sisterly oath of all oaths. "Pinkie swear."

"Now you can have your own room, Sissy," she mumbles.

But it's too real, what she's saying: good-bye.

It's taking Mom and Dad too long. "Mom!" I scream again.

A moment later I hear a screen door twang shut behind me—Mom standing on the porch.

"Ari, what's all your yelling about? Stop acting like a redneck for the whole neighborhood to hear."

"Mom, help!" And that's when she sees me, sees Carli. Mom recognizes the tears and fear on my face and knows

this isn't a childish prank.

Rushing from the stoop, Mom barrels toward us, calling back for Dad. "Burt, get out here! Carli's hurt!" She pushes me aside, inserting herself between us, then cradles her baby girl—her favorite. I watch her sweep hands and lips all over Carli's flesh, searching for the wounds while kissing away the pain. I burn with envy that Mom's never attended me so fervently.

"Sweetie, stay with me. Don't close your eyes," she mumbles frantically into Carli's sweater. "Don't you leave me, honey."

Another twang from the porch. Dad, fresh from the john, is standing in the half-opened screen door, fumbling with his belt.

"Call an ambulance, Burt!" Mom orders, wedged between us sisters, aptly symbolic of our family dynamic. "What did you do to her?" Mom demands, turning her ferocity on me.

"I—I don't know," I stutter.

"What did you do?" Her words are fierce. I blink at the spittle showering my face.

"I think ... I think a car hit her. We were playing in the yard and I pushed her ... and then a car drove up and hit her. Then it left." But Mom knows—she knows.

"Don't lie to me, Ari. Did you let your sister play in the street?"

"No, I swear."

But she's too distracted tending to Carli to hear my answer. She cranes her neck, looking down the empty street for hope. "Why is the ambulance taking so long? And where's your father?"

Mom's murmuring in Carli's ear as if words will draw her away from death's beckoning light. I'm afraid to ask the question we don't want the answer to. "Is she gonna be okay?"

"I don't know. But this is your fault. You should have been watching out for her."

"Mom, I didn't—"

"Just shut up, Ari," she cuts in.

By now I see Dad running toward us with an awkward gait, then drops gravely by Carli's side. "The ambulance is coming. What the hell happened?"

"It's Ari's fault, as usual," says Mom acidly.

I fall back on my hands as if hit by a physical blow. As I rise from my dirt-stained knees, the wail of an approaching siren attracts an audience along Pinewood Avenue. Unnoticed, unneeded, I run inside, leaving Mom, Dad, and Carli in the front yard where we play and sing and fight and tumble. Will it now be where my sister dies?

Entering the living room, on the vacuum-lined gray carpet I see the Barbie we had fought over that morning, the one that Carli had taken scissors to and ruined—the reason I pushed her away from me mere minutes ago in the yard. A doll that was worth more to me than Carli's life when I had examined its butchered hairdo over Frosted Flakes and Scooby Doo. In a hot moment I had wished Carli had never been born—and I told her that too—but I didn't mean it ... did I?

I wished it, and it came true.

Chapter 7

April 7, 2016

It shouldn't be this easy to kill. But even before I did it, I already knew I'd get away with murder.

Josef Alvarez's sloping belly overhung his unbuttoned jeans as he sat across from me, a Hispanic Santa whose own naughty list had caught up with him. I was here to collect on his sins, one in particular. One brown-haired, chubby-cheeked sin named Sophia. He didn't know the reason for the visit as I searched his kitchen cabinets for clean glasses to toast with—no easy task in this pigsty. All I found were two dust-covered shot glasses, but they were perfect for my tequila concoction.

"Dirty glasses. Roach crap on the counter. And your carpet's so filthy you might as well have dirt floors. You're one hell of a housekeeper, Josef," I observed, softening the comment with a light smile. It was hard to play nice with someone you wanted to murder, but I didn't want the son of a bitch to suspect something.

He shrugged a noncommittal answer, his thick shoulders flexing beneath a beer-stained wife-beater. "I don't have anyone to impress."

"It's not about impressing people, Josef. It's about dignity and self-respect."

"I lost that years ago. Besides, once upon a time I had a wife who took care of me, but when she left me there was no point."

"No point to what?"

"Life." He chuckled, as if this were a game.

It was an ironic choice of words, given he was mere minutes from losing the life he didn't even cherish. Yet I had a feeling he'd be more than willing to fight and beg and cry for this same life he now claimed was pointless.

So here we sat, him on the tacky faux leather sofa, legs sprawled out like an eager playboy, and me on the matching chair that might have been beige or cream once—impossible to tell under the grime coating it like a contagious rash. The rest of the sparse furnishings looked like Goodwill rejects or roadside finds. Walter Sallman's *Head of Christ* peered out from the cracked glass of a cheap frame hanging crookedly over a three-legged end table with a broken broomstick propping up the lame end. On the top of the table were seven or eight candles in tall glass holders decorated with colorful pictures of Jesus and Mary and other biblical figures.

I snorted and remarked, "I never knew you to be a religious man, Josef."

"I'm not, but I figure a man should play it safe. Venerate Jesus and Mary and all that shit. Looks good when the roll is called up yonder, as the shitkickers around here say. May God have mercy on my soul. What a crock of *mierda*." He hoisted a fat cheek and farted, as if to underscore his blasphemy. As long as I'd known him, the man never had an ounce of class.

I had to be careful not to give myself away. "That's a good idea, Josef. Play it safe, because you never know when you might wake up ... dead."

I supposed he had chosen to hide out in this hovel in the backwoods of Dunn because neighbors were few and far between. Yet he couldn't hide from me. Not that he knew he should.

Josef raised his glass to eye level. "To new beginnings," he toasted.

I hoisted mine up, a mockery of his truce. "To new beginnings and endings," I agreed. "*Salud.*"

"*Salud,*" he echoed.

Our glasses chinked together, and we downed the spicy liquid in a single gulp. Liquid courage for me, liquid submission for Josef. Sure, life had hardened me plenty, but enough to do this deed? Even I wasn't that cold-blooded ... yet. After today, I suppose I'd be broken in. But at this dithering moment, I needed a boost of liquid courage. The tang of the tequila lingered on my tongue as I poured him another, this time the bottle dosed with my own secret ingredient. It was child's play to palm the tablets into the buffoon's drink.

"You always were a lightweight," Josef commented when he noticed I didn't pour myself seconds. I couldn't tell if he was insulted or amused by my abstinence, but it didn't matter. I knew he'd self-serve until he had both our fill. It was his beloved poison. If only he knew just how poisonous it really was ...

"You know me—can't hold down more than one. Besides, today isn't about me. It's about you."

"Me?" His voice rose with skeptical disbelief as he drained another glassful, then refueled.

"Yes, I want you to enjoy yourself today. You earned it."

His laugh possessed an echoing quality, robust at first, then softening like churned cream by the end. Another drink, another refill. His capacity for booze had always been impressive. "And how did I earn it?"

"You made the ultimate sacrifice."

His dark brown eyes narrowed to guileful slits that had witnessed too much misery in his life tethered to loss. I wondered how he could live with himself ... but he wouldn't any longer.

"What kinda sacrifice you talkin' abou'?" The slur of

his speech meant the pills were working. His bloodshot eyes struggled to focus. His eyelids dropped heavily and sprang comically open again like a cartoon character's.

"Your life, of course." I said it so matter-of-factly that Josef gave vent to a belly laugh that shook his whole body. But my stoic expression must have revealed my absence of humor.

"He-ey, didya give me something'?" His voice rose an octave in fear and confusion.

"Yes, and it's going to knock you out in a minute. Then I'm going to kill you, Josef."

He still had his wits about him and jumped up from the couch and shambled toward me. His feet struggled to find solid ground, feeling his way like a tightrope walker. I knew the floor was shifting beneath him by now like trick stairs in a funhouse. I sidestepped him with ease, relishing my advantage.

"I don' understan'..."

"Let me show you."

And I knew it was go time.

He was almost pathetic now, pawing uselessly at double images of me. It felt too effortless pulling the knife out from where it had been tucked into the cushion of the chair, its metallic glimmer hidden from sight. Even easier turning the point of the blade toward him. Then with a swift thrust, I witnessed the knife surging through epidermis, fatty tissue, muscle, and organ, like carving a pumpkin. I felt it all, reveling in the initial pushback as the blade bent in resistance, but once through, I heard the teeth tearing, the suction of wetness as I punctured his insides with ease, leaving only a delicate exterior mark of my handiwork.

But the blow didn't take him down, not yet. Wobbly he stood, gasping for life-giving breath, clinging to an eroding consciousness as his eyes closed.

THE ART OF FEAR

I wondered what he was seeing, what graphic images flipped across his mental screen. A collage of his many indiscretions? The faces of those he sent to hell?

I hoped we weren't done yet.

I wanted to show Josef the art of fear.

Luckily for me, the only thing more stubborn than death was Josef's will to live.

Chapter 8

Ari

Thirteen days until dead

The seams of my eyes were sewed shut with deep sleep. I woke up that morning in a violent tangle of sheets. They bound my legs, stifled my arms, wrapping around me in a cocoon. I wondered who I kickboxed in my dreams last night to make such a mess of my bed. Typical of me—the fierce sleeper.

Oddly enough, Carli's face was the first one that came to mind.

Don't get me wrong. I never got physical with Carli. Being sisters, sometimes we'd get so mad at each other our disagreements turned into laughable slap fights, our only contact being the occasional brush of hands mid-swing or a hefty push. The sting was enough to call a truce so we could battle it out with our wits.

I always won.

But my anger never lasted long.

She made a lasting feud impossible.

Carli Wilburn's personality was as bouncy as her head of red curls. As far as I was concerned, it was the one redeeming quality that made up for her being a full-time pain in the butt. I could love her—despite her breaking my toys, winning my friends' attention away from me, playing on Mom and Dad's affections, and otherwise robbing me of my chance to be their favorite—because Carli was pure charm. Her winsome smile would melt the heart of the crabbiest Sunday school teacher or the most incorrigible neighborhood bully. And those darn cheeks—chubby well past her toddler stage, with pinkie-sized dimples—were the irresistibly pinchable delight of every prune-faced old lady in town. Even I, her most outspoken critic, fell for the act. The kid was adorable, and she knew it.

From the time I had an opinion about things, April had always been my favorite month—the first taste of outside-all-day weather perfect for tag and hide-and-seek after a suffocating winter spent mostly indoors. No more stifling layers of sweaters and coats. No more frozen cheeks and chapped lips. No more numb fingers that sent us inside to binge watch TV all day. I wanted adventure, and in our house growing up, it was severely lacking. Outside, however, excitement and uninhibited freedom were in endless supply.

But one fateful Saturday morning many years ago, all innocent pleasures would be stripped from me for all eternity, never to root in my heart again. I knew jealousy had snaked its way through me since Carli first arrived home with Mom from the hospital, a wormy bundle of demanding, persistent screams that I couldn't compete with. I was only two, but already I knew the torture of envy, the constant need to wrench my parents' interest away from my baby sister's effortless cuteness and incessant squalling with crayon-scribbled pictures or an impromptu song and dance. When that didn't work, wall art and finger painting food on the furniture got their attention, usually in the form of a good scolding, and sometimes a spanking. But despite my best efforts, I stayed invisible, inconvenient.

The details of that morning remained hazy all through my childhood, still hidden in the fog of my mind throughout adolescence. By adulthood they had been buried so deep and for so long that the bones of the memories were little more than shards and fragments.

But occasionally a vision would peek in on me, rousing my memory from slumber, as if skulking after me and waiting for the right moment to attack. Of course the anniversary of her death was always an opportunity worth taking. And also on days like today, as I rustled up the courage to recite my suicide story to a roomful of strangers.

Morning broke into afternoon, and afternoon poured into early evening.

It was our second meeting, and it had skipped off to a good start when Tristan Cox greeted me from across the fellowship hall with a boyish smile and made a beeline toward me with his unwavering hair and rimmed eyelids. Any chance of something happening between us wilted, though, when I realized he was better dressed and better looking than I was. Men's—or possibly even women's—black skinny jeans squeezed his knobby flamingo legs, and a stylish white v-neck clung to his sexy chest like a second skin. He was thinner than me, damn it, but perfectly so. The braided leather cuff on his wrist met a tribal tattoo on his forearm, which snaked up his arms and hid under his shirt. I could only imagine what that tattoo was doing to the rest of his body. At the "garish" sight of him, my prim mother would have been criticizing his choice to mutilate himself. Not that she gave a damn about my falling in with the "wrong crowd"; she just detested tats and piercings. A generation gap thing, I guess.

Tattoos added an automatic hot quality to any male, in my book. Perhaps in any bad-boy-lover's book. I had always been drawn to deviants like me, I suppose.

I eked a wobbly grin back at him, nervous as a girl

before prom. Not that I would know anything about prom, since me and the girls in juvie lived vicariously off rumors of such rites of passage. Instead, we "insiders" decorated our hallway with obscene graffiti using a stolen can of spray paint while "outside" girls were dressing up for their dates in silks and sashes, doted on with corsages and limos. At least we didn't know what we were missing, we'd been there so long.

"Hey, Ari. How you doin'?" Tristan asked, resting a hand on my shoulder. I willed it to be a protective claim over me, but in all likelihood he was simply touchy-feely. I'd take it, happily.

When was the last time I had been touched? I couldn't remember. Oh, right: Tina had hugged me; it had been awkward, but it felt damn good. But the last time I'd been touched by a man? Shit, what year was it?

"To be honest, I'm too scared to piss," I blurted, immediately regretting my word choice. "Giving my spiel today." I nodded toward the circle of chairs as we ambled over.

"You don't have to be nervous. Worst you can do is mess up, piss yourself from embarrassment, and never be able to show your face here again," he said with a sly grin. "Just messing with ya. Come on. I'll be rooting for you." His grin felt like a booster shot of euphoria. "Just remember that we've all been there with you, in some way or another."

"Thanks."

The noisy chatter around us had crescendoed and fallen to a few whispers as people took their seats. Somebody's chair scraping across the vinyl floor made a flatulent sound that fetched a couple of snickers. Then, an expectant hush.

"I think that's your cue," Tristan said.

"Yep, I guess as the leader I'm supposed to do

something." I chuckled, and he laughed with me.

"Well, see you after, right?"

"If I don't bolt beforehand," I joked.

"That'd be a shame. How would I ask you out to dinner?" Before my brain could process his words, he winked and headed toward the chairs. If my heart hadn't been thudding hard already, I was now officially wading in a sea of palm-soaking anxiety.

I took my place in the circle and offered a warm greeting, my nerves relaxing as I fixed my eyes on Tristan's smiley-faced gaze.

"Thanks for coming back, everyone. I wanted to start off today by sharing a little about myself so that you know where I've come from. Just remember this is a safe place. Anything we share stays here. Cool?"

A roomful of bobbing heads and mumbled affirmations bade me to continue.

"As you might remember, I'm Ari, and I'm a suicide survivor. My story begins with my sister, who died fourteen years ago when we were kids. After it happened, because of stuff I don't need to get into, I landed in a string of group homes, foster care, even ended up in a juvenile detention center, tucked away with other so-called bad kids that needed love and understanding, not isolation. Anyways, the police felt I might be a danger to myself and others, so that's where they put me so society wouldn't have to deal with me. I became severely depressed and tried hanging myself from a sheet after just two weeks of being there, not realizing how hard it actually is to kill yourself with bedding. Movies are so full of shit."

My heart thumped with a dangerous rhythm, like I'd just taken a huge hit of laughing gas. But then I glanced at Tristan, the calm of my anxious storm.

"Anyways, after that incident they moved me to the

56

THE ART OF FEAR

Boys & Girls Homes of North Carolina where I could get better treatment. And that's where I stayed. They tried to help me, but how do you repair a broken child who believes all of the world's wrongs are her fault? That's when it happened again ..."

In the pregnant pause I took to collect my words, my visual memoir swept in through my psychological barrier, rehashing every painful detail.

They say when you hear the knocking, don't let the demons in. Well, it was too late for that now.

Welcome to death. It's a beautiful sight, the last thing I'll ever see. One hundred and forty acres of sprawling country and lakeside calm. Pecan trees lining the campus, ripe for the climbing, sunlight dancing on Lake Waccamaw's lapping waves, butterfly kisses of breathy wind frolicking through burnt orange leaves that bid summer adieu. It's my home—and yet it isn't.

The cottage I share with four other girls is quaint, but it's not where I should be. I shouldn't be bunking with Chelsea or borrowing clothes from Lindsey, both girls carrying emotional garbage bags that fall apart during Lindsey's fist-swinging outbursts or Chelsea's midnight sobfests. I shouldn't have been passed along from facility to facility like an unwanted fruitcake. A twenty-something residential counselor named Naomi shouldn't be raising me. I should be with Mom and Dad, Burt and Winnie Wilburn, who tossed me aside after their love was spent on their dead daughter. Lucky for them, today they'd have two dead girls.

It takes a lot of self-discipline to get to this point where I can finally win against myself. Harboring a collection of aspirin for weeks in a pair of balled-up socks. Plotting just the right timing when I'd be alone in the house, which felt like a lofty goal on the group home campus.

But I won.

So here I stand, gazing out the window of my home away from home, pills in one hand, water glass in the other, at the ready. Then a momentary pang of guilt swats at me for the mess I'm going to leave Naomi to clean up—a bed with a body and comforter covered in puke. Nothing a scoop of laundry soap can't cure, I suppose.

I sit with my legs Indian-style on my pink-and-green-striped bedding. The room's too dark. I want to see the sunlight one last time, so I part the faded yellow curtains just an inch. I toss back the handful of chalky white tablets, swish them down with a cheekful of water, wincing at the bitter taste that follows the pills to the back of my throat and down, down, down where they'll divide and conquer each cell until the point of surrender.

Waiting to fall into the black abyss of unconsciousness, I think back to my day of reckoning. It's been almost four years now since Winnie—she and Burt lost the titles of Mom and Dad long ago—last set eyes on me, and yet I remember her parting words with the clarity of a pithy epitaph on a tombstone ... which they were, in a way.

"It's your fault Carli's dead," she had said. And Burt, his mustached lips trembling, stood idly by offering no defense. "I know you were jealous of her." Her voice was cold but calm, an icy winter breeze that snatches your breath. "You've always resented her, and I know you pushed her in the road when that car was coming. You killed your sister. I can't prove it, but I just know it. And I told the police the same. I can't even stand to look at you anymore."

And the police believed her. She saw me do it, she told them. And Burt mutely agreed. And soon even I believed it was true.

THE ART OF FEAR

So it was best I leave, taken into the custody of professionals. Get help. Fix me, please. But the guilt, that everlasting plague that gnaws at your flesh until you're a walking corpse, burrowed its teeth in me. I couldn't leave my own psyche. I couldn't start over. I abandoned my sister. My family abandoned me. It was a sadistic cycle set on my destruction. But I'll have the last laugh.

I withhold my tears. I feel more courageous this way.

The world begins leaning, heaving and groaning, its heaviness jerking me in wide circles. I feel a shiver of disconnect as the memories crawl out of their crypt. They've been asleep so long, awakening to say their final good-bye.

It's a forsaken place, one's deathbed. An uncertain journey, like being lost in a mist. I wonder if I'll ever have consciousness again in a better place, or if it's lights out forever. As the drugs course through me, I feel my skin shaking over my bones in frenetic waves. Nausea clenches my stomach, threatening to purge my poison. I roll up in a ball, gripping my abdomen as if holding in the contents. Life slips into slow motion, blurring in and out, until I close my eyes.

The annals of my memories flip in random sequence. A fatal thump that shoots Carli's body across a sea of green. Sobs stabbing the suburban tranquility. A swarm of curious, well-meaning neighbors—cranky Mrs. Finch, Carli's classmate Benny from next door, babysitter Becky— invading our yard as waves of red lights strobe across our horrified faces. An ambulance carries my sister away, with Winnie gripping her motionless hand while crying into Carli's lifeless chest.

The last of my consciousness drips into a sea of unknowns as I embrace the darkness.

Chapter 9

Ari

Thirteen days until dead

The fifth season of *American Horror Story* had made multiple rabbits run across my grave—my grandmother's quaint Southern expression for the willies. I flicked off the TV during a particularly intense scene and caught myself checking the corners of the living room for spooks. The cranky sofa—a curbside deal—groaned as I rose to make a grilled cheese sandwich. My mind was restless, which made my stomach grumble. Josef Alvarez was an albatross that suffocated my thoughts, drilling question after question into my skull. Clearly his specter wasn't going to let up tonight.

Tina had left the case file with me after I dropped her off at her Duke Manor apartment following the meeting. I'd almost invited her to stay with me until we blundered into a junior league drug deal going down between two punks—one black, one white—in the parking lot. The encounter left no doubt Tina could take care of herself.

"Dudes!" she hailed them. "This is where I live. How about taking your dope deal somewhere else, like good little boys."

I shot Tina a WTF look. "Are you crazy?" I whispered. "Don't antagonize them."

Ivory spoke up. "You bitches mind your own business, ah-ite?"

Tina was unfazed. "But it *is* my business. Like I said, I live here, and I don't like to see douche bags effing up my neighborhood."

That pissed Ebony off. "Bitch, you gon' be sorry you said that."

We stood in the glow of a streetlamp. The two punks sauntered out of the shadows toward us. The light revealed them to be fifteen, sixteen tops. Ebony kept his hand cupped on his package, which was easy because his pants were on the ground. Ivory tried his damnedest to project cool menace—no small feat for a guy with a mullet.

"One bitch for me, one for you," said Ivory. "What's your pleasure, ladies? Doggie style?"

"Or mebbe y'all be likin' two in the pink, one in the stink," Ebony added.

They collapsed on each other in idiotic laughter. Recovering, they started circling us like buzzards.

I wasn't prepared for this, but Tina was. The look on her face said she was afraid of nothing. "You punks have no idea how disgusting you are. Do your mamas know you talk like that to ladies?"

"I don't see no ladies," said Ivory, "just a couple hos what need a good drillin'."

They were only a yard or two from us now. I started to yell, but I wondered who'd come to our rescue in this neighborhood. I'd made up my mind that when either one of them got close enough, I'd serve up a swift kick to the nuts. Meanwhile I looked at Tina. Her expression said *I've got this.*

Standing her ground, she reached inside her purse and displayed the grip of a pistol. "There's more, gentlemen. Want to see it?"

The punks took a step back.

"Be cool, mama! Put that shit away," said Ebony. "We vamoosin'. Come on, man."

Ivory couldn't resist a parting shot. "You skinny ugly hos couldn'tve taken our snot rockets anyway."

"True that," said Ebony. His hand left his crotch long enough to shoot us a bird.

When they'd disappeared down the street, I found the tongue that I thought I'd swallowed.

"Damn, Tina. You're a regular Dirty Harriett!" I shot a glance at the grip, still sticking out of her purse. "You got a license to carry that thing?"

"Don't need one." She whipped it out. It was a replica .38 special with an orange stripe on the barrel to indicate it was non-functioning. "Looks real, doesn't it? Actually I hate guns, but a girl has to look out for herself. These punks are all talk and attitude. Usually all I have to do is show 'em the handle and they take off with their tails tucked between their legs."

"Too bad, the white dude was kinda cute," I deadpanned. "But the black dude probably has a bigger ... uh, snot rocket."

I'd expected hilarity to ensue, but when a cloud passed over Tina's face, I knew I'd struck a hidden nerve.

"There's nothing funny about it, Ari," she muttered. Then she made a feeble excuse about being tired, shoved the case file at me, and beat a hasty retreat for her apartment.

I had a newfound respect for Tina after the encounter; she was definitely no shrinking violet. Perhaps we had more in common than I realized. We were a couple of streetwise bitches—and I use the term affectionately—that had seen and done it all. Me in juvie and the foster home system, and Tina in the mean streets she'd heretofore only dropped vague hints about. Obviously it had something to do with some hang-up about men, or with sex in general. I knew she'd come around eventually and didn't dwell on it.

As I rounded the blue peninsula—a lasting tribute to

the pastels of the 1990s—jutting out of my kitchenette wall, a cockroach scuttled at my feet, harrying me back two steps. The damn things were as large as mice, and just as fertile. But it wasn't on account of poor housekeeping, since I kept my one-bedroom apartment OCD neat. Juvie life had trained me to keep my things orderly, lest they end up amongst your roommate's possessions without you knowing. Truth was, I lived in a cesspool of a neighborhood where police sirens serenaded you night and day and overgrown grass littered with fast food wrappers attracted vermin. Being on the first floor, my place was an accommodating hideaway for a myriad of critters.

After slathering two slices of bread with a heart attack's worth of butter, I cooked up a grilled cheese sandwich in a cast-iron skillet I'd been preheating. *Mmmm.* Tastes so good, it makes you want to slap your mama—another of Grandma's witticisms, and not a bad idea, considering what a bitch Winnie was. One of these days, I vowed to learn how to make a decent meal that a decent man—like Tristan—would appreciate. But today wasn't that day. Today something else plagued me.

The brown folder with the gruesome details of Josef's death lay in front of me. I heaved myself up into a lone stool and flipped it open, careful not to grease up the paperwork.

A photocopy of a typed formal police report.

Copies of several crime scene photos.

A preliminary autopsy report.

A copy of a suicide letter.

I hadn't expected Teen Cop to be so generous.

Licking my fingers clean, I leafed back to the police report, which covered the basics:

At 8:47 p.m. on April 7, 2016, a 9-1-1 operator took a call from Tina Alvarez saying her father, Josef Alvarez, had been stabbed. When officers arrived on the scene at 813 Gregson Road, they found a Hispanic man wearing a white T-shirt and blue jeans, sitting upright on the sofa with a kitchen knife in his hand, and covered in blood. Dead on arrival. Driver's license found at the scene preliminarily indicates the decedent was Josef Alvarez, aged 40; positive ID forthcoming. A canvas of the neighborhood produced no witnesses, possibly due to the remote location of the house and the dense tree coverage. No signs of a break-in. A suicide letter was retrieved from the scene, and an empty bottle of tequila and several bottles of beer indicate he had been drinking. Preliminary evidence points to suicide. A tox screen forthcoming.

It seemed pretty cut and dried to me, but if Tina was indeed correct that it was foul play, what did the cops miss?

Next I pored over the autopsy report. It was too technical for my layman brain, and pages long. I really just wanted the gist of it, which I found on page 1 under the opening summary:

Autopsy: DPD940284-37G
Decedent: Josef Alvarez

Identified by: fingerprints, family
identification, ID at crime scene
Age: 40
Race: Hispanic
Sex: Male
External Examination: Well-developed
Hispanic male with multiple subdural
hematomas, one on right forearm and
one on abdominal region,
demonstrative of a suicide attempt
Toxicology: Blood and vitreous fluid
positive for alcohols; blood positive for
acidic, basic and neutral drugs
(alprazolam)
Cause of Death: Exsanguination due to
multiple stab and incised wounds.
Manner of Death: Suspected suicide

Subdural hematomas. Vitreous fluid. Exsanguination. I
had no idea what I was reading—just a bunch of
meaningless ten-dollar words. Filling in the context, I
deduced that he died from bleeding out. But the other fact
that jumped out at me was the mention of drugs.

Googling *alprazolam*, I read all about the medicine and
its proper use—to treat anxiety and panic attacks often
associated with depression—along with common side
effects I recognized from the breathless list at the end of
every drug commercial I'd ever seen. If I understood this
correctly, they found alcohol mixed with stress meds in
his system—a drug commonly found in the vanities of
stressed-out moms.

Machismo and panic attacks—not something you
associate with a lowlife like Josef Alvarez. Crack or meth,
maybe. Xanax, no.

Perhaps the suicide note would shed more light on what happened. I laid out the photocopy in front of me and read it:

Where can I go, the tick that I am, if I bleed my host dry? The bodies are drained and my belly full to bursting. My indulgence has killed me.

I've come to the end of my game. Once upon a time my life was a thrill ride. The night was always young as I cruised the streets, ferreting out their secrets in the dark places where demons dwell. Ahead is my graveyard with endless lines of stones where bodies molder into lost memories below. Will I be remembered for anything but the insect that I am? I once was free, living a beautiful lie, dining on the carcasses of others, but fate schemed against me, crushing me, popping the blood from my globular gray belly.

No one will mourn me—only the devil as his handiwork becomes dust. Just a pile of bones and meat. I sold my child's innocence for a dollar. A buck that bought me this richly deserved death.

The poetry of his words was extraordinary— unbelievable—given his lifestyle. Almost as if they were someone else's thoughts, someone not quite so wife-beater-and-dirty-jeans. But what did I know? Maybe not everyone is who they seem to be. Or maybe this was the tequila talking.

The note referenced bleeding his host dry, someone he sucked the life out of. If these were indeed his words, then he sure as hell had enough guilt to off himself. But if they were penned by his "host," whatever crime Josef committed against this person seemed to be the perfect motive for murder.

And I had to wonder what the "I sold my child's

innocence for a dollar" remark meant. Tina had said her father kicked her out. This revelation added another layer to her mystery, one I was hell-bent to solve. But all in good time.

Next, I flipped through the pictures, my eyeballs wandering restlessly over images of scarlet blooming across Josef's chest, pooling along the sofa's vinyl fabric, sprawling across the carpet. Rivulets of blood wended their macabre way across a coffee table, fouling snack chip wrappers and a bunch of other paper garbage, before eventually settling around the rim of a bottle of Jose Cuervo that sat amid a collection of dirty glasses and empty beer bottles.

I wondered what his liver looked like.

I didn't have enough ammo to request another look by Teen Cop. They'd read the letter, checked the crime scene, saw all the same evidence I was now perusing, and yet they still ruled it a suicide. What did I know, really? But my vow to Tina was worth something, wasn't it? I'd made a friend, a *real* friend. It was a chance to be human, to be supportive, to bring something to the table other than shared misery. I could help her find answers, even if the truth revealed suicide. That's what I promised. And that's exactly what I would do.

Chapter 10
Sophia Alvarez

San Luis, Mexico
2004

The sun nestled into the horizon, not yet ready to break the day. But six-year-old Sophia Martina Alvarez was already tiptoeing out of her bedroom, leaving her four-year-old brother Killian curled up asleep at the foot of their bed as the sound of hushed voices in the kitchen drew her down the hallway. Mama and Papa were sitting at the table across from a man Sophia didn't recognize.

"*Buenos dias*," Mama greeted her sweetly like every other morning. But it didn't feel like every other morning to Sophia. Not without the smell of cooking chicken and cheese *chilaquiles*, or if Sophia promised her best behavior, a sugary *churros* treat to start the day.

Waking up to the hunger pangs of the past were long gone. After years of dining on the neighbors' leftovers and scraps of beans and rice that her *madre* always frugally rationed, finally they were eating real meals ... at least twice a day, sometimes more. And wearing shoes and clothes of her own choosing, not her cousins' hand-me-downs.

"*Buenos dias*, Mama," Sophia replied shyly, eyeing the strange man in her home at such an early hour.

"We have a special guest today," Mama announced, her words coaxing and smooth. "Josef, how about you explain to Sophia who our friend is while I get some breakfast for everyone?"

Josef waved Sophia on to his lap, settling her against his chest built like a chopping block. "This is George—he's, well, he's a friend. He's going to be watching you for a little while for your *madre* and me. *Comprende?*"

Sophia insistently shook her head. "No, Papa, I don't want a new friend. I have Arturo next door."

"Aw, sweetie, you can never have too many friends. Mr. George will play with you—all your favorite games. Like *el escondite*—you can hide and he'll find you."

"It's no fun playing with grownups, Papa."

"I promise you, George is a lot of fun."

Sophia rolled her eyes in doubt.

"It's true," George said, his voice like cool steel. "I'll make you a deal. I'll play you in a game of *piedra, papel, tijeras*, and if you win, I'll buy you any toy you want."

"For real?" Sophia squcakcd, looking to her father for approval.

"*Si*," her papa agreed. "Go ahead."

Despite her tender years, Sophia knew something about Mr. George wasn't normal. "Mr. George, you're a grownup, so why do you like playing with kids?"

He rubbed his fingers along his thin mustache, caressing the silky hairs with gentle strokes. His eyes glazed over, like he was watching a long-ago idyll replay in his head. "I find children to be ... refreshing," he finally spoke, the words soothing and melodious, like water tumbling over rocky shoals. "Full of vibrancy and energy. Children make me feel young again. Like I can bottle you up and drink in your vigor all day."

A clash of dishes stopped George short as Mercedes frantically picked up shards of clay from the floor. "Sorry about that," she sputtered, wiping at her damp eyes. But the commotion didn't alarm Sophia as her attention was raptly focused on this charming *hombre* and his unusual interest in children.

"I don't know any other grownups who like playing with kids."

"Now you do. So let's play—rock, paper, scissors."

Sophia placed her tiny hand out, dirt rimming her chewed nails, palm down, then George added his own, delicate and fastidiously manicured, across from hers. Together they counted: "One ... two ... three."

Sophia tossed her fist downward and shouted, "*Piedra!*" while George threw his flat hand out, saying, "*Papel.*"

Seeing that his paper won over her rock, Sophia's bottom lip jutted out. "I lost. Paper covers rock."

"Not today, you didn't," George said with a sugarcoated wink. "Today rock beats paper. I'll take you out after breakfast to pick your prize."

"Really? Thank you, Mr. George!" Sophia squealed. At her father's nudge, she hopped down to offer a cautious hug to this odd man-child.

"Mr. George is going to make you a star, sweetie," Mercedes giggled as she set plates around the table. "With your beauty, you're going to make us rich. Then we'll be able to buy anything you could dream of."

"But I don't want to be a star."

"Don't you want your mama to have nice things?"

Sophia nodded wordlessly.

"Well, Mr. George says you are exceptionally pretty and is going to take pictures of you and pay us for those pictures."

"But I don't want to be in pictures. I just want to play with Arturo."

"Honey, you can't play with Arturo forever. Don't you

want to be famous?"

Sophia shrugged halfheartedly. "Not really. I just want to be a kid."

"Being a kid doesn't put food on the table," Josef gruffly cut in. "Times are hard. Jobs are few. You must do what you can to help the family, Sophia."

"Perhaps," George suggested, "Sophia can be a star without giving up the fun of being a kid." He smiled at the little girl, and she smiled back.

Sophia and Mr. George continued to bond over a game of thumb wrestling. Breakfast was served in the usual way, but there was something different—peculiar—about Mama. First she blinked away tears and crossed herself, and then she cast her eyes to heaven. This was strange to Sophia, because Mama was usually only religious on Sunday and during *Navidad*. Then all of a sudden Mama grabbed her and squeezed her and looked her directly in her eyes. Something Mama had never done with such intensity.

"I love you, Sophia. Make me proud, okay?"

"Okay, Mama." But Sophia always tried to make her parents proud. She didn't understand why the fierce hug, the penetrating stare.

They ate breakfast with much laughter and conversation, but to Sophia her mother's enjoyment seemed tinged with sadness. Afterwards, Mama and Papa walked Sophia to Mr. George's fancy American car, each one holding a hand, before ushering her inside the vehicle, releasing her into George's care.

"Have fun, sweetie. Pick out something extra nice for yourself."

"Aren't you coming, Mama?"

"Not this time. Behave."

"I will."

"And remember, Mama loves you, Sophia. Please

forgive me."

"Forgive you for what?"

But no answer came. No answer ever came.

After her father buckled her in, through smudged glass Sophia saw her mama break down in tears. The sobbing face looked huge and hideous pressed against the window, the veins in Mama's eyes like a sea of angry red snakes, and the cheeks wet and the mouth blubbering like somebody had died.

Sophia was scared out of her wits, for herself and for her mother.

She yanked furiously on the handle, but the door wouldn't budge. Fear turned to panic as her small fists banged against the window. "Mama!" she screamed. "Mama, what's happening?"

The last time Sophia ever saw her mother, she was running toward the front door.

Sophia's mouth dropped open. This couldn't be happening. In a daze, she saw Mr. George hand Papa a thick wad of paper—money. She noticed the odd look on his face, the same look greedy kids had when they asked *Santo Clos* for more toys than they deserved, as he flipped through the bills.

"Papa, help! Please let me out!" she screamed at the top of her lungs. But he turned on his heel and left without a backward glance.

"You miserable brat—stop that yelling or I'll give you something to yell about!"

What had happened to Mr. George's pleasant voice? It sounded like he was mad at her. But why?

"I'm sorry, Mr. George, it's just that I—"

The back of his hand caught her full in the mouth. Nobody had ever hit her like that. Not Mama. Not Papa. She was too shocked to cry. She looked straight ahead as Mr. George's ugly voice seethed in her ear.

THE ART OF FEAR

"I told you to be quiet, didn't I? Maybe now you'll think twice before you give me any sass. You will remain silent for the rest of the trip—or else."

When they had passed the *supermercado* where they bought their food, she got up the courage to move. She looked out the passenger-side window and pressed her hand on the glass, tracing her mama's imagined face with her little fingertips. As the car bumped along the dirt road, away from the only home she'd ever known, she wondered how much her life was actually worth to her father.

As the minutes turned into hours and the open fields and towns whizzed by in a blur, Sophia Alvarez knew one thing for certain: No, there would be no forgiveness.

Chapter 11

Creased down the middle, the photograph in my hand was twelve years old, an image of the Alvarez family at a time when they were still whole. Broken, yes, but whole. While the picture had long been tucked in pockets and envelopes and wallets, the image was as crisp as the day it was taken. In front of their orange adobe two-bedroom home stood Rosalita, the doting grandmother who knew all. Josef, the husband who labored tirelessly for his family. Mercedes, the nurturing mother and cook who could make gourmet meals out of scraps. Sophia, the whip-smart daughter snuffed out too soon. And tucked against his sister's side, the handsome son his papa always wanted—the family's pride and joy, Killian.

Once upon a time they had been a beautiful collection of high cheekbones, bright eyes, and dazzling smiles—the picture-perfect envy of San Luis ... until the stench of poverty clung to them like cigarette smoke, that is.

But happiness is a mirage when you're poor. You don't know hunger until you're numb from the constant war within your stomach, the emptiness that has taken up permanent residence within you. Even as you're eating a meal, the hunger bares its teeth, biting into the cavity where food should be. Hunger is fear—a gnawing worry over when you're going to eat again. Rent is fear—a grace period away from eviction. Every moment is fear when you're poor and can't afford the needle and thread needed to repair the holes in the shirt you've worn four days in a row this week.

I understood why Josef did what he did.

The offer for his daughter's service—as a *child model* was how it had been spun—was too opportune to pass up. And with the assurance that Sophia would get a solid education and all the niceties life had to offer, he had convinced himself it was a no-brainer. One year of her life was a small price to pay for the perks Sophia would have access to; then his family could eat well, live well, pay off debts. Then bring their darling girl home to enjoy the fruits of her labor.

If only Josef Alvarez had followed through with just that. Instead, the debts piled up, the frivolous spending on alcohol, gambling, and drugs reeled him into a whirlwind of IOUs. One year of service became two became eleven.

And a father's little girl no longer little, and no longer his.

And yet he still owed.

It was the price of his sins.

So I had collected the debt on his life.

Now it was time for another—eye for an eye, life for a life—until they were all relieved of this burden. Unfortunately, Josef's life was worthless to me. His death didn't pay off his outstanding balance.

I reflected on his last moments. Unsatisfying, that's what it was. The gaping hole only felt vaster as the skin opened up a larger wound. Josef didn't pay; *I* paid *for* him. Did killing him serve no purpose but to quench my thirst?

Perhaps it was because the job wasn't done. Yes, I needed to finish my work to feel relief. That much I now knew. After all, the family embarked on the path together. Thus they all were accountable for the costs. No one had stopped it. No one had attempted to rescue Sophia when the months became years. No one stepped in to pay off the collectors when Josef fled to escape his responsibilities.

Justice required equal retribution, and it was finally mine to divvy up.

But who was next? Deciding was the hard part.

My fingertip traced the faces, one by one, pausing over each image captured in a timeless frozen moment. The girl, so pretty in her pink cotton dress, was only six years old—and mere days from losing her innocence. Her chubby-cheeked toddler brother, adorable in his *vaquero* outfit, complete with cap gun and traditional flat crown hat, beamed next to his sister, blissfully unaware that she would soon be taken away, as his dimpled fingers intertwined with hers.

It was impossible not to be charmed by this dark-skinned cherub with his winning smile and mass of black curls crowning his bulbous head. But twelve years later he was no longer a child. He was accountable for the costs. Not a boy, but a young man. At sixteen a boy can copulate, can create life, can take life. In accepting his sister's servitude, in relinquishing the battle, he accepted her gifts yet repaid none of the debts. Yes, it was time this young man knew what responsibility was all about. Pay what you owe. Man up.

Tapping my finger on the little cowboy's image, I knew it was the right choice.

Oh, pride and joy of the Alvarez family, be ready for me, for I would be coming for you.

Chapter 12
Ari

April 2002

N othing about him—the shiny badge, the navy button-down shirt taut against his slender body, his crispy brown hair, or his vanilla pudding tone—makes me feel protected or served. Instead, I feel like a prisoner as he bombards me with question after question that come at me so fast I can't think straight.

The overhead fluorescent fixture blinks, strobe-like, causing my temples to throb. The thin cushion on the metal chair is as thin as a pancake. I feel every minute I've been sitting here ache in my butt muscles. The interrogation room is as blank as the policeman's face. He looks at me like a spotlight shining on all my sins.

"Can you describe what you remember before the accident? Were you playing together?"

"Do you remember anything from when the car hit your sister?"

"Where was your sister when it all happened?"

"Did you see the car—the color, anything special about it?"

"Could you see the driver?"

Officer Friendly doesn't seem content with the truth. He wants information, even if I have to make it up, apparently.

I tell him the first things that come to mind. I don't know if they're true or not, since I've lost track of the details from *the ordeal of telling and retelling and backtracking.*

"Yes, Carli and I were playing in the yard. Well, we weren't playing together. I was mad at her for ruining my Barbie so I pushed her away from me. But I didn't mean to."

"I remember seeing the car swerve up into the yard where Carli was, and I heard a loud thump *when it hit her. Then just blood. Lots of blood."*

"She was in the grass but kinda near the road."

"I think the car was red, Or maybe orange? I don't remember."

"I couldn't see who was driving. It happened too fast."

I try my best, but every reply only irritates Mommy more. I can feel her angry heat beside me, the tense squeeze of her clammy hand on mine in an unspoken warning that I can't decipher. It's not the tender comforting caress you expect of a mother whose ten-year-old daughter is being questioned in the wake of her sister's hit-and-run death. No, the arm circling my shoulders is the constriction of judgment. Her fingers woven around mine are the grip of accusations, a guilty verdict. Even as a kid I sense it in her wooden movements, like a nutcracker clamping down on me.

The policeman looks at me, his eyes kindly. For the first time I see the hint of a smile on his homely face. "Thank you, Ari. I know this isn't easy for you, but you did a good job." Then he turns to Mommy. "Unfortunately, this isn't much to go on, Ms. Wilburn. I'm sorry, but without more details, I don't know how we can find your daughter's killer. We need something more—a vehicle description, partial plate number, anything."

"What about the neighbors—didn't they see anything?" Mommy wants to know.

"No, no one saw anything. We canvassed the neighborhood asking if anyone remembers anything at all,

but so far we've come up empty-handed. At this point all we can do is hope the driver turns himself in."

"Of course he won't!" Mommy growls, a sound angry cats make. "So that's it? He'll get away with murder?"

"I'm afraid so, ma'am."

Mommy releases me and sits there stiffly. When she finally speaks, her words stick in her throat. "There is something … something I'd like to say."

"Go ahead, ma'am," the officer says.

Mommy swallows so hard, I can hear it. "I saw what happened."

"Are you saying you saw everything? Why didn't you come forward with this before now?"

Mommy glares down at me, her eyes warning beacons to a ship entering stormy seas. "Because I was trying to protect Ari, but maybe I shouldn't anymore."

The policeman sighs and rises, signaling for Mommy to follow him to the corner of the small room. I hear whispers against the naked white walls, a barren room where people's lives are inspected and pulled apart like taffy. It's a dismal room. Cold and redolent of death. An omen that my life holds no future.

Mommy and the officer return to the faux wood table, both looking at me with eyes watching from a new lens. A lens of suspicion and fear.

"Ari, your mother tells me you and Carli fought a lot. Were you jealous of Carli?"

I nod meekly.

"Were you angry with Carli before the accident happened—about the Barbie?"

I nod again.

"Your mother says she saw you push your sister in front of the moving car. Is that true? You can be honest with me. You're not in trouble if you did. We just need to know."

I look from his walrus mustache to Mommy's creased

forehead, then back again. I know what he wants to hear, whether it's true or not. I remember the shove. I remember the fight. But the car ... I can't remember.

"Honey, you need to be honest with the policeman if he's going to be able to help us. Please tell him what you did."

Tell him what you did ... *My eyeballs ache as the image of Carli's body lying in a pool of crimson thrusts itself on me. Mommy's hand cups my shoulder, kneading the truth out of me. She needs me to tell.*

My fingers frantically twist themselves into knots in my lap, and my gaze turns shamefully downward on my untied shoelace dusting the floor.

I don't know what will come after this moment, but I'm afraid of whatever it is.

"Yes, sir, I ... I pushed Carli." *The words snag in my throat as a sob creeps out.* "I killed my sister."

Chapter 13
Ari

Twelve days until dead

Do you have your purse? We're going on a road trip," I had announced to Tina an hour earlier when she slipped into the passenger seat of my Ford Focus. I hadn't come empty-handed, at least, handing her a to-go cup of Starbucks—a caramel macchiato, a recent favorite of mine.

After a night of police interrogations swimming through my dreams, it was a welcome break to have company this morning.

The long drive to Dunn gave Tina and me a golden opportunity to bond over the usual chickish subjects, but I noticed she studiously avoided comparing notes about the rock musicians and actors I considered hot, a long list to be sure. I wasn't surprised, considering how she'd skedaddled after our run-in with Ebony and Ivory—and my admittedly vulgar attempt at humor. But she talked freely about everything else under the sun, and I found her to be intelligent and witty, and fun as hell to be with. Eventually we fell into a companionable silence, and I decided to play my hand.

"Tina, I know we're just getting to know each other, and I don't want to pry, but I can't help but notice you seem to have some, uh, hang-ups about ... guys."

She bristled. "Are you trying to say you think I'm gay? Well, I'm not."

"What? God, no! It's not that at all. I was just thinking about those two punks. You were brave as hell, but I know it upset you. And today, well, you clam up whenever the subject of guys and, uh, sex comes up."

Tina was silent for a long time. I glanced over at her now and then, saw the tears beading in her eyes, her jaw muscles working. She looked like she wanted to say something but didn't know where to start. Finally she found the courage and the words.

"Remember when I said my father kicked me out?"

"Yeah."

"That's not what happened. The son of a bitch sold me … to a sex trafficker … when I was just six."

I was gobsmacked. I remembered the line in Josef's suicide note: *I sold my child's innocence for a dollar.* It all made sense now. "Oh, Tina, I'm so sorry. I don't know what to—"

"Don't say anything!"

The waterworks opened up full blast. When she was able to talk again, Tina told me the whole incredible story of her shiftless father's betrayal in one long, impassioned, uninterrupted confessional. Details of the unimaginable life of a child prostitute she didn't provide, and I didn't press. I didn't need to hear them to know the degradation she'd endured.

Afterwards I sat in silence, searching for something, anything to say. Suddenly I knew just the right thing.

"Now I know why you hate your father. Alright if I hate him too?"

She chuckled, and then laughed outright. I joined in. There was no doubt now that we were soul sisters.

THE ART OF FEAR

The route to Josef Alvarez's house took us down a rutted dirt road, a glorified cow path with deep ditches on either side. I lost count of all the castoff furniture and appliances, too shitty for a discriminating connoisseur of roadside treasure like I was. Once we came bumper to bumper with a puke-green GM truck, 1970s era, tricked out with humongous mud tires and off-road lights. Squeezed abreast into the cab were four leering good old boys; a huge Confederate flag flapped from the bed. Somebody was going to have to yield the narrow road, and it looked like that duty fell to me, because chivalry was obviously dead here in the butt crack of North Carolina. I eased the Focus into the ditch to let the rednecks pass.

"Lookin' good, ladies!" the driver yelled, stopping alongside our car to salute us with his Budweiser. His buddies joined in with lascivious hoots and hollers. The driver tipped his John Deere cap, gunned the engine, and peeled out in a cloud of dust, exhaust, and gravel.

"I don't know about you, Tina, but I'm impressed as hell," I remarked, piloting the Focus back on the cow path, which I could barely see through the smoke.

At last we came to the sign, riddled with gunshot pockmarks, for Gregson Road. Josef Alvarez's house was situated at the dead end, down a long, curving gravel driveway. We hadn't passed a neighbor's house for probably five miles, and Josef's place, nestled in a sea of pines and the odd hardwood, was hidden from the road. The man obviously liked his privacy.

The house and grounds were from the Early Shithole period. A bald truck tire was marooned on the catawampus roof, and a ratty mattress leaned drunkenly against the puckering vinyl siding infested with cancerous patches of green and black mildew. Tall fescue, littered with crushed beer cans beyond count, grew in scraggly knee-high patches in the muddy yard.

"Listen, did you hear that?" I whispered to Tina.

"What?" she replied in alarm.

"I thought I heard banjos playing."

"Ha, ha."

The yard's focal point was a bottle tree unlike any I'd ever seen. These uniquely Southern curios are small trees or posts ornamented with colorful bottles. No two are alike. They can be whimsical, elegant, kitschy—the only limit is one's imagination. Josef's was a rotting landscape timber decorated with a willy-nilly collection of tequila and beer bottles, some broken, hanging on rusty nails. All still had the labels on them. At the top of the post sat a deer skull with twin Mexican mini-flags jutting proudly from the eye sockets.

"I see your pop was an artist," I observed wryly. "You know, bottle trees are supposed to ward off evil spirits."

"Yeah? Guess the old man's didn't work."

I parked behind Josef's creepy white van, which would have been right at home in *Silence of the Lambs*. Bull thistle, dog fennel, and a butt-load of other unsightly weeds thrived among the neglected lantana bushes and canna lilies growing around the front porch, upon which sat a derelict Kelvinator fridge with the door open to reveal a half-empty twelve-pack of Pabst. We crunched up the gravel driveway to the front door.

"Are we allowed to be here?" Tina whispered.

"Sure, why the hell not?" I answered matter-of-factly.

"Because it's a crime scene, isn't it?" she answered.

"Not according to the police. Besides, you're the next of kin, aren't you?"

Tina nodded.

"Well, then it's your place now."

The screen door groaned in agony as I opened it and tugged on the front door handle. Locked.

"Got a key, by chance?" I asked, eyeing the lock.

"Sorry. Didn't think I'd ever need one."

"I wonder if he left any windows open," I mused aloud.

"Some investigators we are, showing up with no way of getting in," Tina said, rising on tiptoes to peer through a crescentic window.

"I didn't say I couldn't get in. It'd just be a hell of a lot easier with a key, that's all." Tugging a bobby pin from my hair, I held it up and smirked. "Voila! The enterprising gal's lock pick."

Tina chuckled and rolled her eyes. "You're a regular Veronica Mars."

Bending the metal pin, I jammed one straight end in the lock and twisted it until I heard a faint *click*. Thank you, juvie. Moments later we were skulking into the living room, where the scene of Josef Alvarez's death lingered undisturbed. On the coffee table whisky and beer bottles, glasses, and dinnerware sat like timeless heirlooms. A hodgepodge of Mexican religious candles, oddly out of place, stood vigil on the junk store end table. The whole room gave the impression of a museum exhibit, missing only Josef's corpse slumping on the bloodstained sofa to complete the macabre scene. But his presence was there in the general filth and the odd smell in the air that made my nostrils flare. Like pennies smelled after you'd clutched them in your sweaty palm. The coppery stink of blood.

It was a horrific thought, dying like this, and leaving nothing behind but a shithole of a house and crusty bloodstains in the carpet as your legacy. Oh yeah, and a daughter that didn't give a rat's ass about you—and why should she? It was beginning to make sense to me why Josef might have lost the will to live.

"So, what are we here for?" Tina asked.

It was a good question, one I didn't quite know the

answer to. "Clues ... about his death. Something telling us what happened."

"What kind of clues?"

"If this wasn't a suicide, there's got to be evidence that shows how he was killed."

"The police have the weapon—the knife. No fingerprints but his own on it, or anything else, for that matter. What else is there to look for?"

"Well," I sighed heavily, knowing I was treading in water over my head. I had no idea what I was doing here, but I had to try. "Wasn't he supposedly on medication for depression? Let's see if we can find a prescription bottle or something from the doctor. Some kind of medical record or insurance coverage. You go through any paperwork you can find and I'll check the bathroom cabinet."

"Sounds like a start," Tina agreed.

I ambled around the sparse two-bedroom dwelling, finding the place bare of anything but the essentials. The spare bedroom was empty except for a beanbag chair spewing its beans in the corner and a shadeless lamp on the floor.

Josef's bedroom was a step above this, just one though, with at least a dresser holding a lamp. His bed was a solo mattress tossed in the middle of the room with a pile of crumpled sheets spilling onto the floor. The closet's bifold door hung open, revealing a handful of shirts hanging from a crooked metal pole haphazardly attached to the walls. I headed into the "master bath," which consisted of a blue ceramic toilet—in whose disgusting bowl floated a Godzilla-sized palmetto bug, thankfully drowned—and a matching sink. A child-sized shower stall had been shoehorned into the cramped space. Opening the vanity above the sink, I found the personal hygiene paraphernalia of the average male: Barbasol shaving cream, Gillette Mach3 safety razor and blade refill, tweezers, nail clippers, and something unexpected: a thirty-six-count box of Trojan Ultra Thin condoms—unopened. That's the spirit, Josef; always be prepared. But no prescription bottles, or medicine of any kind.

Whiskers covered the sink and floor, and tufts of curly hair circled the shower drain—typical slobby bachelor. Under the sink I found a short stack of clean towels and a pile of skin mags next to the can. Well, at least the old boy had a hobby. So I headed back down the freshly vacuumed carpeted hallway toward the spare bathroom. It was completely empty, unused, except for the eye-watering odor of bleach coming from the bathtub. No hand towel, washcloths, or towels to be found. It was all I could do to refrain from writing "wash me" in the thick layer of dust on the vanity mirror, like Carli and I used to do to dirty cars when we were little. Why did I have to remember that? I felt a dark wave sweep over me and headed back to the kitchen.

There I found Tina rummaging through the cabinets, with a stack of bills splayed out on an otherwise empty kitchen table.

"Any luck?" I asked.

"Nada," Tina reported, slamming the last cabinet door shut. "Just some bills, fast-food receipts, junk mail, address book."

"Shit." I picked up the address book, flipped through it, and pocketed it. I could look later for any information or contacts that might be helpful.

"Oh, and his latest bank statements. Of course he's dead broke—no pun intended. At least he could have left me enough to pay for the propane gas here, you know? But other than useless paperwork, nothing medical-related. You find anything?"

"Nothing showing if he had any prescriptions or doctor bills." I wondered if there was another way we could find out if he had a prescription, then I had an idea. "But I think I know how to find out his medical history."

Pulling out my phone, I searched for the closest pharmacy and found the name and number. If he was in their system, I'd dig until I hit pay dirt.

A nasally pharmacist answered on the third ring, spurting a rush of words—I thought I heard *pharmacy* among them—I could barely decipher.

"Hi, I was wondering if you had a prescription ready for my dad—Josef Alvarez? I was going to come pick it up in a little while."

"Let me see, honey. One sec. Um ... I only have an expired prescription for doxycycline on record."

An antibiotic? "My dad's kinda tightlipped about his ailments. Would you mind telling me exactly what that medicine's used for?"

"Oh, honey, it's an antibiotic for general bacterial infections. It's also used to treat urinary tract infections and"—the pharmacist paused for dramatic effect, and I thought I heard her snigger—"social diseases."

Naughty Josef. Should have used those rubbers. "Nothing else on file? Dad said his antidepressants were running low."

"If that's the case, he doesn't get them filled here. I'm not sure where else he would fill them, though. We're the only pharmacy for miles around."

"Thanks. I'll figure it out. He must have given me the wrong pharmacy information."

"You're welcome, honey."

"Well?" Tina said when I'd hung up.

"Looks like your saintly pop might have had an STD at some point."

Tina humphed. "Big surprise there."

"Yeah. It was most likely the right pharmacy, though, since his name and medical history were on file, but he apparently wasn't taking anything for depression. That could only mean one thing."

Tina looked at me expectantly.

"Looks like your dad was drugged," I said.

"Whoa, so that's big, right?"

"Yeah, damn right. I think it's important enough to ask the police to follow up on. And I also came across something else that seemed ... peculiar." I tugged Tina's hand and dragged her to follow me into the living room. "Look at that—the carpet still has vacuum lines. And get this—the spare bathtub was recently bleached clean. Look around—this place is more disgusting than a pigsty. I can't picture your father on his hands and knees scrubbing his tub."

"You think the killer cleaned up after he was done?" Tina asked, one eyebrow rising with intrigue.

"I think he washed the blood off himself after he killed your dad and then bleached to make sure there were no traces of blood. If they found blood in the tub, it wouldn't be a suicide, would it?"

"Makes sense," Tina agreed.

"And as for vacuuming, maybe that was to make sure he didn't leave any hairs or footprints in the carpet that could be traced to him. Better safe than sorry, right?"

Totally coincidental details.

Pure speculation.

But it held weight enough for me to buy murder.

"It would seem that way."

I leafed through my mental catalogue of details from the scene: the pictures, the autopsy report, the suicide letter ...

The suicide letter. It had been scrawled on a yellow piece of lined notepad paper, but I hadn't noticed any notepads lying around.

"Hey, did you happen to come across a yellow

notepad?" I asked Tina.

"Mmm, nope."

If the tablet he had written his last words on wasn't here, where could it be? Would the person who forged it have taken it to avoid leaving any DNA behind?

"It's just odd," I observed. "Your dad lived like a monk—a very nasty and depraved one. No creature comforts to speak of except for that piece of shit TV. This place is at the ass-end of nowhere. The perfect spot for somebody to hide out—"

"—until his killer managed to track him down."

Tina was on the right track. And I had an idea who the killer was.

"The sex trafficker, the scumbag your father sold you to—"

"George Battan." Tina spoke his name as if it tasted like shit.

"Yeah. I think we've been ignoring the handwriting on the wall, Tina. A man like that wouldn't have any qualms about murdering your dad, especially since you say he was in debt to these people."

Tina sighed. "Maybe. But you don't know Battan like I do. He's a creepy child predator—and you know why he preys on kids? Because he's a pussy. A cowardly freak. I just don't see him being able to take my dad on."

"Doesn't he have guys who work for him that could?"

Tina rubbed her hands across her face. "Yeah, I just didn't think they'd kill my dad over me escaping. I assumed it was someone else my father had done dirty business with. But if Battan is behind this, Ari, he'll be coming after me next."

"That does it, Tina, you're staying with me tonight. That guy could strike at any time."

"Don't worry about me. I think I've proven I can take care of myself. And I'm not putting you in harm's way,

Ari."

I shook my head. "You're a stubborn bitch, aren't you?"

"Takes one to know one."

Chapter 14

Ari

Ten days until dead

It's a frightening thing getting that unexpected call—the late-night ring that means either someone died or is about to.

I'd never been someone's emergency contact before. My vibrating phone jarred me up at around eleven o'clock midway through an REM cycle and a sexy dream about Tristan—*banish the thought!*—and yet the voice on the other end was calmly professional and polite. Not a hint of urgency to be found, but too ambiguous to be trivial.

The vaguer the message, the worse it usually was.

"This is Duke Hospital psychiatric care. May I speak with Ari Wilburn?" The sweet but shaky voice sounded like an elderly church lady—someone who might have been my grandma in another life.

"Speaking," I answered warily, waiting for the bomb to drop.

"I'm calling because you are listed as the emergency contact for Tina Alvarez."

It took a dull moment before the name sunk in. I kicked myself for leaving her alone, for not forcing her to stay with me the past two nights while the specter of her trafficker hung over her head. She said she was a big girl and could take care of herself, and I was naïve enough to believe her. For all her bravado, something had pushed her over the edge.

"Oh my God, is she okay?" I blurted before Church Lady could elaborate.

"She attempted suicide this evening and was brought in. She's stable, but we'd like for you to come down to speak with the doctor."

"I'll be right there." I jotted down Tina's room number—402—scraped my hair back into a ponytail, tossed on sweatpants and a sweatshirt, and hopped out the door with one flip-flop on and the other in hand.

By the time I'd found parking at the hospital and got lost in the maze of hallways and medical wings half a dozen times, it had taken me almost twenty minutes before I tiptoed into Tina's room, finding her lying upright in a hospital bed, her eyes closed and hands folded peacefully across her chest like ... Oh, God, was she—?

Get a grip, Ari, you morbid idiot. Her chest's moving up and down. She's just asleep.

I shuffled to a stiff chair beside her bed, settling against the uncomfortable plastic, which parted in protest. Her brown eyes peeked open at me.

"Hey," she squeaked.

"Hey," I whispered.

We sat in silence—her watching me, me waiting ... for what, I wasn't sure. For starters, an explanation of what had happened between yesterday and today that would make Tina want to cash in her chips.

Finally I spoke. "Pills? Been there, done that. It's no fun when they come back up."

"Yeah, nothing like a nurse shoving charcoal down your throat to kill the buzz." She smiled weakly, but my lips formed a stern line. "I'm sorry, Ari. I don't know what else to say except that ... I'm sorry."

It sounded sincere, felt genuinely heartfelt, but it wasn't enough. No, if there was one thing we had agreed on, one thing that we bonded over during the car rides and lunches and one-on-one talks these past few days, it was the pain that suicide caused to those around us, those left behind. The complete and utter destruction it left in its wake. She knew this. We agreed. We'd both been there, but that was *before*. This was *now*—and *now* meant we learned from the *before*. Shit! She wasn't allowed to hurt me like this ... not this way, never!

Yes, it was only a handful of days since we'd become fast friends, but we were intimate in that forever besties kind of way. We'd shared our secrets, silent moments, chitchat, and laughter and what I thought was a true friendship ... perhaps my only taste of something real since Carli. So yes, while a week normally wouldn't entitle one to full disclosure of someone's innermost thoughts and feelings, in our case I felt it did.

All I could think was *how dare she?*

But all I said was a simple "Why?"

Wordlessly, she pulled out her cell phone and pressed a couple buttons, then handed it to me. "Listen," she ordered simply.

I pressed my ear to the phone and heard a man speak in a cloying voice that instantly creeped me out:

"It's been a long time, I wanted to say hi. I admit, I was hurt when you left without saying good-bye. We had been getting along so delightfully lately, Sophia. Or should I call you Tina now? The name doesn't become you, dear."

In a seismic shift, his voice grew harsh and deep, like gravel and splintering wood. An alter ego climbed out of him, like a demon shedding his human skin. "Time's up, Tina. It's your reckoning. A name change wasn't going to throw me off your track for long. You still owe another year to pay off dear Daddy's debt, and I'm coming to make sure you deliver on what you owe. Your father, sad to hear he's gone. He'll be missed. And I'm sure you don't want to end up like your old man, so understand that I'm watching you. Waiting. I'm coming for you, and I expect it to go smoothly. You know what you have to lose—and that I don't bluff. Oh, and I'm sure you know by now that if you go to the police, it will not end pretty for you or your new bestie, Ari Wilburn." Then back to sickly sweet as if he was bidding his beloved mother goodnight: "Look forward to seeing you soon, darlin'."

Up until I heard my name, the message felt movie-scene distant, like I was watching a horror flick where the serial killer toyed with his prey. Then my name. He knew my name. How the hell did he know my name?

Afterward, I felt exposed, naked. If ever there was a time for an anxiety attack to overpower me, now would be it. But an alien calmness pumped through my veins.

"Don't tell me. Your sex trafficker?"

"One and the same."

Before Tina had spilled her guts on the ride to Dunn, I had never really thought sex trafficking existed anymore. At least not in my reality, in my little corner of the world. But here before me was a real-life victim of a sordid underworld of vicious pimps and kinky johns, and the little-girls-lost that fueled the trade. I couldn't even imagine the living hell she'd endured—and I had a very vivid imagination from growing up in the foster system.

"Yes, it's him. But I can't go back to that ... life, slow death, whatever you want to call it. I'd rather take my own life on my own terms than die a little each day at his whims."

"Tina, I promise I won't let this sonofabitch get to you," I vowed.

"You have no idea what you're dealing with. Didn't you hear him? If there was any doubt in my mind before, it's gone now. He killed my father because dear Dad received money for services I never rendered. I skip out on him and my dad dies—a coincidence? No. He's going to kill me if I don't follow orders. And you too, Ari. He knows your name!" By this point Tina was hysterical, her voice peaking and wobbling with sobs.

"Sweetie, this isn't a reason to kill yourself. Why would you—" I tried, but Tina cut me off.

"If I was dead, there would be nothing to collect on. And my dad's dead, so Battan won't be getting his money back from *him*. So there'd be no reason to go after you if I was gone. So you ask why I wanted to die? That's why, Ari."

"No, no, don't say that. We can put him behind bars where scumbags like him belong."

"Jail? Ha! He deserves more than rotting in a cell. He deserves the death penalty. He stole my innocence. All of my memories consist of years trapped in a hell of revolving men, each with their own sick, perverted impulses. They turned me into a shell of a human being while I endured endless suffering and torture at the hands of psychopaths. Ripped from my family, sold by my own parents for an easy buck, brought to America—the land of freedom! Yeah, right. Freedom to rape and molest and abuse a child as the world turned a blind eye."

By now Tina's fear had exploded into a diatribe of repressed rage that needed to pour free. She needed to vent it all, so I let her.

"What's ironic is that sure, I attended school, and from the outside my life appeared normal. Except that I was hiding bruises and emaciation beneath my clothes and got pulled out of school for more sick days than any other kid in my class so I could service clients. And if I didn't do as I was told? No food. No water. A beating or two or ten. Or good old-fashioned rape."

She drew a deep breath, tears streaming in the wake of her pause. The curse was reeling her back into the nightmare—the memories. I never could figure out how to outrun them.

"So I stayed silent and alone," she said, her voice now a whisper. "Did anyone even care or wonder why I had no friends? Why I was so shy? Why I was always sick? Why the smile of a man made my skin crawl, or the touch of another human made me jump? I will never know the joy of being a carefree kid lying on my back in the grass, looking up at the clouds in the sky and letting my imagination turn them into animals. Instead my childhood was a daily fight for my life, a life that my own family— even my own brother—saw turning to shit, and they benefited from it."

Tina—or Sophia, I wasn't sure what to call her now— had dwelled in a house of tears and lies her entire life. I had no words of condolence, no apologies or empathy or sorrow to offer. It was too horrible to process. So I stood there, dumbfounded, waiting for the hiccup of lost time to pass over us until I could figure out the right thing to say. Only questions came, like bubbles popping in my head.

"You know his name and where he lives. Why can't we go after him and turn him in?"

"I can't. I just can't. You don't understand."

"Like hell you can't, Tina. I'll go with you."

"No!"

Well, that sure as hell sounded final.

My brain skipped through possible solutions, backtracking and fast-forwarding through the information. It was only then I heard what she had said—*really* heard it.

"Wait—you have a brother? I thought you said you

didn't have any other family." I was pretty sure she'd said as much in our first conversation. I admit, I was good at detecting inconsistencies in stories. I'd told my fair share of them as a kid.

"You're assuming we speak. I haven't seen him or talked to him since I was six. I don't really count someone who left me to pretty much die as *family*."

Over a decade-long schism between them? It sounded like my family didn't have a monopoly on grudges after all. "Does he even know you're here?"

"Don't know, don't care."

She had a sibling and she didn't even want him. I would have given anything to get Carli back, and Tina just tosses her brother away. I couldn't help but hate her just a little in that moment, but I pushed past it. Clearly she had damage even I couldn't understand. Who was I to judge her logic?

"Your brother—" I finally spoke. "Maybe he can help?"

She snorted at the suggestion. "Killian? Yeah right. I'm sure he's been profiting off my living nightmare. Who do you think benefited from the money they sent my family all those years? He was an only child and probably loving it. Hell, he's probably the one who turned me in when I escaped—once the paychecks stopped coming. I'd bet anything he gave them my new name and told them how to find me. Nothing like handing your own sister over to sociopaths to line your pockets," she said with a sneer.

"Your brother would really do that to you?"

"I guarantee it."

"How do you even know this if you haven't spoken to him?"

She shrugged. "I heard things."

"From who?" I wasn't letting her off that easily.

"It doesn't matter. All I'm saying is that he's part of why I was forced into hiding. He never once came to my

THE ART OF FEAR

aid, never offered to help pay off whatever debt my father got into. If you ask me, I don't have a brother."

The vague details about her family relationships were really starting to piss me off. How did she expect me to help her when she was hiding every aspect of her life?

"Tina, if you haven't talked to him, maybe he doesn't know what's going on. You should at least see what he knows, see if he can help."

"Back off, Ari! Even if Killian did want to help, he's sixteen. What can he possibly do? If he's not already involved, I definitely don't want to drag him into it. He should be concerned about partying and finding a girlfriend, not rescuing his sex-slave sister."

Sixteen? He was just a boy, really. And at that age, probably just as helpless as Tina. "Sounds like you might still care for him ... a little," I ventured.

"Maybe I do. So what? The bastards may have turned me into a screwing machine, but they didn't steal my friggin' humanity." She started to sob quietly.

I wished I'd kept my mouth shut. I'd forgotten she'd just tried to kill herself and was in a psych ward. Not to mention she was a refugee from a sex-slave ring. The poor kid. I'd been through some shit, but it couldn't hold a candle to Tina/Sophia's story. I waited for the tension to drain out of the room before I spoke again.

"Do you have any other family?" I asked. "Someone I should call?"

"Well, there's my grandmother, Rosalita. She knows the basics of what's going on with my situation ... and about my dad. He was her son. She's kept tabs on everyone except me all these years. Luckily I found her contact info in his cell phone or else I would have lost touch with my whole family."

"Is she supportive?" I hated to ask. But it was a reasonable question, considering Tina's father and brother

99

had both thrown her to wolves.

"Yeah, she wanted to come see me. Reconnect. I figured once things calmed down I'd take her up on it."

"Well, I think now's the time," I suggested. "Maybe they'll let you out of here sooner if they know you're going to have ... company." I hoped breaking out of here sweetened the deal enough to get Tina to agree.

"I'll just tell them I don't have insurance."

"Ha! They won't be able to wheel you out of here fast enough."

"Alright, I'll call her and see if she's up for a visit."

The idea of a doting grandma watching over Tina lifted a corner of the blanket of stress weighing on me. But there was still so much more to worry about.

Even with the insinuated risk to my own life and the mountain of half-truths I'd need to trek through, I still wanted to help Tina. Maybe even *needed* to. I couldn't explain it if I tried, but helping her was helping me. Crazy, I know.

If there was ever a time when I felt a bludgeon to the head trying to knock some sense into me, it was now. I needed a purpose in life, and one was knocking. I couldn't save Carli. I couldn't save myself. But hell if I couldn't save Tina. Even if it cost me damn near everything. People like me didn't have shit to lose anyways.

Chapter 15
Rosalita

San Luis, Mexico
1997

The creamy white gown hung on Mercedes Estrada like water rippling down a bronze sculpture. A simple heart-shaped bodice held up by angel hair-thin straps flowed effortlessly into waves around her ankles. Gossamer dreams of the wedding feast, piles of gifts, and dancing the night into morning played on her ruby lips in a blissful smile. Toying with an upswept hairstyle, she spun playfully in front of the dusty mirror in Rosalita's bedroom, admiring the satin clinging to her curves.

"What do you think, Mrs. Alvarez—or can I call you *Madre* now? It's only a week until we're family."

Rosalita Alvarez offered a tight-lipped grin. "Yes, dear, a week away. You must be nervous, no?"

Mercedes's eyes flashed at Rosalita from the full-length mirror. "*Si*, I have butterflies in my stomach. But I adore your son. Josef's perfect, don't you agree?"

But Rosalita didn't agree. It was true that she'd begun to love Mercedes like a daughter years ago when she and Josef held hands for the first time as childhood sweethearts. Their early courtship was filled with carefree idylls that had warmed Rosalita's heart. Josef took

101

Mercedes for walks down their packed dirt street to the market where he treated her with Mazapan, a sweet crushed peanut confection, or a Pulparindo, whose medley of sweetness, saltiness, and chili pepper fire made her little rosebud mouth pucker most charmingly. Sometimes Rosalita would watch them playing on the rickety swing set in the backyard, matching each other's feats of daredevilry, and rejoice to see them stealing adolescent kisses mid flight.

Any mother would find such innocent demonstrations of affection endearing. Until that first sobering glimpse of reality. Rosalita knew the truth, saw the darkness peering from the corners, watched it unfold in a dangerous crescendo that would overtake the beauty of love and destroy everything in its wake.

Josef hung in the shadows, and Mercedes foolishly accompanied him.

It all started with a deception. A harmless lie. But it wasn't so harmless, was it?

He had broken into the neighbor's house and stolen their grocery money. None were the wiser about his involvement until Josef came home one day sporting flashy new sneakers. Shoes far beyond their means.

Where did you get those? Rosalita had asked him point-blank.

I found them, he snapped back.

But she knew. Money missing yesterday, fancy sneakers today.

Eduardo was no help, instead turning Rosalita's accusation against her, questioning her sanity ... yet again. And thus it was an unspoken secret between mother and son that neither would speak of again.

Little things like that throughout the years. Little things that kill your morality bit by bit. Little things that drag you into the mire of sin until it fills your lungs, suffocating you with evil. This was the path Rosalita now saw them on, but she dared not voice it.

Any union with Josef was lethal, but she was forbidden from saying as much, at her own peril. Her husband Eduardo would never abide any threat to the perpetuation of his genes. Within a year Mercedes would likely be birthing the first grandson, and to Eduardo, the promise of vigorous progeny was worth burying the secrets, the lies, the sinister companion that would haunt their family for generations to come.

Josef wasn't the only one cursed. The chicken was coming home to roost, and Mercedes was that chicken. A mad one at that.

It hadn't been all too obvious at the start. Small things, really. Rosalita noticed the lighthearted bickering between the young lovebirds but laughed it off as childish antics. Eventually harsh words were exchanged for heated fists on both ends, and the toxicity bled through in bruises and tears. It bubbled and popped under the surface, eventually erupting in off-again on-again relationship drama. The couple would drive each other away with their tempers, then Mercedes would lure Josef back with her *chocho—Dios, forgive me for my language.*

Discord. Seduction. It was the cycle they lived by. Certainly they would wear thin and part ways, Rosalita assumed. Until it didn't. Until the proposal.

Asking for his *abuela's* wedding ring, Josef had announced his plan to propose. Eduardo cheerfully clapped him on the back, praising his manhood. Rosalita, however, pleaded that they were too young, still needed to see the world before making such a big decision. And were they sure they were compatible?

"Aren't they too young?" Rosalita exclaimed over a dinner of *chimichangas* that evening, turning to Eduardo for aid in thwarting this nonsense.

"He's twenty-one, Mercedes is nineteen—they're hardly children. Certainly old enough to live on their own," Eduardo argued on his son's behalf.

One less mouth to feed—that was Eduardo's agenda.

"But the fighting. Love shouldn't be so ... violent," Rosalita had further tried to reason.

"Oh, Mama, we bicker. That's all. About stupid stuff," Josef said, underplaying the truth of it. "But we love each other deeply. We love, we fight. We're practically married already!" he laughed.

"There's nothing wrong with *pasión,* my boy—it's good for making babies," Eduardo had said with a mischievous wink, squeezing Josef's shoulder in approval.

"You don't think they're a bit aggressive with each other?" Rosalita had prodded.

"Enough!" Eduardo had turned on her, the word terse. "You know how you get when certain thoughts enter your head." He tapped her skull, referring to her paranoia that caused her to say and do things she'd later regret—things that he had threatened to hospitalize her for but relented upon her assurance she would behave. "Those are lovers' spats. Nothing to worry about, dear." But Rosalita was not so easily pacified. When their volcanic hatred eventually erupted, it would either kill their marriage, each other, or their future children. One way or another there would be victims.

These were the thoughts passing through Rosalita's mind as she sat on her bed watching her future daughter-in-law twirl like a fandango dancer, basking in prenuptial bliss. Try as she might to hide her doubts, the urge to speak them became overwhelming.

"Mercedes, you know I love you, yes?"

"*Ciertamente,*" she said, mid-spin, then waltzed to Rosalita and hugged her. "You're the mother I always wanted. If only my mother were alive to see this day, she would be so happy. But at least I have you."

"Yes, dear, you do have me. And you trust that I'll always be honest with you, yes?" She grasped Mercedes's hands in a gesture of affection, hoping it would show her sincerity.

"Of course." Mercedes sat on the bed next to her, eyeing her with mingled curiosity and wariness.

"Then I must speak truthfully with you now."

"Okay ..." Mercedes sounded doubtful.

"I fear for your marriage to my son. While I care for you both, it is not a healthy relationship. No mother wants to watch her child enter into a destructive relationship. You both have too much brokenness to heal together. Your loss of your mother, and your father the way he is ..."

She didn't want to touch on the inescapable facts of Mercedes's father's abusive behavior or his excessive drinking. Somehow they would eventually poison everything Mercedes touched—including Josef and any children they had.

"And then Josef isn't without his issues, as you know. His urges and anger issues ..."

Daring not to say more, Rosalita left it at that. Certainly Mercedes was familiar with Josef's outbursts—and her instigation of them. Couldn't the girl see just how ill fated their marriage was?

"I know we're both flawed, but we love each other. We can work through whatever problems we face. I wish you could accept that. Eduardo has. Why haven't you?"

"Eduardo wants Josef out of the house. That's his motivation for his decision. I actually care what happens to you both—that you both find happiness. Do you think you and Josef can give that to each other?"

Silence reigned for several moments, until Mercedes lifted her chin and narrowed her eyes. Then standing above Rosalita, she looked down on her with a face twisted into ugliness by contempt.

"Mrs. Alvarez, I'm only going to warn you once. Do not attempt to sabotage our wedding or else you will regret it. I would hate for your husband and Josef to hear about your ravings and delusions in graphic detail. We both know what will happen to you if you can't keep your sanity in check."

The question of her sanity was the last thing Rosalita wanted to revisit.

If they wanted misery, that's what they'd get.

She could be sure of that.

Flipping her hands up, she rose, shaking her head. "You win. I've said my piece. No need to threaten me with hospitalization or medicine or treatments. It's your funeral. Go ahead, take him. Mark my words: You may come to find that *having* him is not so pleasant a thing as *wanting* him!"

With that she stormed out of the room, bustling toward the kitchen where she needed to busy her hands with preparing *pollo con arroz* for dinner.

To hell with them all, she fumed as she wiped down her prep table. *Let them ruin each other. I just hope I can protect my grandbabies from the nightmare they're sure to be born into.*

And that's the moment when Rosalita Alvarez wished she had never brought baby Josef back to life.

Chapter 16

Ari

Nine days until dead

The vacuum of silence after my announcement popped like a bubble as the questions pelted me:

"Is Tina still on suicide watch?"

"Is she recovering okay?"

"Does she need anything?"

"How long will she be in the hospital?"

"How can we help?"

The floodgates were opened, and the compassion was pouring in. It was unreal, unexpected.

It wasn't an easy discovery, though.

Earlier that morning, dawn had tucked away the night's black edges, awakening me next to Tina's hospital bed. Rubbing sleep from my eyes, I had suddenly remembered the group meeting today. And whether Tina believed it or not—and she certainly did not—she needed help. She needed support. Two things I had never experienced, but something told me the suicide support group was different from the callous world I was used to. I needed to share, yearned to break free from yet another secret that held me captive.

So after arguing with Tina that it was the right thing to do, that it must be done, I stood before the group and explained in brief detail that Tina had attempted suicide the night before and needed their prayers. No one asked why; they didn't need to.

There often wasn't a *why* worth dying for. Sometimes it was an abundance of whys. Sometimes it was the lack of why that was reason enough. The group didn't ask, and I didn't tell. And it was a relief.

"She'll be under observation for a few days, but it's for the best," I explained. "And if you want to visit her, she'd appreciate it. For those of you who don't know what it's like after a suicide attempt, it's awful. It's lonely and yet invasive. It's demeaning and humiliating. All in all, it just sucks a bag of dicks. Any emotional support you can offer in person would be awesome. Thanks, guys."

A gaggle of voices planned out who would visit which day until it was time to head home. Tina would scold me later about the horde of visitors, but I knew she'd be genuinely glad to see them, no matter how many cuss words she lobbed at me.

Exhausted from today's events and the stabbing pinched nerve in my neck from sleeping crookedly in a hospital chair all night, I stifled a yawn as I began folding chairs. Mid-yawn, a warm hand rested on my shoulder. I turned as Tristan pulled the metal chair from my fingers, and he gestured for me to let go.

"You look like you could use a break," he said, then carefully added, "And maybe a coffee after this?"

"More like a massage and a nap," I said, smiling grimly.

"Long day, huh?"

"Yeah, too much emotion per hour today. Don't know how other chicks do it. I'm spent."

"Well, maybe some food will recharge you ... or at least help you sleep better."

I knew something that would help me sleep better tonight. I heard a hum come out of my mouth, as if I was

108

actually considering it.

"What if I brought you dinner to your place tonight? Then you can eat and crash." As if that wasn't convincing enough, he topped it with an extra dose of charm. "C'mon, give a guy a chance to do something nice for a pretty girl."

The offer was out there, hanging in limbo, waiting to be caught. And I wanted desperately to take it. Despite my longing for bed, I couldn't turn this down. An attractive, thoughtful guy interested in *me*? It was revolutionary getting something more than a stranger's whistle or a pat on the ass. But what did I really know about Tristan Cox? Nothing other than that he made skinny jeans look good. He could be a criminal in a hot guy's clothing. And suicide survivors weren't exactly known for being levelheaded and "normal."

Then I thought back over the two years I'd lived in my apartment. Not once had I invited a guy to my place. How was it even possible that at age twenty-four, I had yet to entertain a male in my home? Fear of commitment and a stubborn independent streak had turned me into a perennial wallflower in the dance of life. I skulked through my empty evenings and vacant social life while other girls my age were being wined and dined. It was time I joined in the fun—and damn the anxiety to hell. But dating someone from my support group ... something warned me that it was a big no-no and only headed for heartbreak.

Clearly sensing my hesitation, Tristan quickly added, "Not a date. Just food. We all gotta eat, right? If it makes you feel better, I'll leave your food on the porch, knock, and then run away."

It seemed innocent enough ... for now. At least until I could figure out the risks of getting involved with Tristan, and what kind of demons I'd eventually unearth.

"Um, okay, yeah, that sounds good," I agreed, barely able to push the words out. "But no funny business, got it?"

He laughed, and only after I realized I sounded like an old fart did I join in.

Despite Tristan's casual coolness, my nerves were sizzling in frenzied panic, but I had to keep them at bay. I hated the idea of mood stabilizers—or "Mommy's candy" as I remember my mother calling them—but when my anxiety crept into every corner of my life, ruining every good moment that I stumbled upon, a Xanax sounded pretty damn good.

"What're you in the mood for?" Tristan asked.

Drugs, I thought to myself.

"Options include Italian, Greek, Chinese, or burgers."

In typical girl fashion, I knew I wouldn't be able to eat a bite in front of a hot guy, and my appetite would be kaput the second Tristan set foot in my apartment, so it was better to waste cheap food than good food.

"How about burgers? Is that okay with you?"

"Sure thing. Just give me your address and we'll meet at your place after I pick up the food."

After we exchanged information, I noticed Mia Germaine, one of the women in our group, idling nearby, clearly waiting to speak to me. I told Tristan I'd see him in a bit and headed over to Mia.

"Hey, Mia. How are you?"

"I'm doing a lot better each day, thanks. I'm moving past the pain. Finally getting my life back on track after everything."

I remembered vague details about her past year— particularly her part in catching the "Triangle Terror" serial killer that plagued our humble town of Durham with a string of murders.[1] Knowing that Mia was behind the scenes of a major news event was cool ... in a horrifying,

---

[1] See *A Secondhand Life* by Pamela Crane at
http://www.pamelacrane.com

scary way. Amid avenging several murdered young girls, Mia nearly lost the love of her life, her job, and her friends as she faced down a killer. She redefined stress for me. But on top of all that, to lose someone you care about to suicide … I wondered how she was still standing. I doubted I would be.

"I'm glad to hear you're recovering. If you ever need anything, let me know." And I meant it.

"Well, I'm actually here to offer *you* something."

"Me?" I wondered aloud. I never asked for anything. I made it a point not to.

"Earlier you were talking about having memories about your sister's death. That isn't unlike what I experienced—hazy memories of events, but too hazy to make sense of. Does that sound right?"

I nodded feverishly. Finally someone who understood. "Yeah, exactly like what I've been having."

"So, I know this will sound crazy," Mia began, and I could see her blushing with embarrassment, "but I went to a dream psychologist who helped me immensely. Dr. Avella Weaver. She's not some voodoo psychic type of person. She's an actual doctor," Mia added hastily.

"Huh," I mumbled, curious but skeptical.

"Dr. Weaver was able to help me focus on the details of my dreams and break through the haze to see what was happening. It really helped clear things up for me, get me answers. I just thought I'd mention it in case you didn't know where to turn."

"Hell, I'd be willing to try anything at this point. Thanks, Mia."

"No problem. I hope you get some answers."

As I headed home for my non-date with Tristan, I reflected on what had become of me. My brokenness. My crippling anxiety. My loneliness. I couldn't put together the puzzle of events that got me here, but here I was. Was it my part in Carli's death? Was it my parents' fueled anger toward me? Or the foster homes? Juvie? Or the lack of healthy relationships? Where was the breaking point when I went from whole to shattered?

I felt like a riddle I couldn't solve.

But today I was proven wrong about one thing. I wasn't alone. I had support. I had a whole room of people who genuinely cared, who were reaching out to me. I felt like I had exchanged my bitterness at the world for the balm of friendship. They were my lighthouse in the storm—appearing out of the fog when I needed them. When Tina needed them.

Closing in on my apartment, I barely remembered to breathe as my stomach turned somersaults. Tristan would be arriving at any moment. With his effortless cool. His smoldering sexiness. The way he slipped into my skull, overpowering my thoughts and emotions—dammit, he was like a bad drug I should stay the hell away from. But I wanted him. Wanted to do unspeakable things to him. And him to me.

Tonight I would put my heart all in. Let myself fall.

As I pulled into the parking lot, my cell phone rang, showing Tristan's name.

I knew when I saw it that he wasn't lost. He wasn't calling to reconfirm the menu. Before I picked up the phone, I already determined there was no point trying to win at life. I was destined to lose.

Sure enough, I hung up two minutes later after his mysterious cancellation due to "something at work coming up" and a dozen apologies and promises to make it up to me. As fragile as my heart felt at the postponed non-date, I realized I had no idea what "work" entailed. Maybe I didn't want to know. He was a virtual stranger. So why did I feel so shattered?

I was tired of broken promises, being left behind,

becoming forgotten. Screw him.

Logically it shouldn't have been a big deal. He cancelled, shit happens. No biggie. But to me it was a biggie. I had gotten excited about it. I shouldn't have. I should have said no in the first place. *No* is stoic. *No* is impenetrable. *No* is tough. *I* am tough.

That's what I needed to be—cold to the world.

Tristan got his chance and blew it. He was officially on my shit list.

Chapter 17
Ari

April 2002

The accident wasn't the hardest part of losing Carli. After the car tossed her like a Raggedy Ann doll across the yard, the ensuing minutes had been a whirlwind of activity, of lingering hope that she'd make it through. The exact time when they confirmed her death wasn't the hardest part either. I was too much in shock for it to register. I hung on a dream. Even the funeral I managed to get through, open casket and all, because I could see her, talk to her, plead with her not to leave me. She was still here, among us.

Now it's the night after Carli's funeral—and this is the hardest part of losing my sister.

The silence.

My universe shifts.

The sweet contemplation of bygone hide-and-seek games mixed with morbid thoughts of her dresser, her toys, our memories collecting dust. Dust that she is now part and parcel of.

With her body buried beneath six feet of dirt, down with her went any chance that it had all been a nightmare I would wake up from. As I lay in bed, I watch frames from the past week flip by, like snippets from a filmstrip. I rehash every tear-stained moment of the funeral, the casket placed stoically up front beside a picture of my smiling *dead sister, the sobbing congregation, the praiseworthy eulogy that can't bring my sister back, the procession, the cars in a sad slow line to the cemetery, the rain pelting me as I watch them lower her in, the flowers falling on her, the salty tears mixed with raindrops, the firm grip of my parents dragging me away.*

I thought I would wake up to find it was all a bad dream, but it's real. And it's my fault.

Our bedroom—no, my bedroom—decorated in Pepto-Bismol pink ruffled curtains and flower petal bedding, is anything but cheerful now. Carli's matching twin bed is barren, the covers stiff, as if mourning her. My room has become a mausoleum where my fond memories have gone to die.

A voice like a foghorn breaks through my foggy thoughts. It travels down the hallway, through my open door. It's Dad yelling at Mom. I can tell they're in their bedroom with the door open.

"It's time we come clean, Winnie. It's just not worth hiding anymore."

"Are you serious? You would go to jail, Burt." Mom's shrill voice pierces my eardrums like a siren. "Then how would I pay the bills? And Ari—would you expect me to raise her on my own? No, you know as well as I do that turning yourself in isn't the answer."

"So instead you want our daughter to take the fall?" Dad thunders.

"Yes, because she's to blame. She was supposed to take care of her sister, but I saw them fighting. I know Ari pushed Carli into that oncoming car."

My heart spasms. Mom's words shred the muscles of my heart as I taste my failure as a sister, a daughter, a human being.

"You really believe Ari caused this? You don't think it has anything to do with my ... extracurricular activities?"

By now Dad's words become softer, but they're still audible between the mere feet separating our rooms.

"The whole thing was an accident, Burt, not someone out to send you a message. You're getting paranoid. Just stick to the plan and let things smooth over." When Mom insists something, we listen. Even Dad knows not to argue.

"Fine. But promise me you won't let Ari get caught up in this."

I don't hear Mom's reply as their door slams shut, but I already know my head is on the chopping block as far as she's concerned. It always has been.

Each breath becomes more strained, like a fish on the shore, gasping for life. I won't be sleeping tonight, so I sit up in bed, gasping, and look out the window to center myself. I'm surprised to find the pink blush of morning kissing the landscape awake. Night's starry party is over, until it's time to come back out and play.

I catch a puff of oxygen, hold it in, and release. Soon the panic wanes like the tide going out. I lay back down and curl up under the covers—a lost little girl in a big bad world. I wonder if I can sleep the rest of my life away and resolve to try ...

Chapter 18
Rosalita

Rosalita Alvarez felt like death warmed over. Her neck ached from the stiff, last-minute trip to Durham, North Carolina—the last place she should be right now. Her feet were swollen with what felt like miles worth of walking from the Greyhound station through the dark streets, searching for a bus line that was still running and would take her to the nameless cheap motel with several slamming one-star reviews she'd found online. After dropping off her luggage, she Ubered her way to Duke Hospital and its labyrinthian stairwells—of course the elevator would be out of order when she needed it most—and at last she now wandered the halls in search of her granddaughter. She was exhausted, irritable, and worried. All she wanted was her bed.

When she finally found room 402, she peeked around the door and saw a girl—no, a *young woman*—watching a home improvement show on a television perched high in the corner. Disheveled spikes of hair sprung up like a cave full of stalagmites. A tattoo crept out from under the neckline of her sagging hospital gown—a butterfly, perhaps? Was her little granddaughter already grown up? She couldn't be.

In her mind, she'd always be the six-year-old, curly-haired mischief-maker she'd never gotten to say goodbye to.

"Sophia?" she asked as she entered. The lights were dim, shrouding the bedridden patient in a subtle gray. Her steps were tentative, uncertain that she had arrived at the right room.

The girl turned at Rosalita's voice.

"*Abuela!*" Tina shrieked, arms outstretched for a hug.

Rosalita scurried to her, drawing Tina to her pillowy bosom. How she had craved cradling a child to her chest!

"Look at you," she exclaimed, holding Tina out as she examined her with a doctor's scrutiny. Despite the passage of years, time hadn't stolen their familial bond. Blood never forgets. "You're skin and bones, Sophia! I will get you some *real* food, yes?"

"No, I'm fine. Sit, please. I'm so glad to see you." Tina patted a chair next to the bed. "I go by Tina now, by the way."

"Tina? Why? Is it because of those ... *monsters* who took you?"

There was no other word to describe them.

Tina shook her head. Clearly there were details between the lines that Rosalita sensed were best unspoken. Horrors that she couldn't—and shouldn't—imagine.

Rosalita knew a little something about horrors. Their persistent vengeance. Their unwavering grip. Even now her decades-old nightmare taunted her. The *splosh splosh splosh* of water. Then an eerie nothing. A panicked rush of limbs. Then numbness slipping over her, slithering down her body, eating her whole. The unforgiveable sin was born. She shook away the memory.

"Long story, *abuela*. Another time. How was your trip?"

"*Asi asi.* I don't want to talk about me, though. You're in a hospital and the reason why worries me." On the way here Rosalita had vowed to keep conversation pleasant, but there was nothing cheery about the situation. A niggling worry followed her to Durham: Was Sophia's plight her fault? Was Sophia's life a punishment for Rosalita's past? With bony fingers the skeleton she had buried again and again continued to claw its way out of a mound of loose earth.

Seeing her only granddaughter like this, knowing she had tried to kill herself, even God Himself couldn't stop the outpouring of concern. It was a grandmother's duty to tend to wounds.

"You tried to hurt yourself. Is this because of your father?" Her nurturing tone grew stern at the mention of Josef.

"No, it was not because of him," Tina insisted.

"Because if it was, he's not worth it. He got what was coming to him."

"*Abuela!*" Tina chided. "That's your son. Certainly you don't feel that way about him."

"And you don't—just because he's your father? If you even want to call him that. A man who sold you as a child. A man that set your value at a meager few hundred pesos and cashed in on your suffering year after year. A man who—"

"That's enough!" Tina cut in. "I don't want to talk about him anymore." A strained silence passed before Tina spoke again. "Have you heard from Killian?"

"Nothing more than a brief update. He's as bad as your father. Won't return my calls. You know he lives here in Durham, don't you?"

"I didn't know that for sure, but I suspected it. Why hasn't he tried to contact me?"

"Because he's selfish and he doesn't value family. He was living with your father for a little while, so I can only imagine the bad influence Josef had on the boy. I fear he's going to end up just like him."

From the moment of Killian's birth the resemblance

hadn't escaped Rosalita's attention. They shared the same brooding intensity and identical swaths of curls framing handsome faces. But what neighbors and friends counted as mischief in their eyes, Rosalita recognized as sinister intent. She saw it corrupt and destroy her own son, but how could she rescue her grandson from the same doom? Was it too late for his salvation?

"You can't trust Killian, dear," Rosalita warned, patting Tina's hand until her palm came to a rest on top. "Keep your distance. I don't know if he had anything to do with your father's death, but I wouldn't put it past him. The boy was hung up on fame and fortune, and with greed as a guide, he's capable of just about anything."

Rosalita imagined Josef as the disgruntled ferryman Charon transporting Killian's soul deeper into the Underworld with steady paddles across the River Styx. It wasn't stretching the imagination far enough.

Tina sat silent, their hands a motionless connection. As Rosalita observed her, a sense of dread permeated the room. She saw her granddaughter's unspoken pain—the tremble of her lips, the vacancy of her eyes, the tension in her limbs. Rosalita hoped she wasn't broken beyond repair.

Watching her granddaughter hide her pain, Rosalita was reminded of her own past. Her own buried secrets that kept uprooting from her psyche, tormenting her on a whim. There was no escaping one's mind—especially when it was so damaged.

The evening passed in pleasant chitchat, growing into a comfortable familiarity as they watched a group of attractive *gringo* handymen convert a back porch into a palace on TV. A home repair show Rosalita had never seen, nor cared to see again. They only looked up when a young woman walked in, blond ponytail swaying, Chiclet-white teeth greeting them.

"Hey, Tina. Oh, you have a visitor. I just wanted to drop off the best damn chocolate-peanut butter milkshake you'll ever have—from Cookout. I can come back tomorrow." The girl inched closer, setting a tall Styrofoam cup down on the rolling food tray.

"Thanks, but don't leave, Ari. This is my *abuela*—my grandma, that is. Come meet her." Tina reached out for the girl, as if tugging an invisible rope between them. "*Abuela*, this is Ari Wilburn, a friend who's been taking care of me since Dad's death."

"Any friend of Tina's is a friend of mine," Rosalita said, sidestepping Ari's outstretched hand in favor of a hug instead. She'd always been a hugger among a family of non-huggers, and she loved that her touchy-feely nature drove them nuts. "Thank you for taking care of my *nieta* during this difficult time. If I wasn't staying in a motel you know I'd insist on her staying with me."

"I'm happy to have her once she's out of here," Ari said. "And if you need a place to stay, we can make room at my place. There's no reason you should be staying in a motel."

"Oh, that's nice of you to offer, but I'm comfortable where I'm at. It's not too far from here—out on 98."

"If you change your mind, I'll be glad to have you. I've grown close to your granddaughter these past few days."

"At least she has someone looking after her until she's well enough to be back on her own. Losing her father—my son ... well, I'm just glad she got to say her goodbyes before he died. I wish I'd had the same opportunity. Though I would have given him a piece of my mind, so maybe he's better off this way."

Ari stood there with a quizzical cock of her head. "Huh, I thought you didn't get to say goodbye, Tina." The challenge in her tone was crystal clear.

"Did I say that?" Tina asked, her voice wavering. "I

must have misspoke. It was all kind of a blur, you know."

"When did you see him?" Ari probed.

"You saw him the day he died, didn't you?" Rosalita interjected. "At least that's what you told me."

Obviously it was the wrong thing to say as Rosalita caught a glare from Tina. Meanwhile, Ari stared at her like a laser beam marking its target.

"Yes, I saw him before he died," Tina caved with a sigh.

"Wait, let me get this straight. You talked to him before he died. Then you found him dead and called the cops. It sounds awfully suspicious, Tina."

Rosalita's eyebrows shot up. "Tina, what is she talking about? Is this true?"

"I swear it's not what it looks like," Tina contended.

"Then why the hell did you lie to me—*again*? Why cover it up?" Ari demanded.

Tina's breaths sounded weighty, as if the truth was heaped upon her chest. "Isn't it obvious? I was the last one who saw him alive. That would make me a prime suspect. And I'm sorry I didn't tell you from the start. I needed to confront him about why he sold me. Why I was so worthless to him."

By now tears were trickling down Tina's cheeks, drawing Rosalita in to offer comfort. It didn't matter to her why she lied. All that mattered was that Josef was dead and gone.

"I'm sorry, I don't mean to press," Ari soothed. "I just don't understand why you felt you had to lie. If you didn't do it, there's nothing to hide."

"Oh, like you didn't hide from me what happened to your sister," Tina muttered.

Ari's face crumpled, like she'd been slapped. "Maybe I should go."

"Please ... don't!" Tina's hand shot out, grabbing Ari's wrist. "I'm sorry. I don't know why I said that. And I don't know why I hid it from you. I guess when I later found him dead I was afraid to tell the cops about seeing him. I didn't want them to think I had something to do with his death. So I just stuck with the same story for everyone."

"Even me—after I tried to help you?" Ari sounded wounded. "It makes me wonder if ... never mind. I just wish you'd been honest with me. I have a hard enough time trusting people as it is. Being lied to doesn't make it any easier for me."

"I know. I know because trust doesn't come easy for me either. We're alike, you know." Tina clumsily pulled Ari toward her into a hug. "You know what he told me? He said he loved me, that he never meant to hurt me, but that they were broke—the brink of starvation broke—and this guy assured him I was being cared for. Do you think that's the truth—that my dad cared about me?"

"I don't know what the hell to believe anymore," Ari whispered, "but I'd like to believe it."

From where Rosalita stood, it didn't sound like the son she knew. But like an agreeable grandmother, and from years of practice, for now she'd keep her tongue in check.

"Look," Ari said, abruptly pulling back, "I'll let you two catch up. I gotta get my ass to an appointment. I just wanted to check in on you. It was nice meeting you, Mrs. Alvarez."

"Nice meeting you, dear."

Ari waved a quick goodbye and left, the air softly rustling the curtains as the door swept shut behind her.

In Ari's absence was a calm as the strain of tension drained. Rosalita didn't dislike Tina's friend, but she didn't like her either. Something about the girl's brusque manner and emotional demands on Tina grated on her. And why was she so inquisitive about her family's affairs?

Rosalita Alvarez never took to nosey people sniffing around her family's business. There were lines—and Ari

123

was crossing a bold one.

In what world was it unfair for Tina to keep her demons under wraps? And why was some fast friend trying so hard to exorcise them? Was Tina's life really any of Ari's concern? She wasn't family.

Family knew how to keep secrets.

Ari shouldn't have been invited in.

"You better keep track of your stories, *Tina*," Rosalita warned, "or else the lies are going to take you down with your father."

Chapter 19
Ari

Eight days until dead

After my visit with Tina at the hospital the night before, I felt my brain splitting at its hem. Why the hell had she lied—twice now—about her father? First she hadn't seen him at all. Then she saw him postmortem. Now she spoke to him? There was no escaping the possibility that she had something to do with his death. The motive was more than enough to push a girl over the edge. Then the lie—make it a double—on top of it aroused suspicion. Tina's insistence to the cops that it was murder, not a suicide, was her only solid defense, as far as I was concerned. No one would purposefully dig her own grave. No one in her right mind, at least.

Shaking my mind off this track, I glanced down at my GPS. I had taken Mia Germaine's advice and called Dr. Avella Weaver to make an appointment. While the whole idea of dream therapy sounded like a crock of shit from a *Ghost Whisperer* episode, Mia swore by her results. Anything was worth trying once.

When my GPS directed me between an antique shop and an upscale restaurant in downtown Hillsborough, I found a nondescript door with a brass plaque bearing Dr. Avella Weaver's name. A bell chimed with a retro-sounding *ding-dong* as I entered an office teeming with unusual knickknacks and an overpowering perfume of incense.

Sculptures of various exotic animals tempted me to knock them over—a compulsion toward chaos that I'd struggled with since childhood. The atmosphere felt mystical, like I was about to meet magic for the first time. What was I getting myself into?

The vibrant fuchsia and teal fabric chairs caught my eye, and I wondered where she bought them. Rather than sit and wait, I perused the abstract artwork on the walls, admiring the woman's taste. It certainly lacked the usual sterility doctor's offices were known for.

A moment later a woman in a purple silk dress appeared around the corner, her curly gray hair cut boy short—a "mom cut," I called it.

"You must be Ari?"

"That's me."

She offered her hand and I shook it, her grip surprisingly firm despite its boniness.

"It's wonderful to meet you. I'm Avella. If you'll follow me, we can get started."

I trailed her down a hallway with wooden tribal masks hanging on the walls, and my thoughts immediately went to Tina hiding behind her lies. I couldn't help but feel betrayed.

At the end of the hallway we entered a candle-lit room where she pointed me to a burgundy sofa across from two beige chairs. Ocean waves crashed in the background, with an occasional sharp peal of a seagull—an ambient soundscape piped in from unseen speakers.

"Have a seat over there and I'll join you in a moment."

I sat on the sofa next to an end table holding more carved animal figures. I picked up a whimsical giraffe and toyed with it, keeping my compulsive fingers busy.

"I have coffee, tea, water, and juice," she offered, returning from the kitchenette.

"Coffee, thanks," I answered. She set down a tray with

a steaming pot of coffee and water, creamer, and sugar packets on a beautiful little credenza. I dumped a handful of sugars in the mug she handed me, then added the coffee and creamer until it was a milky brown.

After steeping herself a cup of tea, she sat across from me.

"So," she began after a sip, "tell me about yourself. What brings you here today?"

"A friend referred me—Mia Germaine?"

Avella nodded enthusiastically. "Oh yes, Mia. I'll have to thank her. So you're friends?"

"Yeah, I guess we are." I was still smarting from the recent snag in my budding friendship with Tina, but I figured sharing the same psychiatrist with Mia counted toward intimacy.

"And why did Mia refer you?" Avella set her teacup down and folded her hands on her lap.

"I've been having dreams about something that happened when I was a child—a hit-and-run that killed my sister. For years I blamed myself for her death, but lately I have questions about what actually happened. I want answers. I want to know if there's more than what I vaguely remember."

"You've come to the right place. And I want to reiterate that this is a safe place, and everything we discuss is confidential." Avella patted my leg and smiled warmly.

There was a trustworthy grandmotherly appeal to her. "Thanks. I appreciate that."

Avella leaned forward, placing her chin on her hands, intent on watching me. I felt oddly at ease.

"To begin, tell me what you remember about the accident."

In the past I had always clenched up when therapists burrowed for information. I wasn't trying to be difficult; I simply couldn't break through my own barriers to access the memories. They had become untouchable to everyone but me. But lately I had reached a breaking point, and the past was endlessly flooding my psyche. Closing my eyes, I just needed to direct the flow toward Avella.

"I remember having a fight with Carli about a Barbie earlier that morning. Then we headed outside to play and I think I pushed her into the street. And just as I did that a car drove by, hitting her. I was screaming for help and my mom came out. After that, I don't remember much."

I opened my eyes to find her tender smile and gentle gaze.

"Very good, Ari. I think you're ready to find those answers you seek. First I need to know what details you're looking for from the memory. I want to attempt to recreate the event with you so that we can siphon out what we need."

"I don't really know what I'm looking for. Maybe the car that hit her? We never found her killer, but if I knew what the vehicle looked like, I could possibly find the driver."

She nodded encouragingly. "Perfect. That's our focus—the car. So, here's what I'm going to do. We're going to practice what's called wake induced lucid dreaming. It's going to feel like a dream, but you'll be awake and can control it. I'm going to help you recreate each detail until we can see the vehicle. Does that sound good?"

"Yep."

She stood and guided me to lay back on the sofa, resting my head on a velvet down-filled pillow.

"Close your eyes and breathe in ... and out. In ... and out." Her voice was meditative above me, like an angel speaking down through the clouds. The relaxing sounds of crashing waves and chirping birds took me in their embrace.

The melody of her words continued. "Imagine yourself

at home in your bed. Allow yourself to surrender to sleep, but as your body relaxes, your mind will stay alert."

She talked me through releasing my body and embracing my subconscious awareness. I felt myself melting into her words. "As you inhale and exhale, you'll begin to feel your limbs grow heavy and your mind chatter will fade. Allow the sound of my voice to transport you into a state of tranquility."

As I felt myself being swept into a deeper state of mental and physical relaxation, I noticed a subtle hovering sensation. My body drifted along freely, as if timeless and unguarded.

"I want you to empty your mind and gaze into the blackness. If a thought comes into your mind, don't focus on it. Allow it to pass. You may start to feel like your body is softening, or floating. As you soar, think of the dreamscape you want to envision. Detach yourself from the real world and visualize yourself stepping into your dream state—your past. The day of the accident."

The darkness enveloped me, its weight almost suffocating, until colors started filling in the blackness. The swirling patterns began to hypnotize me, drawing my awareness away from Avella, from her office, from Tina, from the present.

"Imagine your childhood home. You're looking down on it, hovering above that day. Now stop and descend into the front yard. Visualize your sister."

With her prompting, my flesh numbly sank into the sofa while my mental state let go. Soon my internal dream world evolved into what felt like a tangible place.

I heard Avella's voice resume, distant now, remote. "The scenery ... explore it. Imagine the grass under your feet. Imagine the open sky. What do you smell?"

The more I let go of my current reality, the more I submerged into the alternate one, instead of viewing it from above. Once I dropped out of my lucid state, I felt a vibration, like electricity pulsing through me, its static drowning out Avella's words. Then I found myself in my old front yard, and Carli was playing just outside of arm's reach. The smell of freshly mowed grass filled my nostrils as I heard the mechanical growl of a neighbor's lawnmower.

"You are playing with your sister. Visualize each moment. What do you see?" Avella's soft voice broke through, conjuring up a more vivid Carli, our bickering. But I didn't push her into the street. Instead I tapped her and fled, teasing her into a game of tag. Then I heard the squeal of tires and a spongy *thump*—but Carli was still standing, chasing me. The sound was from the front tires riding up over the curb, then chewing up our yard.

Then another sound, deeper this time—two thuds, one after the other, as the front bumper hit Carli, and Carli hit the ground. I ran to Carli, hearing only my own screams drowning out the car's getaway as it smacked back down on the asphalt road before speeding away.

"Can you see the vehicle, Ari?"

I looked up and watched it drive away, a burnt orange hatchback. Like a gaping mouth, the oversized rear window reached from the roof to the bumper in my child's-eye view, the two rectangular brake lights blinking at me.

"I see it," I mumbled.

But the sequence of events faltered, and from the front door I viewed my mother huddled beside Carli while my father hobbled down the porch steps toward them, his limping figure blurring out of focus.

In a tidy instant the dreamscape faded, and I was back in Avella's office staring at the ceiling. Finally I found what I'd been searching for.

And then some.

I got a mental picture of the car, but why the hell was

my father limping?

Chapter 20

Ari

Eight days until dead

Since the advent of smartphones, tablets, and e-readers, I wondered if people even used libraries anymore. I hadn't stepped foot in one in ... well, shit, ever. Not being the most studious kid in the world, my local library served solely as a brick shield from windy drafts so that I could light whatever off-brand cigarette I was smoking at the time during my adolescence.

But when my Google search for information took me in circles, and I couldn't access the local paper archives without a paid subscription, I figured it was time to see what all the library hype was about.

The Durham County Library's aisles were pretty well marked, enough so that I could avoid talking to the grinning bald man at the help desk whose eyes followed me behind his large wire-rimmed glasses, like two fish inside a fishbowl. The way the frames slid down his oily nose made me think of sweat, and sweaty old men made me think of ... well, gagging.

"Can I help you?" he nearly yelled to me across the room in a nasally voice.

I smiled stiffly, giving him a thumbs-up that I was fine. *And please, please don't ogle me like that anymore.*

After wandering between floor-to-ceiling bookshelves packed with every subject I could imagine, I meandered to the front left corner of the building where a line of windows led into a separate room with the word ARCHIVES on it.

The door clicked shut behind me, sealing out the tap of fingers on keyboards and the whispers of huddled students presumably talking about their history project research. I knew the truth—that high school romance was in the air.

Upon entering the glass room full of periodicals, I ran my gaze along the spines of vertically arranged bound volumes until I came to *THE NEWS AND OBSERVER*—APRIL 2002. Sliding it off the shelf, I set it on the table and flipped until I came to April 9 edition—the day after the accident.

It was a little disappointing, to say the least, that my sister's death did not make the front page. No, the article took up just four column inches at the bottom right of page A-8—easily overlooked next to the newspaper's fold; a tacky half-page ad for a tire company dominated the page. A child dies and she doesn't even get decent news placement.

I read the article, sickened by how short it was—much like Carli's life:

EIGHT-YEAR-OLD DURHAM GIRL VICTIM OF LETHAL HIT-AND-RUN

Durham, NC

Carli Wilburn, age 8, died Monday morning after a vehicle hit her while she was playing in her front yard with her sister at 22 Pinewood Road. Her father and mother, Burt and Winnie Wilburn, called paramedics after an unidentified car crushed Carli, causing a severe head wound and internal bleeding. Paramedics transported the youth to Durham Regional Hospital where she was pronounced dead on arrival due to her injuries.

Police investigators are currently searching for information on the make and model of the car that might lead to the apprehension of the driver.

Carli was a student at Holt Elementary, which her sister also attends. A memorial will be held April 11 at 10:00 a.m. at Cornerstone Bible Church on Guess Road.

A picture of my old stomping ground, captured in the minutes after we had already headed to the hospital, accompanied the article, showing crime scene investigators already processing evidence, and several knots of gawkers. The patch of grass where I last saw my sister alive. The tire tracks left subtle impressions in the dirt, not deep trenches. A rear-wheel drive car, maybe? My eyes traveled to the maple tree mere feet from where Carli was thrown. I looked closer, as if the image was one of those optical illusions that would pop out a clue in 3D.

A skidmark stretched up across the curb, but at an odd angle. Almost perpendicular. If it had been a drunk driver mindlessly swerving off the road, it should have been almost parallel to the curb. But this was clearly deliberately aimed. And if that was the case ... was it possible I had nothing to do with Carli getting hit? Was Carli a *target*? And if so, why?

After folding the volume back up and returning it to its shelf, I needed a drive. Some air. And someone to talk to. I dialed Tina, but I ended up in her voicemail, leaving nothing but a hang-up. There was no one else ... unless ... no, I couldn't. I wouldn't.

And then I'd be damned if I did.

Fingers have a mind of their own sometimes. It happens when you're drunk dialing. It happens when you're emotional in the middle of the night eating from a tub of ice cream watching a sappy movie. It even happens when you're bored out of your mind. In my case, it was happening in a moment of desperation.

I dialed Tristan up, and to my embarrassment, he answered.

"Hey, Ari." His voice sounded sheepish or freshly woken—I wasn't sure which.

"Hey, Tristan. I was wondering what you were doing right now."

He paused. "Uhhh … hanging out with you, I hope?"

"Good answer. Mind if I pick you up and we go for a drive?"

"I don't know. Last time I agreed to something like that, I ended up on the side of a back road in Oxford with no pants on. How do I know I can trust you? How do I know my virtue will be secure in your hands, or that you don't have some kind of nefarious intent?"

Laughing at his boyish wit, I instantly lost any regret about calling him and decided he might have even charmed himself off my shit list and earned himself a speed-dial spot on my phone. I wasn't sure if I was fickle or just incredibly lonely. Probably a little of both.

Or maybe I was just being a girl.

"Keep dreaming. I'll see you in ten."

The first few minutes in the car with Tristan felt like a stuck clock hand, ticking the same second again and again. But once I started showcasing my carpool karaoke skills, and entertained him with a game of dodge the pothole, the conversation soon flowed effortlessly—despite residual whiplash from my kamikaze city driving.

"I think the point is to try to *miss* the potholes." Tristan rubbed his neck with an exaggerated wince.

"Bite me," I playfully retorted, followed by another

thump! thump!

"Seriously, though, do you want to go get an alignment now, or wait until you hit every pothole in Durham? I think there's only two left. We can swing by and hit them, then be done with this game in a jiffy."

"You'll be done in a jiffy," I retorted, trailing off. I must have left my wit at home today.

"What was that?" Apparently he noticed I was off my game.

"Shut up." But I didn't mean a single word of it.

We laughed, we bantered, we poked fun, and yes, we even got whiplash together as I drove. It was refreshment to my lonely soul. I felt at ease with him, more so than I had any business feeling with a man I knew so little about. Something about him was just so ... disarming. This could be bliss, or it could be dangerous. Who was he? Why was he in the suicide support group? What skeletons did he have jangling around in his closet, and how ugly were they? Something told me that no matter how damaged he was inside, I could love this man.

Love? What the hell was I thinking? But my malnourished heart was already leaps ahead of my more rational brain; there was no backtracking now.

I had shamefully opened up to him, going into way more detail than I should have for a first non-date. I told him about the hit-and-run driver who got away with killing my sister, and why I needed to find him, and to my surprise, he wanted to help.

"Everyone needs closure, Ari. I wanna make sure you get that."

I snorted. "Really? That's what the cops told me too. Instead they locked me up in juvie. Protect and serve, my ass."

"I'm so sorry. But not all cops are bad. Their actions were probably based on what your parents were saying.

136

And when it comes to child services, it's not the cops who make the decisions. It's the social worker. They clearly didn't think you were safe in the care of your parents."

Or that my parents were safe with me.

After all, my mother accused me of willfully killing my sister.

"Hm, I'm pretty sure all cops are self-serving pricks. But whatever. Water over the bridge, or under the dam, or whatever. As you can see, I'm not bitter." I didn't want to go into the nasty details of how juvie kids were pushed around, berated, loathed by those hired to look out for us. He didn't need to see that side of me, as long as I could hide it. And I was extraordinarily good at hiding things. "So how do you expect to help me?"

"I have my methods."

I batted my lashes and purred sultrily, "Oh, I'm sure you do, big boy."

My mock seduction wasn't lost on him as his smile deepened and eyebrows rose, lifting a head full of gelled exclamation points. I imagined him on stage jamming with a guitar.

"You'd be surprised what kinds of connections I have. I'll have to tell you my secrets sometime."

"You show me yours, I'll show you mine." The flirting was running full steam ahead and I couldn't, wouldn't stop it. Was this what *fun* felt like?

"I think I already know a few of yours."

"Oh really? Prove it." Despite the playful repartee, my challenge was for real.

"Okay. You obviously feel responsible for what happened to your sister. You want to make amends for the past and help others heal from theirs. You're a loner, but you don't want to be. And you're strong, but you should allow others to carry you once in a while."

His words were feathery, lifted on the breeze and

floating down around me.

"Oh, and you're a terrible driver," he added drolly.

"I am not! Everyone else is! I'm an excellent driver." I lifted my chin with a mock snobbish air.

"I've never been to a chiropractor before. After today I think I need to start."

"Oh really?" *Thump! thump!*

"Okay, okay! I give! I give! But seriously, your singing ..."

"Oh, now I think you're just trying to get in my pants with all this flattery," I said, swatting at him.

"The horror!" he exclaimed. "Never. I'm a gentleman."

"Oh, let's face it. All men really care about is getting laid."

Tristan clutched his heart in mock insult. "You think I'm in this just for the booty? I can't speak for the entire species, but yes, some of us ego-driven, one-track-mind males care about things other than hooking up."

"Oh, cars. I forgot you care about cars."

"Exactly. But don't forget booze. Women, booze, and cars—in that order. That comprises the entire male mind. Oh, and sports. Don't forget sports. So, women, booze, cars, and sports. Or is it women, booze, sports, *then* cars ... I can never remember. It's so subjective. It's definitely one of those two, though ... unless it's not."

"Prove you have substance. Tell me your story," I challenged. Everyone at the suicide support group had a story. If you faced death, thought about death, yearned for death then you had something to tell. I'd yet to hear his.

"I guess I grew up with a pretty normal family. Nothing interesting about me, other than that I'm a dude who wears leather and arm bands."

"You mean bracelets?" I teased.

"No, girls wear bracelets. Men wear arm bands. Arm bands are cool. Huge difference. Ask Johnny Depp.

Anyways," he winked as he continued, "nothing traumatic happened to me, other than that I was an outcast growing up. Got picked on a lot."

"Probably because you wore bracelets, Tristan."

"Shut up about the bracelets ... er, I mean arm bands. Do you want to know my story or not?" He pinched my arm playfully.

"Sorry. Go ahead."

"So I didn't have many friends growing up. We lived on a farm, so that kind of isolated me."

"You're a farmer?"

"Was—*was* a farmer. City boy all the way now. Living in that kind of isolation plays hell with a growing teen's self-esteem. It got worse as I got older and lonelier. And my job—well, I like what I do, but I see a lot of shit in the world. It gets depressing. So I go to group to help keep my head clear. Get some perspective, y'know?"

"What is your job, by the way?" Finally I was getting to know him.

"Let's just say I work with a lot of lowlifes."

"Oh, so you're in politics."

"Heh, yeah."

"Hey, as long as you're not a cop, we're cool."

"That's good to know."

"Okay, Bracelets, you said you wanna help me? I'm gonna put you to the test. Help me get some answers today."

"That I can do." Then he winked at me. "In fact, for you I'm pretty sure I would do anything."

And ... I was smitten. Maybe he was a little smitten too.

When we pulled up to 22 Pinewood Road, Tristan laid a comforting hand on my shoulder.

"So this is it, huh? Where you grew up."

"Yep." I couldn't push more than that simple word out

as my throat constricted with emotion at the memories washing over me.

I parked along the street a couple cars' lengths past where I remembered Carli getting hit. My former home hadn't changed much, despite changing hands a couple times. Too many memories drove my parents out shortly after I left: "This was where Carli colored the wall with my lipstick. This was where Carli took her first step. This was where Carli spilled an entire gallon of milk. This was where Carli caught a spoon on fire in the microwave."

I wondered if they had any *"This was where Ari ..."* moments.

The white siding was a subtle gray, and the green shutters were now a blinding royal blue, but everything else, down to the pansy flowerbeds and budding rosebushes, looked the same. Even the thick maple tree out front with *ARW* and *CLW* etched into the bark still held out low branches, perfect for little legs to climb. The only difference was that it seemed much humbler—not the impressive yard and massive house that I saw from the eyes of a child. The yard was shorter, the house more modest. It's odd how a child's outlook can magnify things ... or perhaps an adult's perspective sucks all the majesty out of life.

"Looks like a nice place to grow up," Tristan said. His voice cracked, as if he, too, were afraid to disrupt the poignancy of the moment.

"It was, for a time." My voice was hushed, distant.

Despite never leaving the same town I grew up in, I hadn't visited this place in all that time since I had left. Carli's ghost kept me at bay.

As we stood there in numbing silence staring at the yard, a couple ran past decked out in matching neon spandex, tiny backpacks bulging with water bottles, and patches of reflective tape all over their bodies. They looked ridiculous and utterly annoying.

"Professional runners? Is that the new trend—God-awful eye-blinding spandex? And that dude's not even wearing a cup!" Tristan whispered after they jogged out of earshot. "I so want to punch them in the face right now."

"Me too!" I laughed. "Though I'm a little curious why you noticed his cuplessness ..."

"I wear leather pants, Ari. What do you think that's saying?"

It was then that I realized Tristan got me. A laugh during a solemn moment—that was all me. Inappropriate laughter was my salve. A kid fell and broke his leg? I laughed ... after helping him up, of course. When Mom slipped on a puddle on the ceramic tile floor? I laughed ... after running to my room covering my mouth so she wouldn't hear. I adored that Tristan could chop the head right off of the tension with one swift joke.

We had been standing for a solid couple of minutes, and I wondered if anyone was at home calling the police about two stalkers casing their house right now.

"We should probably stop staring at the house. I wonder if Mrs. Salinger still lives next door."

"You wanna go find out?" Tristan offered. "It's better than doing jail time for loitering here all day."

"And share a cell with you? Hell no. Let's go."

We walked along the street—Tristan on the grass and me with arms spread out while tiptoeing along the curb like it was a balance beam—toward a perfect replica of my own house with no noticeable difference other than the color scheme. I knocked on the door, grateful Tristan was beside me. There was no way in hell I could ever knock on a door to the unknown and still be there when they opened it.

Yes, I had no balls.

A sharp, incessant Chihuahua bark—I knew the breed

by the compulsion to plunge a screwdriver into my eardrums just to make it stop—at the door was followed by a scolding—*Sprocket, you stop that!*—then the yapping receded into the depths of the house somewhere.

Sprocket. I remembered the name and was pretty sure it was the same dog from when I lived next door. God, that thing had to be close to twenty years old by now. My bet was that it was too mean to die, like those grumpy old fossils who lived to be over a hundred, their longevity fueled by vitriol and hate.

A moment later the clatter of the door handle was followed by a *swoosh*. A spindly woman with not enough brown hair dye peered through a head-sized crack in the doorway. Her skin overlapped itself like a head of lettuce. It took a moment for my brain to unlock the face from my mental catalogue, but sure enough, it was Mrs. Salinger ... looking way older than she did when I'd last seen her fourteen years ago.

She'd been an old mom even back then, having her son Benny in her forties. It was a fad many moms were hopping aboard, waiting until financial and career stability to have kids. For some reason it took forever to get there, which made for a lot of only-child families in this neighborhood.

"Mrs. Salinger?" I asked, assuming she'd have no clue who I was.

"Oh my gosh! Ari—Ari Wilburn?" she squealed.

"Yes," I chirped, dumbfounded by her recollection.

In a rush of arms and hands, she pulled me into a hug and shook me like I needed resuscitating. After that hug, I just might have.

"And who is this handsome young man? Your hubby?" She waggled her eyebrows like we were sharing a juicy secret.

"Tristan Cox. Nice to meet you, ma'am."

THE ART OF FEAR

I appreciated how he avoided the marital implication. No need advertising my single status to the whole neighborhood, which was exactly where the news would travel if left in Mrs. Salinger's care.

"Well, come in, come in!" Every word was accentuated, pulsing, and eardrum splitting. I had forgotten how her tinny voice carried. She pulled us through the door, then pushed us into a living room reeking of mothballs. "It's been ages since I've heard from your parents. I tried keeping in touch with them, but they moved so much, I gave up on updating my address book. And you ... just look at you! As gorgeous as ever. Benny's going to be so disappointed he missed you."

"Benny still lives here?" I asked.

"It only made sense. He'll be finishing up with college at the end of this year, God willing. As long as he keeps his grades up. Spends too much time with the video games, if you ask me. I'd love for him to bring a girl home one of these days. But boys will be boys, I suppose."

Boys will be boys. Except Benny was a grown man of twenty-two.

While Benny had been in the same class as Carli, he'd had a most obvious crush on me for as long as I knew him. A googly-eyed, drooling, tongue-numbing crush. Any time I'd invite him to play outside, he came down with a severe case of shyness that sent him into hiding, struck dumb, on his front porch. A weird kid, and it sounded like he hadn't changed much.

"So what brings you out this way?" Mrs. Salinger—for I never knew her first name—babbled on, avoiding even the slightest conversational pause. It was like a moment of silence literally pained her.

"I actually wanted to ask you something. I was wondering if you remembered anything about the accident ... like the car that hit Carli?"

Her face fell into a frown. "Oh, sweetie, I'm sorry, but I didn't see a thing. I didn't even know what happened until Benny came running in screaming about it. The police came around asking questions, and I wish I had more to tell them, but I only heard about everything after the fact. And most of that was from Benny."

I could imagine her disappointment at missing out on the tragic details of the latest gossip. It was what she lived for back then, her stock-in-trade.

"Wait—Benny saw it happen?"

"He sure did. But he clammed up the moment the police came around. Petrified. I guess a man in uniform can be intimidating to a child. Plus he was a shy boy, you know. Even a glimpse from you and his little jaw just clamped shut!" She laughed as her memory swept her somewhere else in some faraway time, but I was stuck on something right here, right now.

Benny.

Benny saw what happened.

Benny saw the car.

"Do you think Benny would remember what he saw?" I asked hopefully.

"I dunno, but you can come on by anytime to ask him yourself. I'm sure he'd like that. He's got classes all day today, but he'll be around tomorrow if you want to drop by."

I thanked her a million times over and vowed to return the next day. Was it possible the answer to my lifelong question had been next door all along?

As we headed to my Focus, Tristan playfully hip-checked me. "You did good in there, kid."

"Thanks."

"Do I need to be worried about you and Benny being alone tomorrow?" He chuckled, walking me to my driver's-side door.

144

"Hmm ..." I thoughtfully stroked my chin. "Plays video games. No job. Lives with his mommy. Uh, how could I pass up that gem? Not sure I'll be able to restrain myself."

And if Tristan didn't watch it, I'd be losing my restraint on him too. But I locked that temptation away. At least for the moment. And yet I found myself standing there beside the car, waiting ... for what, I didn't know.

Or maybe I did.

Our eyes met, held, and I forgot to breathe.

Tristan must have found the key to my desire, because a moment later I felt the air relax, then stiffen between us, a contraction of time as the silence gasped for breath. Then suddenly an electric charge jolted my heart. I could feel it—the moment before our first kiss.

As he tilted my chin upward, every cell vibrated at his touch. I reached for the fount of his love, thirsted for it. I yearned for his passion to collapse upon me, pulling me under.

His kiss was thrilling, supple, uncertain, masculine. Everything a kiss should be.

Gripping my waist and pulling me into his, I shuddered against his firm body, fully aware of the shockwaves racking every nerve. I was certain my synapses were firing at a deathly rate, but at least I'd die happy. His hands on my body were an ocean—pulling me in, then pushing me away as his Cupid's arrow pierced my heart.

We were leather meets lace. Even if the lace—me—was a little yellowed.

Perhaps kissing Tristan would be that regrettable Craigslist impulse buy when I got home, but right now he was the balm for my aching heart. Just what the doctor ordered.

Chapter 21

Ari

Seven days until dead

I don't know where exactly Cloud 9 is, but I had set up camp and planned to stay a spell. After yesterday's kiss, I didn't know what to do with myself after I arrived home—alone. Feeling fidgety, I needed something to focus on, other than replaying the kiss for the next several hours.

I ended up whiling away the time by looking through Josef Alvarez's case file. Upon finding nothing, I pulled out the address book that I swiped from his house. He was probably the one guy left in a million who still used a tangible address book. There were barely a handful of names in it—Rosalita Alvarez, George Battan, Pedro Luis—until one in particular caught my eye: Killian Alvarez, complete with address and phone number. Luckily the info wasn't as outdated as the address book.

Calling him during my lunch break at work, my floor supervisor Florence and the kids' department associate Gloria caught wind of the masculine voice on the other end and teased me mercilessly—and with way too much innuendo, which felt ickier given that they were both in their early seventies:

"It's about time you found a man to release all that pent-up horniness with."

Ew.

"When's the last time you did the horizontal tango?"

Double ew.

"You're overdue for some hard salami in your diet!"

They screeched with laughter while I shushed them in the background, praying Killian hadn't overheard as I explained who I was and made plans to meet after work. After hanging up I yelled an exaggerated "eeew!" and scolded them, explaining how he was a sixteen-year-old boy who was the brother of a friend. Of course that's when the crude cradle robber comments had started, forcing me to hide out for a while in a changing room.

The oversexed old bags were still ragging me when I clocked out of work five minutes early, thanks to my short lunch break, and headed to the Waffle House on Hillsborough Road, nervous about what I would say to Killian ... and wondering how much Tina would kill me for doing so. Most likely she'd be dismemberment mad.

The Waffle House's yellow sign looked cheery and inviting against the gray concrete block exterior. The red awning shaded me from the sun scorching my winter-white arms. If I had any chance of surviving the fast-approaching summer, I'd need to get started on my base tan, as it was only April and we were already hitting the mid-seventies.

Inhaling a deep, calming breath, I opened the glass front door and an icy blast of air conditioning tousled my hair and clothes. Damn, they kept the place cold.

Inside, only a smattering of people sat in booths, making it easy to find Killian—the only Latino adolescent in the place amid the mostly elderly patrons. Like his sister, his features boasted perfect symmetry and shine. In the way he nodded his head at me in greeting, I instantly saw a ladies' man.

"You Killian?" I asked.

"Yep. And you're Ari, right?"

"Hey." I nodded and sat across from him.

He tossed me a menu—more like flung it at me; it slipped through my fingers and onto the floor, making me feel foolish, even though it was his fault. I stooped to pick it up, bumping my head on table on my way up. After we had placed our drink orders, a syrupy residue from the menu clung to my palm, attracting shreds of my napkin to my skin as I wiped at it. I was officially annoyed now.

Already this was going so well.

"So you know my sister," Killian began, slathering ChapStick on his lips before finishing his thought, "Sophia—er, Tina."

"Yeah, which is what I wanted to talk to you about." The door was open, but I had no idea how to step through. Did I simply slam him with *Your father may have been murdered by sex traffickers and they're coming for her next?* I'm sure there was some kind of etiquette involved, but when it came to manners, I was clueless. I blamed the foster system for that.

"I don't know how much you know, but Tina's in the hospital right now."

"What? Is she okay?" He jumped up from the booth as if ready to bolt to the hospital right then and there.

I patted the air in front of him in a *sit-down-there's-more* gesture. "She's fine now. But the reason she's in there is because she got a threatening phone call. Are you aware of what she's been through?" I had to tread carefully if I wanted to maintain Tina's confidence while helping her.

"Yeah, I know about it. The traffickers. My dad told me. That's why I'm in America. Me and my dad came to find her to get her out."

"Really? What happened?" Clearly they hadn't succeeded.

"I found out dear old Dad got into more debt while we were here and they were gonna take it out on Sophia. I wanted my dad to pay them off to free my sister, but Dad had other plans. We ended up having a fight about it ... a falling out or whatever. Haven't seen him since."

Shit. He hadn't seen his father since ... when? I sure as hell hoped I wasn't the one who would have to break the news to him about his father's death. Unless Killian was the reason no one would ever see Josef again.

This was not going as planned. "Do you know about your father ...?" I couldn't finish the sentence, and thankfully Killian wasn't going to make me.

"Being dead? Yeah, I'm aware."

Thank God I dodged that bullet.

"I'm sorry about your loss," I muttered as sincerely as I could force it.

"Wasn't no loss for me. Good riddance, old man."

He was clearly overcome with grief.

"So you're okay that he's dead?"

"The man sold his daughter for some quick cash, then dragged me here away from my life and my friends, only to run up more debt and leave me hanging. I had nowhere to live, had to get a job, never even finished school. What am I supposed to do now? He leaves me homeless, no cash, no nothing. So yeah, I'm cool with him killing himself."

"Tina and I think he might have been murdered."

"Fine, then I applaud whoever killed the *bastardo*." He slapped his palm on the table, causing my glass of water to tremble and spill a few drops. Now that was unsettling, laying his endorsement of his pop's murder out like a royal flush.

The waitress apparently took Killian's outburst as her cue to take our order. I shooed her away with an impatient gesture.

As Killian's hand rested on the table, something

sparkled in the sunlight pouring in through the smudged window. His watch, bedecked in diamonds. And a gold ring adorned with red gems. I scanned upward, noting the gold chain hung around his neck and a diamond stud in one ear.

Penniless, huh? Bullshit.

I called his bluff.

"And your bling?" I glanced down at his hands so he could follow my gaze.

"You think I'd sell my sister for some jewelry? This stuff is from my sugar mama. I don't even like gold. I wear it for her. I'm just as much a victim as Sophia. They came after me too. Threatened to hurt me, but they know they can't touch me."

Typical teen machismo.

"Who's *they*?" I needed more. He was telling me what I already knew.

"Some prick with a lot of cash, but I don't know his name. Dad kept it all hush-hush. Just ask Sophia. She can tell you."

But Tina wasn't talking. Afraid that I would go after the guy, she kept her secrets sealed. How was I supposed to help her find her father's killer if she insisted on protecting him?

"I've tried. No luck. So you say you care about your sister, but why haven't you tried reaching out to her?"

"I did! I got her number from my grandmother, left a bunch of messages, but she won't talk to me. All I'm trying to do is look out for her, but she's convinced I'm out to get her. I want to see her, if she'd let me."

Had Tina lied about that too? I was starting to wonder what the truth really was … and if Tina was playing me for a damn fool.

"Look, let me talk to her." Maybe if I helped ease their estrangement I could dig down to the truth. "I'll see if I can mediate between you two. Since your grandmother's here too, it might be a good time for a family reunion."

"Good luck with that. You clearly don't know how stubborn the Alvarez family can be."

Family dynamics weren't exactly my forte as my own track record clearly demonstrated, but if there was any chance I could help them—and claw my way through all of Tina's fabrications, something I knew a bit about—it was worth a shot. If anything, the whole investigative thing was a fast cure for my anxiety. Ever since playing detective for Tina, I'd talked to more people than I had in the past decade.

"The secrets your sister tried so hard to bury keep coming out of the woodwork, and your father was killed because he kept pissing off the wrong people. I have a pretty good guess at how stubborn your family can be."

Killian walked me to the door, then halfway through he looked at me. "Which hospital did you say Tina was at, again?"

"Duke Hospital—on Duke Street."

"Thanks."

I regretted sharing my intel as soon as I said it.

Chapter 22

Josef

San Luis, Mexico
2013

Josef was a man who took matters into his own hands. It was the reason he hadn't always made the best of friends. It was why he leased out his daughter to pay the bills. It was why Mercedes left him all those years ago. But this—the horror his eyes were witnessing—could not continue. It was time to take back what was his.

Before this moment, porn was just a movie to get off on. A fifteen-minute fling with the imagination when he was bored or horny or tired. It was a hot chick and a faceless dude—as far as Josef was concerned—consensually getting it on so that Josef could, well, get off. The women got paid, the men got pleasured, and the customers got relief. Win-win-win.

But when he stumbled upon a "hot new release" that was taking his favorite porn hub by storm, he just had to look. See what the fuss was all about.

A mouse click. Buffering.

Pregnant chick porn.

Nah. Not his cup of tea.

Well, maybe one more look.

Then shockwaves.

The girl in the film wasn't some busty bitch he'd seen a

million times before. But she was familiar. Too familiar—in the familial way.

Though much older than he last saw her, he recognized the almond shape of her eyes. The way her cheekbones angled upward. The arc of her pulpy lips that used to kiss his cheek goodnight.

It was Sophia. His baby girl. And judging by the swell of her belly, about six months pregnant. She was not the baby he remembered. She was a woman, but not quite. Despite her full breasts and long limbs, there remained the bloom of adolescence in the innocent face, contrasting with the abject fear in her eyes. She blushed in cherry blossom pink embarrassment and shame, and squinted away the reality of what was happening. It clearly wasn't a choice.

He counted the years ... if memory served, she was way too young to be pregnant, way too pure to be doing *this* while a man moaned and groaned over her. Was this what she was commissioned to do now?

He had never asked questions when George Battan offered a large sum of money to recruit Sophia for his services. Just one year of her life, that's all.

"Some light housework and cleaning, but otherwise she'll live a normal life. Have friends, go to school, play with other children. She'll just be helping our customers do things they need done around the house," George had assured him.

And without hesitation Josef accepted it. No questions asked. No follow-up needed.

Until the year was up. When Josef threatened to tip off the police, another exchange was made. Another lump payment for another year. Hell, Josef even offered to help recruit more girls for George when needed.

And so it went. An unconventional arrangement, George had explained, but he was a fair man.

Josef didn't want details, not then nor every time he received his payment for Sophia's continued service. And yet somehow in his subconscious he knew why he asked no questions, hadn't bothered with details.

Because of this. Because of what he innately knew she would become.

Yes, he knew, and never stopped it.

Until today. Seeing it for himself, her fate was suddenly real. His love and fidelity for his daughter took over.

Not my mija, no. Not my nieto.

Pausing the video, he found his address book with George's number and pounded in each number on his cell phone, nearly cracking the screen with each jab. It rang, eventually going to voicemail.

"George, I just saw my daughter in a porn—and her unborn baby. You promised me she'd be taken care of. Call me back or I'm coming to find you myself."

Hanging up, he breathed a little frantically—both from residual shock and unleashed anger. He needed to kick someone's ass.

George's, in particular.

But how could he find him? He was in the States somewhere, probably hiding out. But maybe the film had answers. Unfortunately the filth he watched didn't feature credits full of names and locations, but there had to be something. There just had to.

He replayed it from the beginning, turning off the volume and blinding himself to his daughter's nude body with an imaginary censor bar. The scene took place in a warehouse of some sort. Bare brick walls, exposed vents hanging crookedly from the ceiling, naked lightbulbs dangling precariously from thick wires. A stained mattress offered the only comfort in the room. The typically squalid setting for the XXX porn Josef liked to wallow in.

Behind the figures was a two-person-tall window looking down on a sports stadium. Pressing his face closer to his computer screen, he looked for something in the scenery beyond. Any visual that could help. It was there. If it took him until his last breath to find, it was there.

A perfect close-up angle widened his view.

Pause.

A two-story brown cow stood in the left-field corner of the stadium, and from there his eyes wandered ... until he found the words "Durham Bulls Athletic Park."

Toggling to another screen, he typed in the name of the stadium and traced it to Durham, North Carolina. He already had a valid visa—a little thank you from a friend at the U.S. Consulate who owed him. And plenty of cash—ironically, thanks to George. If the movie had been filmed recently, perhaps Sophia would still be there. And if Josef was lucky, George Battan would be too.

Until Josef killed him.

.

Chapter 23
Tina

Her eyes were a pleasing mix of brown and blue as Tina gazed adoringly at the infant in her arms. She'd always wanted a little girl, even as a little girl. Dressing up her dolls in rags she managed to pin together into mismatched outfits, then cradling them and soothing them and feeding them … but for young Tina, it wasn't just a childish pastime. It was a life she dreamed of, down to the boy who would become her beau: Arturo, her best friend. He was handsome enough, in a dirt-and-spit kind of way. He knew the games she liked to play and how to let her win without it being obvious, which was all that counted in her little world.

Plus he always shared his treats with her. There was no better criteria for a husband than that.

Her fantasy life clung to her index finger with a baby-sized fist. Dimples dotted each meaty brown knuckle as she counted one, two, three, four, five tiny fingers wrapping around hers, squeezing with a force that said, "Mine!"

Yet in this dream there was no Arturo. Only a blur of a face—or many faces, all blank and empty like a cantaloupe skin. There was nothing warm about them in this dream. The only tenderness came from the wriggling sack she carried, the puckered lips searching for nourishment—just a few sips to fill the baby's belly.

She watched a line of men pass by, searching their

faces for recognition, but they were far too old. Far too white. Far too horrifying. The haze masked the demon behind each one.

In a blink the scene grew cloudy, and as Tina consciously tried to force it back into alignment—mentally grasping for the pixels to coalesce—the moment faded into a dark oblivion, and the baby in her arms slipped into shadow.

Yet the weight of the bundle remained. She searched for her baby, growing frantic as her surroundings drifted off into the void. Then a face came into focus. A man's face. A nice enough face. A trustworthy face. The face of a father, but not her father. Not her baby's father.

He stepped into a spotlight, and that's when Tina noticed his arms carrying something. A whimpering something. Her baby! She ran to him, grabbing the infant from his arms, but when she gazed down at the face, it was a child's face.

A young girl's face.

Marla's face.

Her green eyes pleaded with Tina. "Help me!" she sobbed into Tina's chest. Tina clutched her firmly, but the heat of Marla's body became intense. Too hot to touch. Until she melted away.

"Marla! Please come back," Tina shrieked into the emptiness.

But all was nothing. And all was lost.

❧❦

A squeezing sensation on her shoulders shook Tina awake. Except that she was literally already shaking.

"Ma'am, wake up." Tina's eyelids sprang open like two retractable blinds and she stared at the too-close face staring down at her.

"You okay, honey?" the lady asked.

Tina glanced around, the confusion still potent. Nothing looked familiar. Where was she? How did she get here? All she could remember was Marla. She had to get to Marla. "Marla?"

"No, honey, I'm Delores."

But the woman's words fell in a jumble. "Marla?" Tina called louder. "Where's Marla?"

"Is Marla one of the nurses?"

"No, I need Marla!" Tina felt her lips moving, but she couldn't recognize the sound of her own voice, and it was terrifying.

Cold—her body shivered with a clammy chill. Her hospital gown was drenched in sweat, her hair slick to her scalp.

She saw her arms swinging, her fists punching, and heard her screams rising, but she couldn't control it. She couldn't control anything—not herself, not her nightmares, not even what happened to Marla.

Another face materialized beside the lady's, this one instructing her sternly. "I'm going to give you something to calm you, Tina. You need to relax."

A sharp pinch later, a tranquility oozed through her like ice melting into her bloodstream. Of their own accord her arms flopped down at her sides and her fists unclenched. She felt her body relax into the mattress and her breathing normalize.

"You're okay now, Tina," the nurse said, patting her arm.

"What happened?" Tina wondered aloud. Her fit felt like an out-of-body experience.

"You had one heck of a nightmare. You were screaming and carrying on about some Marla. I was afraid you were gonna go into shock or something."

Marla. Another nightmare. She had to get her

158

subconscious under control before ... before what? Before she went crazy? She was already in the psych ward. As the nurse advised her to get some rest, Tina wondered if she was ever going to be allowed to leave—this hospital, or the nightmare.

Chapter 24

Ari

Seven days until dead

Some people never change. *Star-Trek*-loving nerd, virgin-for-life, pimple-faced Benny Salinger was one of them. He was the kind of geek that the mathletes and brainiacs felt sorry for because he had nothing to show for it.

Poor Benny—still the same loser.

Not that my aspirations had been any nobler. My back ached from a pinched nerve hauling a vacuum down a set of warehouse steps today—despite my temptation to just roll it down and let gravity do the work—because the conveyer belt was broken yet again. If I was lucky I could move up in retail, but given that I wasn't the motivated type, I'd probably never make it to a floor supervisor.

Guess I'd be living off of generic mac 'n' cheese for a long time.

Sitting across from me, Benny's tubby belly poured over his drawstring sweatpants, quivering with each breath. At least he was eating well. Maybe next time he wouldn't buy a Mr. Spock T-shirt two sizes too small for his fat Kirk body.

After Benny dragged his yapping, snapping rat-dog *Sprocket*—what kind of name was that, anyways?—into a bedroom and closed the door, we got reacquainted on his mother's floral couch, in his mother's mothball-ridden living room, in his mother's prim home. I discovered Benny was just as lost as I was.

Dog whines and the clatter of pots and pans provided ambience as his mother cooked something that smelled like fried chicken. Even the air felt sticky with oil. "You just have to taste my chicken!" Mrs. Salinger yelled from the kitchen, at least twice during our conversation.

We caught up on school and jobs, whined about my parents' disappearing act, tiptoed around my relationship status, and avoided the topic of future dreams altogether. I patted myself on the back for navigating the conversation perfectly without a single anxiety attack.

"I'm so glad you stopped by. It's good seeing you, Ari," Benny said after we covered the basics and entered a gawky stranger silence.

"You too, Benny. I actually had something I wanted to talk to you about."

"Yeah, Mom told me. You wanted to know what I saw ... that day." His voice was high and thin.

Anything more than a generic reference to *that day* was like uttering a curse. Everybody avoided the words *the day your sister died,* as if saying them aloud brought the curse upon themselves. Those words were the *Lord Voldemort* of my life.

"I'm looking for anything you can remember. Anything at all."

"It was so long ago, and we were just kids. I don't remember much from my childhood, except the other kids picking on me—and my crush on you." He chuckled shyly, clearly hoping I'd take the bait, but I sat stoic and unsmiling, waiting for something. Anything. "Uh, yeah, but I do remember that day. Nothing huge, but I remember the car swerving into the yard. I remember thinking how odd it was, that it was going so straight and fast, then suddenly swerving off the road like that. And then Carli flying toward the house in slow motion—not really, it was just a perception thing, know what I mean?—at a crazy angle."

He stopped. His piggish little eyes looked moist. Even for him the memory was crippling.

I hadn't thought the angle of Carli's trajectory that weird as a ten-year-old, but now as a reasonably rational adult, it made a huge difference. Benny testified to what I had deduced from the picture—the driver had to have jerked the wheel pretty damn drastically. It wasn't an accident, and I now had eyewitness testimony. Once I found this guy, he wouldn't know what hit him.

"What about the make or model or color—anything?"

"Orange. It was definitely throwback 1970's orange. And a hatchback. A Chevy Vega, maybe? Or a Ford Festiva? I'm not much of a car guy, but one of those types. I remember it looking like a clown car to me back then."

An orange hatchback. Exactly what I saw during my session with Dr. Weaver. So it wasn't a creation of my mind. It was real. How many people owned hideous orange hatchbacks in 2002? There couldn't be many people that would willingly drive a rolling eyesore like that around in public.

My first real, official lead.

"I really appreciate this, Benny."

"No problem. I'm sorry I wasn't much help back then. I guess I was scared, shocked …"

"It's okay. We were kids. Besides, you're helping now. I'm gonna find who did it—who killed Carli. I'm going to bring her justice, give her peace."

"I hope so." Benny sighed as I rose and grabbed my overloaded hobo bag, my pinched back nerve seizing as I bent down. I desperately needed a new job. Anything but retail or annoying customers or demanding bosses. Did such a job exist? Doubtful.

162

"Oh, before you go," he said as I took my first step toward the door, then stopped and turned. "You may want to talk to your parents about the night before. It was late, because I was looking outside from my bedroom window, supposed to be sleeping. Your dad was talking to some guy in the front yard, and they started yelling when the guy kicked him in the knee and stomach a few times. It looked real badass."

The limp. Yes, now I remembered my father was limping for almost a week. Too much had happened for it register at the time, but my unathletic, couch potato father hurting his knee? It's not like watching TV was an extreme sport.

"You get a look at the guy?"

"Not really. White. About the same height as your dad. Not much else I could distinguish about him in the dark."

I hugged him and planted a kiss on his fat cheek where a splotch of red suddenly pooled and spread down his neck.

"Thanks, Benny."

"Sure you can't stay for dinner? Mom's making homemade fried chicken."

"Not tonight." I smiled and touched his arm. "But let's keep in touch, okay?"

"I'd love that."

And I hurried out of there before giving his mom a chance to chase me down with a drumstick.

Chapter 25
Ari

2002

The soundless scream a dog whistle makes—that is my mother. I admit that the rebel in me snuck out to play more often than it should have, but I'm lost. I'm a kid abandoned by her best friend. I'm coping the best I can. But I can tell by the way Mom gawks at me—the way her lips curl in disgust, the way her brow crinkles and her eyes narrow to slits as she watches me, as if calculating my next move—that she will never, ever forgive me for Carli's death.

It's been a handful of days since it happened, and the policeman and Mom have been discussing a group home as a temporary option for me. There's too much tension at home. I'm acting out. It's not good for anyone. Just something temporary until things cool down.

This is what I overhear them saying. But foster homes are for good kids in bad situations. According to Mom, I'm a bad kid causing a bad situation, thus not worthy of foster care criteria. So it's a group home for me.

I know I've been reckless. I throw tantrums. I break things. I run away for hours. I unleash a side of me I never met before. But Mom is no help. Because she fights back. She breaks my will. She doesn't come looking for me when I'm gone. And she's unleashed a side of her I've never met before, either.

164

Accident or not, I don't feel safe at home. I don't even feel safe in my own skin. Mom subjects me to what feel like round-the-clock verbal assaults, and Dad does little more than hold the punching bag for Mom to hit—that being me. I can't go to school, because the kids will stare and whisper. I'm the girl who pushed her sister into an oncoming car. I'm the girl who killed. So it's me and Mom at home—two strangers made of the same flesh and blood, unable to find common ground.

Compared to what I don't really know about group homes—but have gleaned from Mom's Lifetime movies and tabloid TV talk shows—home feels like heaven. God only knows what the kids would do to me in those places. The only self-defense I know was eight weeks worth of karate lessons when I was six.

I can't leave the protection of these four walls. I'll die if I'm tossed into a roomful of kids who had stolen cars, stabbed people, or beat up old ladies for their change purses. My signature fighting move is spinning in circles with my arms out. I'll be dead within a day. Though maybe that's what I deserve.

The brief discussions between my parents about sending me away keep growing into full-blown conversations.

"Do you think she's safe here at home?" I hear Dad pose to Mom.

"Her sister was murdered, Burt—murdered by someone! You tell me if safe is ever going to be a possibility."

I wince, unsure what exactly Mom means by that. Does she think I'm out to kill them too?

Knowing my doomsday is coming, I don't know why I did it, especially since it was a surefire way to incite Mom's fury ... yet again. I can't explain why I decided to knock over Mom's most cherished vase, scattering dear old Gram all over the living room carpet. Mom broke down trying to vacuum up the ashes while I fled to my bedroom in a fit of tears and screaming sobs.

That's the last straw for Mom.

One call from Mom and DFCS shows up—just until things calm down at home, they assure me, but it's no assurance. My only certainty is that I don't want to live anymore. The caseworker tells me the tension is too intense, and with my unchecked anger and Mom's grief boiling over, it isn't healthy for me to remain at home anymore, so off I go.

With a heavy duffel bag strap carrying all the possessions I could fit inside pinching my shoulder, I'm led to an unknown car, with an unknown lady, to an unknown destination. As the caseworker pulls out of my driveway, I stare at my home where I hope to see my parents, arms around each other, crying at my departure. Maybe even running after me with a change of heart. But the front porch is as empty as my soul as the car bumps down the street.

I have no idea where I'm going as we head into a part of town I've never been, but the lady explains that with no emergency placements available, I'll be staying at a group home until a foster home opens up. If it even comes to that, she adds. She tells me it's a nice place, with lots of activities and a private school and kids just like me. I'll fit in, I'll have fun, I'll feel much better about it in a few days.

All lies.

In the backseat of her car, I feel so alone, just me and some mismatched clothes, a folded picture of me and Carli, and my favorite Richard Adams books—all that remains of the life I leave behind.

The group home is everything I dreamed it would be, and then some—if dreams were nightmares.

We arrive at a small campus dotted with brick buildings. The sign is written in a simple black font against a pale blue backdrop with unkempt grass sprouting up around it. No flowers, no kids' toys strewn in the yard, nothing to indicate kids actually have fun here.

Nothing homey. Nothing charming. Nothing comforting to a lone ten-year-old snatched away from her parents.

I step into a spacious lobby where a bunch of kids sprawled on a sofa, their limbs pretzeled into crazy shapes, watch cartoons on a wall-mounted TV. It's impossible to judge from their impassive expressions if they're bored or unhappy or just tube numb. Next I drop off my bag of meager possessions for a staff member to inspect, then I'm shown my room. A ten-by-ten square with a single bed and a dresser.

I'm guided back into the nucleus of the building where we pass a room decorated in homemade art, with a girl pounding out discordant chords on a console piano. I'd partake in art projects and group therapy sessions in this room, I'm told. Next is the dining room and kitchen, where all the kids contribute to meal preparations and cleaning. I'd only ever helped my mom make macaroni and cheese once before, and I still overcooked the noodles and over-milked the powdered cheese.

As we circle back to the row of bedrooms, I hear a girl crying behind a partially closed door. I wonder how long she's been here, how many days she spends crying. I can't be that girl.

The only comfort I have as I curl myself into a ball against the wall beside my new bed is that I don't have a roommate to torture me. I feel myself slipping, losing all will. How can I overcome this? Closing my eyes, I picture Carli and me, hand in hand, skipping through some never-never land with unbridled joy.

For her, for Carli, I must survive.

I decide then and there that if I'm going to survive, I need to be tough. I need to turn my anger and hurt inward and be stoic and strong. What do I even know about strength, other than what the school bullies have shown me throughout my childhood? I must shed my old self and be reborn. I'll rebel, I'll defy authority, I'll search for the loophole that will keep my spirit alive.

But it wasn't enough to drive away the fear, or the desire for death.

Chapter 26
Tina

2014

Sophia Alvarez's breaths misted the chilled afternoon air in floating, frantic puffs. She had been walking until her legs grew numb, avoiding all the major roads where she could get spotted. Months of planning had gone into this moment, but now she was regretting her newfound freedom—and her decision to do this in the dead of winter. Soon night would fall and she would be homeless, foodless, freezing, and alone.

Not that starvation was foreign to her. Even at the suspicion of Sophia "squaring up"—or fleeing—her pimp would withhold food for days. Sometimes even water if he was feeling testy. But rather than putting the fear of God in her like his threats did to his other girls, it only trained Sophia to be tougher. To push her endurance. The if-you-can't-beat-them-join-them flock mentality of her "family" of victims had never set in. Adapting wasn't an option. Fight or flight. Fight *never got her anything but a brutal beating and loss of privileges—like school—so* flight *it would be.*

It was a miracle she'd gotten this far. Her weeks of uncharacteristic deference should have been a red flag. But he must have just assumed she'd finally—after ten rebellious, punishing years—broke.

Then it came. The perfect opportunity.

For nearly a year Sophia had been his one and only

169

until just months earlier, when he picked up another girl— twelve years old. Marla. That was when it happened. The decision. The turning point. It was one thing for Sophia to be worn out, tossed aside, overpowered, and beaten, but watching another child go down with her ... her resistance was born. She'd escape and come back to rescue Marla. Meeting the girl's emerald eyes, it was a promise Tina made to the child the first night she arrived, cuddling into Sophia's arms and crying herself to sleep.

One might conjure an image of a shoddy apartment building in a ghetto red-light district. One might imagine dim, flickering lights and screams echoing down a hallway lined with drug addicts passed out along the floor. One might even envision a bare mattress with soiled sheets balled up in a corner while rats scurried under their feet.

Life wasn't actually like that for her.

Sophia was "elite."

Some perverts liked their "dates" young, and pre- pubescent girls like Sophia had once come at a higher price. Dollars dictated better hygiene and living conditions. Her pimp certainly didn't want to live in filth, and she lived with him, so there you have it. Sophia didn't know it yet, but the creature comforts she "enjoyed" would vanish little by little as she matured into adolescence, putting her in the streets with the other "wifeys" turning tricks.

But George favored her.

Not every girl was so lucky.

It was a suburban house. One story. Three bedrooms with actual bed frames and clean linens. She'd had the same Hello Kitty bedspread since her first day there, a gift for being a good girl and doing what she was told. Until she stopped doing what she was told.

She learned quickly to adapt to survive.

Blending in to avoid snooping neighbors was how she survived. She attended school, but friendships were forbidden. Extra-curriculars, forbidden. Speaking about her captors, forbidden.

She was to act shy, he was to be called "Daddy," and that was that. She'd be rewarded for compliance and beaten for defiance. A six-year-old doesn't call a bluff when a man threatens to gut her and then kill her entire family if she ever tells a soul. Especially when he's followed up on his threats of pain and torture.

So she obeys. Without a second thought.

And thus her world turned, a student by day and a rape victim by night.

Until it stopped, mid-rotation.

Sophia was now sixteen and on a do-or-die mission. She'd plotted the where and how, but needed the when. She rode the bus to and from school now—a recent privilege earned by her indulgence of George's every wish. The route gave her a glimpse of the sprawling town and the side streets that she could travel on. In computer class she scoured resources for local victim shelters—she didn't trust cops—and mapped out her journey in feverish handwriting on a piece of notebook paper she hid in her pocket. Leaving when school let out at 2:15, it'd be a bit of a walk, but doable.

As Sophia's had been, Marla's "seasoning" was accomplished through a series of moves meant to intimidate, manipulate, beat down, and destroy self-will. Her little brother's life was the chess piece used to coerce Marla to obey. She was old enough to understand George wasn't bluffing and that it was her job to protect her long-lost family—by any means possible. Even with her own life.

And when she cried for Mommy and Daddy? No food. Cried louder? No water. Days on end locked in her room, isolated. It was an effective method, a mental branding.

After years of subhuman treatment, it was hard to break free from the cycle.

But Sophia was doing it right now.

As she glanced at her paper and then the approaching street sign, she had one turn remaining. She was going to make it before dark!

Humming Tina Turner's "What's Love Got to Do with It" while her steps quickened, she felt a freedom she'd never know.

The door was unlocked when she arrived at the shelter.

"Hey, honey," a black woman greeted her behind a folding table. "You here for a room?"

Sophia nodded, her trained shyness suddenly muting her.

"You got a name?"

She hesitated, then said confidently, "Tina."

"Welcome to a new life, Tina."

The present
9:03 p.m.

Sophia's eyelids fluttered in a restless sleep as I stood over her, watching the contours of her forehead gently slope into defined cheekbones, all wrapped in smooth brown skin. Her hair matted to her scalp in a sweaty mess that I wanted to touch, but didn't.

I wondered what she was dreaming of, if the nightmares followed her here. The time for mercy had come. I knew what Sophia suffered. I knew it was a burden no girl—no woman—should bear. It was time to give back what I had promised her so long ago—her innocence.

I had betrayed her, so it was my responsibility to fix what I had broken.

They would call me a heartless monster, the media.

172

But I knew better. I worshipped on the altar of her flesh. She was mine, and I was hers. We belonged together. Others would shudder with revulsion at my aid, shrinking far from me as I passed, but not Sophia. She would understand.

It felt spontaneous, standing here in this moment. I hadn't planned on this. Sophia hadn't been on my list—not yet, at least. But her suicide attempt was an echo from a long-ago cry for help. This was the only way I knew how to help her.

I brought peace. I brought an end to suffering. I was her sentry at the gate of liberation.

Not all good deeds can be on a schedule.

The thick pillow filled my gloved palms as I held it with outstretched hands. I sucked in a cleansing breath, then placed it over Sophia's face, holding it down with the entire weight of my body as she violently clawed at me, kicking fiercely, while I listened for any approaching staff footsteps beyond the locked door. Her muffled cries got no further than the pillowcase fibers, and I knew my window of time was closing before someone knocked to come in.

The knife I had placed next to her glinted in the glow of the television on the wall. I grabbed it and caught myself for a beat—for I loved Sophia in my own unique way—before I plunged the blade into her side. The flailing stopped, and I fought with the urge to stay. No, the risk was too great to wait for her last heartbeat, for her last living moment to be with me.

With a chaste kiss on her hand, I uttered a placid "I love you." I had backed up my love with action, no cheap words would suffice. Feeling the electric shock of her touch, her skin felt like a trembling flower opening, soft and serene as her hand fell. Although her petals were crushed, she would bloom again on the other side.

I pocketed the knife and slipped out the door, letting it

stridently swing closed behind me, whispering a mournful good-bye as I walked out of the hospital.

Chapter 27

Ari

Six days until dead

Nine twenty-one.

A phone call that late made me jump. This time I recognized the number.

This time the words were dire. Cryptic, which only unleashed panic in me.

Tina Alvarez is in critical condition.

No answers. No information. Nothing but an order for me to come down to the Intensive Care Unit where they would fill me in.

Had she attempted suicide again? God, I hoped she hadn't succeeded this time.

I ran two red lights and sped fifteen miles over the limit. But when I got there, Tina was unconscious.

Damn it, this was my fault.

I flagged the nurse on duty, demanding a play-by-play of what exactly happened. The twenty-something fresh-faced recent nursing school grad stammered her way through the details she knew, which were vague. Her blond ponytail swung like a cheerleader's as she waved her arms to accompany her words—a hand talker. Tina had a visitor in the psych ward that evening, but as they didn't keep a log of who came and went, Newbie Nurse wasn't sure who he was.

The next thing they know, a night nurse comes

running out of the room yelling for help. Someone had stabbed the patient in room 402 in the abdomen. She never even got a chance to cry for help, as they found her with a pillow over her head and unconscious.

No one saw his face? I drilled her.

Just another nameless, faceless person passing through the hallways. There were so many of them every day, no one could ever keep track.

What about the security cameras? I demanded.

The cameras only caught grainy, foreshortened views of a baseball-capped individual entering and later exiting the wing—providing no face shots or identifying features— and there were no cameras near Tina's room down at the end of the hall.

No one knew who the visitor was.

No one saw anyone else come or go.

No one could tell me if Tina would make it.

All this caring, all this friendship, all for naught.

Why did everything I touch turn to shit?

This killer, whoever he was, was taking the Alvarez family down one by one.

I hadn't realized it was almost one in the morning when I got home. One twenty by the time I was lying in bed worrying about Tina. Two fifteen when I was tossing and turning, aching for company. Two thirty before I finally dialed the last digit of Tristan's phone number.

"I really need to talk to someone. You busy?" I had sputtered the moment he groggily picked up.

"Time is nothing but a number," he had insisted philosophically after I caught a whiff of my own desperation and apologized profusely for calling him at such a late hour.

I didn't really know him well enough to call him at this hour, did I?

Now he sat on my sofa across from me, his rumpled T-shirt clinging to his chest, his hair a disheveled mess of bed-head peaks sprouting in every direction, his eyes sleepily unfocused but straining to stay alert. I found his fresh-out-of-bed look sexy, and his cavernous yawns did nothing to spoil the picture.

"What's on your mind at three in the morning?" Tristan asked after gulping the Budweiser he had brought with him—a little pick-me-up, he called it.

"Everything. Nothing. Shit, I don't even know where to start."

"Start with what happened today."

My vision lost focus as I stared off in space.

"Tina was attacked today." I was too tired to say more.

"What?"

"Yeah, but at least this is enough to re-open her dad's case as a possible murder instead of a suicide."

"I guess that's a silver lining for ya."

"Except that Dunn has, like, two cops total and the detective on his case is fifteen years old," I snapped. "But I guess it's progress." I *hmphed* my sarcasm.

"Hey, in case you didn't know, I'm here for you." He rested his hand on my thigh in a comforting way, like a friend would. "Anything you need. I'm even prepared for a sleepover—got my jammies and everything I need"—he tipped his Budweiser high—"so we have all night."

On any other day, in any other scenario, I would have imagined a completely different connotation to *having all night* together. But today, today Tina was heavy on my heart. There was no room for lusting after Tristan.

The thickening night pulled and stretched the shadows. Only a dim pinprick of light pierced through the living room from a streetlight that had found the gap between my curtains.

"How could Tina have been stabbed—while in a hospital? And no one saw a damn thing?"

"I wish I could answer that."

"I mean, he waltzed right out of there, Tristan. How the hell does someone slip into a hospital psych ward *unnoticed*, smother a patient *unnoticed*, stab her *unnoticed*, and leave … *unnoticed*?"

He shrugged empathetically. "But she's okay, right?"

"She's in critical condition. They think she'll pull through because they found her right after it happened, but … she could be *dead*, Tristan!" The hysteria simmered as that alternative reality fabricated itself in my head, verging on a boil. I took a deep calming breath.

"But she's not dead. She's strong. She'll be okay." His hand shot up and circled around me, pulling me into him, my back against his body. A protective gesture. A sedative to an unnerved woman like me.

"I need to figure out who did this … and why. I think I have an idea, but it's going to sound batshit crazy."

"Lucky for you I like batshit crazy."

How much was too much to tell? Tina's story was her own, but Tina, well, Tina was unconscious. Tina was almost killed. Maybe it was time to betray my promise to keep her secrets, if it meant saving her life.

"I need you to swear to me that this stays between us. Got it?"

"I gotcha, Ari. My lips are sealed." To prove it, he held an imaginary key in his fingers and turned the invisible lock on his lips.

And then I proceeded to tell Tristan everything. About Josef's death, how I suspected it wasn't a suicide but a murder. I told him about the autopsy report, about the drugs in his system but how he had no prescription on file, how he had been working with a sex-trafficking ring to

178

sell Tina, and when Tina escaped, Josef owed them money. I told him about the threatening message the traffickers left her, about Tina's lies to me and to the cops, about her being the last person to see him alive and the one with the biggest motive for revenge.

I told him about the bleached bathroom and missing notepad from the suicide note. I told him about Killian's fight with Josef, then my meeting with Killian—and my slipup in telling him which hospital she was at—and hours later her attack. I told him about Killian's questionable expensive tastes and about Rosalita's clear ire toward her son and grandson.

I poured it all out in a waterfall of words, then left it all on the table for Tristan to sort through, to dissect, to piece together a sensible picture from it all.

But instead of answers, he just listened. And sat silently when I finished.

"So? What do you think? Do you think it's Killian who killed his father? Maybe hired by Tina's trafficker? Or Tina getting revenge? I don't know what to think anymore. My brain's fried, Tristan."

For a moment he simply watched me.

Then he spoke, carefully. "Wow, that's some stellar investigative work. You work in retail? I think you're definitely in the wrong profession."

"But does it all sound crazy?"

"No ..." he wavered, his voice edging on *maybe*. "But I think you need to step away from this. I think you're in way over your head."

I knew it. There was something murky in front of me, but I couldn't see through the quagmire. Not yet, at least. Perhaps this was bigger than I thought; the excitement of discovery made me tingle all over. "So you agree—there's something going on? I'm on to something, aren't I?"

"Possibly ... yes, maybe something. But if someone

killed Tina's father, then followed it up by going after her, you need to get out of the line of fire. You told the cops. Let the professionals do their job."

I huffed. "Except they already think it's a closed case. Suicide. I'm sure they'll tell me Tina's attack is circumstantial."

"Maybe it is, maybe it isn't. Just please give it a rest before you start wading in too deep?"

Ha! Oh, I left the shallow waters several laps ago and felt the rip current trying to sweep me out to sea. It was scary but thrilling, and I liked it. But I wasn't trying to be confrontational with Tristan ... just yet. We had plenty of time before I should show him my true colors.

"I guess once Tina pulls through we'll find out who hurt her and get some answers. I'll keep my hands and eyes to myself in the meantime."

I hated making promises I had no intention of keeping.

Chapter 28

Ari

Five days until dead

The cushion behind me was cool and empty, the starkness of it alarming. The space that Tristan had filled, the length of my body pressed into him like a hand cupping a hot mug, was now devoid of his heat. Only his musky scent lingered.

The apartment was filled with the silence of abandonment. I wandered toward the bathroom, hoping he might be quietly freshening up so as not to wake me. But the neatly hung towels and untouched washcloths told a different story. He had left in a hurry.

I hate mornings, but a cup of coffee helped tame the beast. Lumbering into the kitchen with the weight of fatigue slowing me down, I saw that the coffeemaker had already been started, with a note tucked under a clean coffee cup set out for me:

Hope you don't mind me rooting through your cabinets, but you don't make it easy to find where you keep stuff. Luckily I randomly opened your freezer, where I found your coffee grounds. I hope fresh coffee makes up for me sneaking out. I got called into work suddenly, but I'd love to see you again soon. Even if it is a 3 AM booty call … sans booty.

Tristan

Like a schoolgirl whose first crush said hi to her in the hallway, I grinned in giddy triumph. He had written!

But my smile faded as quickly as it came when I realized I had no idea what "work" meant for Tristan. Who gets called into work in the middle of the night? Was he an emergency medical technician? Or a firefighter? No—he wore too much leather to be either of those. He looked more like the lead singer of a rock band, but rockers were busy getting laid by their groupies at three a.m., I supposed. Lucky groupies.

It was disturbing how little I actually knew about him, and yet he knew everything about me.

Was he becoming my ... *therapist*?

No way in hell, I couldn't let our potential romance die a miserable death before it even started. Especially if it meant I would be the basket case and he would be the proverbial sounding board. *That* didn't sound grueling— having a baggage-toting girlfriend with more drama than the entire cast of *Days of Our Lives*. But there was hope for us yet. His note meant we were salvageable, so I needed to pull us out of therapy mode, toss my baggage to the curb, and make him fall in love with me, damn it.

With my morning open and an ability to fall back asleep impossible, I decided to check in on Tina before my afternoon shift. I had told the nurse to call me the moment anything happened, if she woke up, but judging how frantic the ICU was with nurses bustling about as if they were on speed, I figured my request got shoved in the bottom of the mile-high pile of other patient requests.

Parking was a breeze before nine o'clock—a time I would usually be entering another REM cycle. I tapped on Tina's closed door and it shifted a crack open. The television was on ... and Tina was watching it! My heart leaped as I ran in, a hot mess of tears and laughter.

"You're okay!" My voice got caught in the salt in my throat. Despite the tears blurring my vision and snot dripping down my lip, I jumped in for a hug and kiss.

Tina wiped away whatever residue I had left on her cheek, chuckling. "Yes, I'm okay, silly. In a crazy amount of pain, but alive. Though when I woke up, I wished I hadn't."

She mumbled a complaint of searing pangs in her stomach and how the nurses couldn't care less.

"You *were* stabbed, dumbass. It's to be expected you're gonna have a lot of pain. Didn't they give you any painkillers?"

Tina frowned childishly. "They're being frugal with them ... because of the whole attempted suicide thing. The dosage they're giving me is barely touching this."

"Do you want me to ask them to give you more?"

"Pretty please," Tina said with a grimacing grin.

I pressed a button that paged the nurse's station.

"While we wait, I wanna know what happened. Did you see who it was?"

Tina heaved, then winced. "I wish I knew. I was asleep. Me and Killian—"

Then she stopped. Just clammed up.

"You and Killian what?"

"He came to visit me."

I knew it, the bastard. He promised he'd let me intervene.

Unless he had planned on going after Tina.

It was only logical if he was working for her trafficker.

But I couldn't say what I was thinking—not with Tina in this critical state.

"We were talking about a bunch of stuff ... he confessed how he came to America to free me, but then after him and Dad arrived they got in a fight about money.

Dad couldn't find work and wanted to leave me with George for a couple more months until he got on his feet, but Killian wanted me out right away. Apparently it got ugly, Killian left, and they hadn't seen each other since."

Until Killian killed him, that is. He conveniently left that part out.

"Anyways," Tina continued, "Killian didn't know exactly how to find me until just recently—thanks to you."

"I'm sorry I slipped up—" I sputtered.

"No, it's okay." She waved me off. "It's good we reconnected. He has a girlfriend—some married cougar, not sure what I should call her—and got his GED. You know he's only sixteen and graduated already? He's really smart."

Yeah, smart enough to get away with murder—the first time. But not a second time, because I was on to him.

"He got a job doing construction—"

Or do you mean sex trafficking little girls? I wanted to say.

"And he's saving up for college—"

"Instead of using his precious savings to get these traffickers off your back?" I interjected, not bothering to mince my words.

I couldn't stay silent a moment longer.

How blind was Tina to reality? Her brother was an asshole. Maybe even a homicidal asshole.

"I didn't bring that up, Ari, and I would never ask him to do that for me. He needs to take care of himself just like I need to take care of myself."

"Whatever. Sounds like a crock of shit to me, but it's your family." How could Tina overlook the clear-as-day fingers pointing to Killian lurking behind their father's death? He conveniently had a fight with Josef right before he died. He was conveniently at Tina's bedside right before the attack. What more did Tina need? She was tangoing with a killer—*her* attempted killer! But instead she wanted to remain oblivious—all for the sake of *family*. Screw family.

"Yeah, it *is* my family. Anyways, we watched some TV and it actually felt ... normal. Like a normal brother-sister visit. Like we were siblings again, like back when we were kids. Kinda surreal." The nostalgia in her voice annoyed me.

"And then what?" I prompted.

"I ended up falling asleep while he was here. I don't know how long I was out, but I woke up to a pillow on my face suffocating me. I fought back—I really tried—but then whoever it was stabbed me and I lost consciousness. Never saw anyone. Next thing I know I'm in intensive care. But hey, at least the nurses are nicer in this unit!" Her voice rose with a chipper laugh that spread like an irritating rash.

"This isn't funny. You almost died."

Tina turned to me, her face flat and deadpan. "You think I care about dying? I think those monsters making me live in fear is my punishment. I've spent two years in hiding, watching over my shoulder, wondering if today will be my last day of freedom—if being chained to dread is really freedom. I'm just waiting, biding time until I'll be passed around from pervert to pervert again like a bowl of spaghetti. So if I wanna laugh, I'll laugh. And when those monsters finally succeed in killing me, then I'll really be free. Because some things are worse than death."

And here I thought I knew all there was to know about life and suffering. I was clueless. I have never known real anxiety.

"We can catch them—the monsters. We can put those bastards in cages so they'll never get out or hurt you. Please help me help you."

"I told everything I know to the police. They said they'll

take another look at the hospital surveillance footage and get back to me. And they scraped my fingernails so hopefully I'll have gotten some DNA that will lead back to who did it. I'm leaving it in the cops' hands; I just want to step away from it."

Exactly the same thing Tristan had asked me to do.

I felt no different than a two-year-old having a fit after her blankie was taken away. But I actually wanted to help Tina. It filled my battered brain with something other than anxiety attacks and regret. What the hell was so wrong with me stepping up to help ... and maybe exorcising my demons in the process?

Chapter 29

Ari

Five days until dead

Y ou're gonna love staying with me," I assured Tina as I fished for my keys in my labyrinthine handbag.

In a momentary relapse, it reminded me of my mom's purse when I was a child. Sitting in church, Carli and I would ask for gum, and Mom would tell us to look for it, always handing her bag to me with its many zippered pouches and silk-lined pockets. For the next thirty minutes at least—through the prayers and the sermon and the Bible reading—we'd busily search for the elusive pack of gum in her cluttered purse. We'd rummage through a collection of tissues, loose change, mom's hairbrush, and an assortment of odds and ends, usually never finding that gum. But it didn't matter. We had fun making a scavenger hunt out of it, which passed the time and kept us still. I now wondered if Mom had set the whole thing up simply to occupy us during those long, boring services that I suddenly ached for.

Carli and I, our bony legs dangling off the wooden pew seat. The choir singing old-school hymns, the rise and fall of our bodies as we knelt and stood in tandem, the message of hope and perseverance delivered from the pulpit. Better days, those were. Innocent days when our family of four wrestled ourselves out the front door in an argumentative frenzy to make it to church on time, then plopped into our usual welcoming corner of the sanctuary, releasing the chaos of the morning into the dusty air.

I had hated sitting through the church service back then, but now I longed for it. The normalcy of it.

The rattle of my keys brought me back to Tina. Although she should have stayed another day or two to recover in the hospital, Tina checked out against medical advice. Even though security had been stepped up since the assault, it was just too risky to leave her there, exposed, vulnerable, just waiting for the killer to come back and finish the job. Her original plan was to live with Rosalita in her rundown motel, but I wouldn't have it. No, she needed a *secure* home to recover in with a full kitchen and home-cooked meals—or my offerings of canned soup and grilled cheese—not some pay-per-night place with a bug-ridden bed and mini-fridge.

I fiddled with the stubborn lock. "It's a quiet complex, and the neighbors are nice enough. I know it doesn't look like much from the outside, but it's not too bad." Little white lies. Did it really matter, though, considering where Tina had come from? I'm sure she wasn't one to judge.

When the door finally budged open, my chatter stopped and crickets chirped. There was a gasping silence as we both stood there—me in shock, Tina in confusion.

"Uh, in need of some housekeeping?" she asked tentatively.

The sofa and coffee table were overturned, the chairs upended, papers and books and movies and junk scattered across the carpet. Some jackoff had tossed my place.

And right as I was assuring Tina of her safety here.

Nice place, my ass. Luckily, my precious TV had been spared.

I threw my arm out as Tina took a step forward. "I

need to make sure no one's here." If the perpetrator was lingering, I'd have a surprise for him. I tiptoed to the kitchen and grabbed a steak knife from the drawer. With stealthy steps I wove around the scattered remains of my possessions, checking each room with my knife aimed and ready to strike.

But the apartment was empty. I was almost disappointed.

"C'mon in. It's safe." I waved Tina in weakly. "Welcome to my shit hole."

My things—my personal stuff. I felt nakedly vulnerable.

"What the ... I don't even ..." No words. No words could capture my fury. I had bounced right past fear and plunged into pissed off.

"Who would do this?" Tina speculated aloud.

"Maybe the same person who tried to kill you? Your traffickers, your brother—"

"Whoa there, girl. Don't go blaming Killian for this. He's innocent."

"Until proven guilty," I added churlishly.

As far as I knew, it could have been any number of people. The trafficking minions were first on the list, but I couldn't rule out Killian, since he was last at the scene when Tina was attacked. Maybe he had beef with me for snooping and this was my message. It was adolescent enough to be him.

Then there was Rosalita, who clearly voiced her disdain for Josef and knew I was helping Tina find his killer. Was this a passive-aggressive plea for me to back off my little investigation side-job? It seemed a little classless for an old lady, but this wasn't exactly the behavior of a well-adjusted person.

"Why don't you call the police while I start cleaning up," Tina offered.

"Why the hell do I need to call them?" It was none of their damn business, if you asked me. It could have been anyone, and it was an easy enough job to break into a no-security first-floor apartment around here. A little jiggling of the cheap sliding glass door on my porch was enough to loosen the lock free. I'd learned this trick after numerous times locking myself out.

"You have to report this."

"Why? What's the point? No one got hurt. Police don't give a shit."

"Because it could be related to my attack. There could be evidence here. Just do it, Ari. But help me with this sofa first. Don't wanna tear my stitches."

We pushed the sofa upright and it landed with a *thud*.

"You sure you don't want to rest while I clean?"

"It's the least I can do for dragging you into this."

But there was no dragging about it. I wanted this. Needed it, even. It felt good to be doing something other than hauling vacuum cleaners down warehouse stairs, or folding and hanging pile after pile of women's fitting room clothes. I needed something more, and this was exactly that.

It was my purpose.

At Tina's nagging I dialed the local Durham Police Department direct and was transferred to an Officer Buchanan—whom I aptly named Undertaker (after the WWE legend) because with a voice like that he had to be a six-foot-four steel-muscled badass … and also because I was running out of witticisms—and told the Barry White baritone what we came home to. I added details about Tina's attack, asking if he could look into whether they had identified a face or gotten the DNA tests back. He assured me he'd check, then advised me not to touch anything, since he'd want to see if anything was missing and check for fingerprints. I doubted whoever did it would have left such a glaring trail, but I obliged.

Upon arrival, Undertaker lived up to my expectation. Towering over me, the pecs on his thick chest stood out like two hams, straining the buttons in his painted-on cop shirt to the max. A neckless head, square as a box, sat upon the widest shoulders I'd ever seen. He had a blue five-o'clock shadow and an old-fashioned flattop graying the temples. A lipless gash served for a mouth and the dark eyes underneath the Frankensteinian brow were cold and unsmiling. He looked like he'd fallen off a wanted poster himself, but damn was he efficient. Sweeping through each room, he did his thing—powdering furniture here and there with black dust, picking up random spewed papers, checking windows and doors—and finished in about ten minutes while I recapped recent events. Nope, no fingerprints, big surprise. After I leafed through the debris strewn all over the floor, I assured him that nope, nothing was missing, so he shrugged his way to the door.

"Looks like the intruder came in through your porch. Easy enough to do. You should have your landlord put in a better lock."

I grunted. "No kidding. The three-year-old in 2B could probably wiggle the damn thing open, and he's dumb as a sack of bricks. Caught him yesterday running headfirst into parked cars."

Not that my landlord cared if I was raped and pillaged at night, as long as the thief didn't steal his fixtures—which would come out of my security deposit, for sure.

"You think this break-in has to do with my attacker?" Tina chimed in.

"There's not enough to say one way or another, but we'll keep our eyes open. If he comes back, we'll be ready."

Ready for what?

Empty promises.

"Oh, and one other thing." He turned to Tina, who sat in an easy chair with her knees pulled up to her chest. "We went through your hospital footage again. We saw your brother leaving before the attack, at 8:32. We spoke with him and we have several witnesses corroborating his story that he left the building. Based on the severity of the wound and how much you had bled out, the stabbing had to have happened a little after 9:00, no more than ten minutes before the nurse found you, which was at around 9:10. She may have even passed the attacker on her way to your room."

He had slipped right between our fingers.

That took Killian off the hook ... or not.

Unless he had circled back wearing the cap.

"Anything found from under my nails?" I heard the hope rise in Tina's voice.

"Unfortunately our DNA swab turned nothing up. Just keep an eye out in case the attacker comes back. Plus, I'm going to have a uniform do a drive-by and check on you a couple times a day, at least until things calm down, okay?"

That sounded more like cops stalking me. Hell no. That platter was off the table.

"With all due respect, sir, no way, no how do I want cops following me. Got it?"

"Even if yours and Tina's safety is at stake?" he urged. "I might have to insist on this. Tina was nearly killed—the killer may return. We need to take precautions."

"I don't give a flying rat's ass, officer, about your definition of precautions. She was in a damn hospital room with people all around, and she still got stabbed. A friggin' cop circling the block isn't going to keep her safe. And I've heard about the corruption in law enforcement. How do I know your beat cop hasn't been hired to hurt her?"

The Undertaker took a step forward. I took one back. He pretty much had one expression, pissed, and now it was turned up to eleven. I braced myself for a verbal smackdown.

"You watch too much television," he said with a sigh.

That was it? This guy was a pussycat. I was emboldened. "I can protect her better than some man in blue too busy stuffing his face with donuts and coffee to give a shit about her. I'll watch her 24-7, okay?"

I knew he was trying to protect and serve and all that shit, but blue uniforms made me feel anything but protected and served. More like guarded and scrutinized.

The Undertaker threw up his python arms. "As long as Tina is okay with that, fine. I'm not going to argue over it."

We both glanced over at Tina to make the call, who shrunk back into the cushions of her chair. When she finally found her voice, she said with shaky confidence, "I trust Ari with my life. I'll let you know, sir, if I change my mind."

"See? We feel safer on our own, thank you very much."

As I prodded him toward the exit, I opened the door to find Tristan mid-knock. And his face pink with alarm.

"Hey, Cox," Undertaker greeted him. "Were you called in on this? I didn't ask for backup."

"No, uh, Buchanan, I'm here on a personal matter."

"Oh, okay. Well, see you at the precinct."

"Later."

The two men shook hands before Undertaker headed out the door.

What. The. God. Damn. Hell.

"So." Arms folded, I waited for Tristan to explain himself, blocking him in the doorway, inwardly fuming.

"So."

"You're a cop."

The writing on the wall looked bleak from where I

stood. He was a *cop*. The one profession that left an acrid taste in my mouth. The same people who named me "criminal" and sent me to a home akin to kid's jail. The same people who yelled at me and shoved me when I walked too slow through the lifeless gray halls. The same people who found me nearly dead and didn't show an ounce of emotion for a weeping, emotionally battered child. Shuffle me off, get rid of me, that was their motto.

Of all the damn jobs, my dream guy picked this one. Just my luck.

"Yep, a cop. But a good one, I promise." Tristan rocked back on his heels, hands tucked in his pockets like a cocksure little boy. "I wanted to tell you, but ..."

"You know I can't stand cops."

"Right, hence me not telling you."

Why the hell did I have to fall so hard for him already? I could cut him loose right now, move on. But ... but he was so damn cute.

No.

I moved to slam the door in his face, but he blocked it from closing with the toe of his boot.

"Ari, wait!" he pleaded.

I knew the slop-fest I was about to witness. *I'm sorry for hurting you. I'm sorry for breaking your trust. I'm sorry for lying.* Ha! I wasn't that girl—the one who fell for fake apologies. And I certainly wasn't that girl who would take him back so easily—or at all. One strike and you're out was how I played the game ... or maybe a couple strikes when it came to Tristan. But no more.

"Save it. And I hope the door hits your ass on the way out." I aimed my palm at his chest and pushed, but he wouldn't budge.

"Please hear me out. I'm sorry. I wanted to tell you. I did."

I held up my hand to spare him the trouble, but he

blustered forward.

"I work undercover, so it's not something I'm used to disclosing in introductory conversations. *Hey, I'm Tristan. I'm an undercover cop. Shoot me, please.* It's not exactly easy to be forthright with someone when you lie about who you are for a living."

"Exactly, you lied. You lied to me. What the hell else aren't you telling me? Why should I believe a damn thing you say?"

"I didn't want to lie. I wanted to tell you the truth, but the closer we got, the more afraid I was of losing you over this. And then too much time had passed, and I didn't know how to anymore."

"I don't even know who you are."

"I'm the same guy you knew yesterday. The same guy who was over here at three in the morning, helping you through a hard time. The same guy who will let you drive despite having spent two hours getting my back adjusted. The same guy who will get in the car with you without a set of earplugs. I'm the same guy, damn it, that likes a girl … the best girl I know."

The best girl he knew? Laughable, but sweet. Either he didn't know me at all, or maybe he liked what he saw, flaws and all. My resolve wavered. Maybe it wasn't so bad. But he had lied from the start. It wasn't so simple to just shrug off. "I just don't know. I need time to think about this. I think you need to leave."

"Think about this."

They say few kisses can match up to that first one, but this one definitely gave it a run for its money. Unlike before where it was tender and unsure, this was driving with passion and desperation, raw emotion. At first I resisted, a cursory attempt with little conviction, more out of requirement to my ire, but as his arm wound around my waist, pulling me closer, and his lips increased their pressure against mine, I yielded completely to him. My resistance spent, my body melded to his, making the spaces in between nearly indiscernible. When we finally separated, chests heaving, loins aching, his profession was the last thing on my mind.

Damn, he was good.

"Fine. I'll tell you what. Maybe we can see how things go, and if I can't get over your cop-hood, or if you annoy me too much, I'll just break your heart. Okay?"

"You got a deal."

He playfully nuzzled my neck.

"Hang on! You're not out of the dog house yet, bub," I chided, gently shoving him away.

His eyes glanced upward behind me, then widened. For the first time since he showed up he took in the scene around him, noticing the mess behind me, then stepped around me to get the full view. He whistled lowly, then muttered something undecipherable as Tina emerged from her bathroom sanctuary, sensing the private and awkward moment had passed.

"Ransacked—and a damn good job of it too. Anything taken?"

"Not so far as I can tell."

"Ari, next time something like this happens, you need to call me immediately."

"Next time? There won't be a next time for this douche bag," I spat.

"I'm serious, Ari. I'm working a string of murders, and if this has anything to do with me and my investigation, I need to protect you."

I rolled my eyes. "You know, everything doesn't always revolve around you men." I heaved as I wondered how long this would take to clean up. "I really don't feel like dealing with this right now. Can we go out somewhere, anywhere?"

Slapping his legs, Tristan said, "How about I take you ladies out to dinner and I'll help you clean up when we get back?"

No argument from me.

"Let's go! Maybe you can tell me more about this murder spree you're working on."

Tristan placed his hands on my shoulders and aimed me for the door. "We'll see."

"Oh, and drinks come with dinner, right, Tristan? I know I sure as hell could use one—or ten."

Chapter 30

Ari

Four days until dead

Benny's last suggestion to me was to talk to my parents. And that's exactly what I was here to do.

No forwarding address? No problem.

The Internet was a wonderful resource.

Thank God for the Freedom of Information Act.

The shock on Mom and Dad's faces when I showed up at their front door was priceless. The repugnance in my mother's eyes as I pushed past them through the semi-closed door, hauling Tina along behind me—there was no way I was leaving her alone except when I was working—I found hilarious.

Yes, Mother Dearest, here I am! Your discarded daughter, home at last. You can't get rid of me that easily.

"Hey, parents! Surprised to see me?" I bulldozed my way through the house with Tina lingering in the entry and my parents trailing me like hounds chasing a fox.

"Ari ... what are you doing here? How did you even find us?" my father said between exasperated breaths as I continued my exploration through the dining room, kitchen, living room, then circling back into the entry.

Not a speck of dust.

Not a knickknack out of place.

Nice and neat, just like the lies they lived.

I abruptly stopped at where the entryway opened into the living room, and Dad nearly bumped into me.

"*Find* you? So you were hiding from me all these years? Didn't want to be *found* by your only kin?"

"I didn't mean it that—" Dad blustered.

"Save it," I spat. "A little stalking can work wonders in turning up information—like a home address."

"What? You're stalking us—?" Dad stuttered.

"I'm kidding, Dad. It's not that damn hard to find an address online these days."

"Oh." His face scrunched up as if calculating a long math equation. "What prompted this visit, darling?"

I could hear the smooth edges of his voice, trying to fake nurture, but he was merely attempting to calm the storm. No actual love hung in those words.

I examined his face, a face I could barely remember any other day, but right now the memories pummeled their way into my head. The creases around his bright eyes, his perfect teeth I didn't inherit, the wiggle of his mustache when he talked. But the mustache was gone, revealing laugh lines etched around his mouth. I wondered how often he actually laughed these days.

"Got rid of the caterpillar, huh?" A pet name I called it as a little girl perched on his knee.

"Yep, wanted a change. I miss it though." He stroked the vacant skin above his upper lip. "So? What brings you here?"

"Just thought I'd say hi. And bring my friend Tina along. Tina," I turned to her, "meet my parents. Parents," I directed at them, "meet Tina."

Mom folded her arms in defiance while Dad nodded a solemn hello.

"So you and your friend are just popping by, huh?"

I tossed my hands up in the air and blew toward a nearby sofa. "You got me! I'm here to talk. And I'm not leaving until I get what the hell I came for."

"Language, Ari," Dad warned.

"Language, my ass," I shot back.

Dad rolled his eyes.

I fell into the fancy microfiber cushions and patted the empty space next to me. "So what's it gonna be?"

With cautious steps Dad chose the loveseat cattycorner me, while Mom hung back in the entryway in a silent standoff with Tina.

"Oh, *Mater*, dear!" I yelled whimsically to her. "Come in the living room. We're gonna chitchat."

Her heels *tap tap tapped* across their professionally cleaned ceramic floor. Even the white baseboards were pristine. *It's the little details,* I could hear my mother's edgy voice echoing from a faraway time and place in history when she set Carli and I about our weekly chores.

"Get to the bottom of why you're here, then you and your guest need to leave." The stern vexation of Mom's voice hadn't changed in all those absentee years.

Tina eventually snuck in and picked a faraway chair away from the cluster where I faced off with my parents.

"What, no cookies or tea, Mom? How rude."

"Ari—" Mom warned.

"Wow, you guys are stiff. I won't bother with updating you on my life, since you clearly don't give a shit. And I would ask about yours, but you want me out of here as fast as possible. So that leaves us with getting straight to the point. I'm here to talk about Carli—the night before the accident."

"Wha—you seriously came all the way here to drag out ancient history, tormenting your mother and I with the past?" When one described a father's voice as *booming*, my father set the standard by which all others were measured. His body shook, the floor vibrated, and anyone within earshot trembled at the sound of his *boom*.

Even scarier was when he rose from his seat upon doing so, towering over you.

That was what happened at that moment. And I admit, I was scared—at first. But the salt-and-pepper hair with only remnants of its former brown aged him. The stooping shoulders, the quivering thin lips—he wasn't the man I used to fear.

Glancing at my mother, her vibrant red hair was dull and lifeless now, a shade of auburn with gray flecks I didn't remember. She had the first signs of a turkey neck, crow's-feet around her eyes, and her hands were frail, veiny, alien-looking things ending in knobby fingers that she flexed ceaselessly from nervous tension. Her fingernails looked youthful, though, and capable of inflicting damage.

They could no longer make me back down. Not now. Not ever again. I stood face-to-shoulder with Dad, daring him to shut me up.

"You're damn right. I came all the way here to do this. You *owe* me. You both do. For lying all these years to me, to the cops, to yourselves. All the shit you put me through. I didn't push Carli, and you know it. That car intentionally swerved to hit her, and you know who did it."

"What? That's nonsense." Mom turned away, raising her chin in avoidance.

"I have proof. So tell me the truth and maybe I'll let it go and move on. And leave you two to your happily ever after without me."

"Proof? What proof?" Dad's challenge couldn't faze me, though.

"A witness who saw you getting beat up the night before. Certainly it would raise suspicion if that information was given to the cops, don't you think?"

The pink vehemence in his face drained into sickly white-gray. He crumbled into a humble heap on the sofa.

"You know about that?"

"Yes, I know about that."

"Who allegedly saw this?"

"Don't concern yourself with that. Concern yourself with telling me what you got into a fight about, and with whom. I know it's related to Carli's death. I guess that means that *you* killed her, doesn't it?" I turned the words against him, attacking him with the bite of accusation. The charge of him being responsible for his own daughter's death.

I never saw it, only felt it. Mom, the pouncing lioness, her clawing fingernails leaving scratches across my cheek in the wake of her stinging slap. I cupped the tingling flesh, keeping my tears at bay.

"What the hell?"

"You don't speak to your father like that!" I cowered at her shriek.

"You want to defend him? Why? And why didn't you defend me?" I screamed at her.

"I wanted to, Ari, but I simply couldn't anymore. You wouldn't understand." Her voice grew softer at the end ... as if she'd exhausted every emotion.

"Understand what?" I was tired of all the cryptic bullshit they kept tossing at me. Years of lies. Years of cover-ups. Years of pushing me away. For what? I couldn't handle being on the outside anymore. I needed answers. I deserved them.

By now the waterworks had burst and streams trickled down my face. Yet my parents remained robotically stoic, watching me crumble. Probably enjoying it, too.

"Ari, it's better for us all if you just stay away from all this," Mom pleaded. "Let Carli rest in peace, go live your life and make the most of it. You're better off without us in it. I'm telling you—it's for your own good."

"Is someone threatening you? Is this all about

202

protecting me from the person who killed Carli?" It sounded ludicrous even as I spoke the words—that my parents actually cared that much about me to lose me in order to save me—but once upon a time they did love me, didn't they? Could all of that love have vanished without a trace after Carli's death?

"Stop with the questions," Dad interjected. "We're done."

"If you want me to stop, then answer me. Who attacked you, and why were you fighting? You worked in an office, not the mafia. Since when do white-collar bank managers get their kneecaps busted up for a clerical error, huh?"

"It's ... complicated." I could see Dad was caving.

"Try me."

Dad sighed in resignation while my mother daggered him with a silent plea, but he continued, regardless of her wordless threat. "I had a friend. Let's call him ... George. Well, he was a ... business associate. I was handling his funds at the bank, but some money went missing. It wasn't me, I assure you, but he blamed me anyway and lost his mind. It eventually got sorted out after our little scuffle."

"Why didn't you press charges?" His story had more holes than a Krispy Kreme store.

"We worked it out. That's all that matters. It's over, and it had nothing to do with your sister."

"What the hell kind of business associate beats up their bank manager, Dad?"

"A crazy one, I guess. What the hell kind of girl eats peanut butter and pickle sandwiches?" he answered so matter-of-factly that I couldn't help but snort at the comic relief.

"It was on a dare, Dad."

His dare. Something he had done a lot when I was a

kid. We had been sitting at the kitchen table making sandwiches. I must have been no older than five or six at the time, and I whined about not wanting peanut butter and jelly for lunch. So he dared me to try something different. *Like what?* I had asked. So he double-dog dared me to eat pickles and peanut butter. I did, and I didn't mind it too much … especially after seeing his face turn a sickly shade of green upon watching me swallow. I got a kick out of eating that in front of him for years afterward.

"You never did back down from a dare …" I could hear the nostalgia in his voice, and for a sweet moment I think we both relished it.

Growing up, Dad's humor was one of my favorite things about him. No matter how spastic Mom was acting, or how intense Carli and I were fighting, Dad's jokes brought us back from the brink of insanity.

"I still eat that sometimes," I said between light laugher.

"You're disgusting, honey, but I love you regardless."

Did he really, though? Or was this an act to appease me so that I'd leave?

"About your questions, that's all I know, honey. I wish I had more to tell you, but I don't. Are you satisfied?"

"No, but women never are, right?"

At Dad's staccato *ha!* I grinned faintly, realizing I was never going to win against them. I resigned and stood to leave while on somewhat decent terms with them— whatever that actually meant. They reminded me to let go of the past and just focus on now while bustling me out the door, leaving no room for misinterpretation. There was no relationship to salvage. Little did they know that the past was my *now*. Until I figured out who was behind it, it would consume my present. And whatever dirt I tilled up, even if it damned them, I would expose it.

"That wasn't awkward at all," Tina said from two paces

ahead of me as she nearly jogged to my car.

"Yeah, you can always count on my hospitable, doting parents to put on a good show."

"Your dad—where did you say he works?"

"He's a bank manager. Why?"

"He looks familiar. I can't place him, but I recognize him."

"He's been in commercials for East Coast Bank. Maybe that's where you saw him?"

I watched an uncertain realization dawn across her face. "Yeah, yeah, I think that's it. Though he was much younger then, huh?"

"Give or take a decade."

The commercials had been filmed back before the accident. Before our family was torn apart. Back when I knew what *family* felt like.

I could never go back to *before*.

Chapter 31

Ari

Four days until dead

Tina's snores growled their way down the hallway from my bedroom, like an elk in heat. The poor girl had been put through the ringer. I hoped she at least had some nice dreams to escape to.

Even I could feel the heat of panic during the quiet moments. First Josef, then Tina. Whoever was behind the attacks relished the taste of blood, and they were clamping down hard. It was only a matter of time until they came back for Tina to finish the job. And then maybe me.

After emptying a box of tissues with a long weep, I had sent Tina to my room for the evening and insisted I'd take the sofa. My mind was too restless for television—even episodes of *Dexter*—and my thoughts too scattered to read. It was too early in the evening to sleep, so I kept replaying my visit with my parents on a loop in my head, each time picking apart their words like a buzzard on a deer carcass.

Something in the conversation waved a red flag at me, but what? We hardly exchanged any words. And Dad's "confession" was bare bones, short on details. I remembered my mother's cutting glare and laughed at how he ignored her and went on.

Take that, Mom!

What did he say, though? The man he'd had a fight with was a business associate. He even hypothetically named him—Jeffrey? John? It was a *juh* sound. It didn't stick to my brain at the time, but now it was utterly, critically, life-or-death important to me for reasons I couldn't explain.

George. That was it.

So familiar but also foreign.

I knew I'd heard that name before, but with so many cluttered thoughts in my brain, some were slipping out.

I tried to shrug it off, but it continued to nip at me. Why was that name so important?

Did I know a George? No face came to mind. Did I see a George written down somewhere? Yes, that was it. I remember the scribbled word. But where?

Maybe the police report.

My unconventional organizational skills came in handy for once, since whoever trashed my house hadn't looked on top of my fridge. I had put Josef's file up there for easy access and to keep my dining room table clutter-free—one perk of having OCD—and it turned out to be a good location, since that file was the one thing I didn't want to lose.

I pulled the folder out, including Josef's address book. Rifling through the papers, I found nothing with that name—George. I began to stuff everything back into the file, until my gut prodded me to open up the address book. Flipping through the sparse scribbled entries starting with *A*, I soon found a *George* listed under *B*: George Battan.

I sharpened my memory, thinking back over the days of conversations with Tina. Wasn't that message on Tina's phone from a George as well?

Yes, Tina's trafficker—George. How could I forget?

Clearly I needed more sleep.

It was an ironic choice of "hypothetical" name for my

dad to pick for his business partner.

Thoughts volleyed back and forth like it was an Olympic sport. Was it possible Dad's George and Tina's George were one and the same? Unlikely. It was such a common name, but a damn wild coincidence. There were hundreds of Georges in town. George Battan was probably a cover he used with Tina, but he probably went by something else with his underlings and *business associates*.

But still ...

In detective stories they called it a hunch, and that's exactly what this felt like.

I didn't believe in coincidence or serendipity. But then again, Durham wasn't a big town. People bumped into one another. Maybe it wasn't big enough for more than one high-ranking criminal named George.

No, that would mean that my father had something to do with Josef's death. That was too far beyond the realm of possibility—my father, a crook *and* a killer. Different Georges, different criminals. That made more sense. I'd find a way to break my father, to get in his head, but the time wasn't now.

Right now I had something else to deal with.

It was too bad Tina had been adamant about me not looking for information on her trafficker, insisting I not go to the police about it, because I hated to go behind her back. But whoever this was had hit me at home. He came on *my* turf, messed with *my* stuff, and hurt *my* friend. The least I could do was confront him about it. Tina couldn't blame me for acting out of self-preservation.

It was only half past eight, early enough for a telemarketer to call, so certainly early enough for me.

I dialed, and to my heart-stopping astonishment, he answered, his tone alert. My heart ravaged my chest as the anxiety began to swell. I hadn't expected him to pick up. Perhaps I hadn't really wanted him to. It was far easier to start something than to finish it.

"Is this George Battan?"

"Who's asking?" he answered. His genteel voice had a girlish lilt, almost a Michael Jackson falsetto, but with a sinister undertone. It reminded me of what a child molester would sound like if I had to give one a voice.

"I'm a friend of Josef's." The simpler, the safer. If he knew who I was talking about, then we would get somewhere.

"Ah, yes, Tina's friend Ari, right?"

How he knew it was me went beyond creepy.

As if reading my thoughts, he added, "You have an easy to distinguish voice, my dear. Though, I'm disappointed. I was hoping Tina would come to her senses and contact me herself, but apparently she likes to play games. I can play games too."

It took a moment for me to accept that I was speaking to Tina's captor. If I just found a way to negotiate with him, I could end the madness. But my brain was fumbling through loose strings of words that wouldn't make sense as they popped in and out of my head. I inhaled a relaxing breath, grounding my crackling brain.

"I'm not calling to play games." I forced a steady voice. "I'm calling to finish things. I want to pay off whatever she owes so she can be free and clear."

"You think it's that easy to release Tina from her ... obligation?"

Obligation? Was that the polite phrase for sexual slavery?

"Isn't it? You want money, I'll get it to you. I just want her to be able to move on with her life."

He chuckled, not the boisterous guffaw of an evil genius, but a soft snigger.

"I don't think you realize what you're getting into. But

if Tina wants her freedom and you can afford it, then I'll agree to your request. But let me be clear: Just you. No cops. No surprises."

"I agree as long as you do the same—I want you, not some hired hand. I want to look you in the eyes when you tell me it's over—that Tina's free. I'm not asking for much—just to see you say it. Deal?"

I needed George, not a loyal lieutenant who would go to jail before snitching on him. I couldn't afford for him to hide behind protection.

He paused, as if considering my motives behind the request. "Alright. It'll be me. But if you can't keep this simple and clean, then I'll remind Tina what's at stake."

"What is at stake, exactly?"

I was betting on another threat of coming after us, of a repeat stabbing, but I would have lost that bet. In two words George shook my world, jackhammered apart everything I thought I knew about Tina.

"Her daughter."

Chapter 32

Ari

Three days until dead

Tina and I hadn't been on speaking terms since our fight about yet another secret she'd kept hidden from me—a baby. A chubby, crying, shitting, crawling secret. And the reason she hadn't wanted me to go to the police or to confront the infamous George Battan.

Her little girl, Giana, would be his next target.

I didn't realize a black market for babies actually existed, but Giana was proof of its reality. Underground deals thrived as the highest bidders kidnapped their spoils. Wealth could buy loopholes, bypass red tape, delete a paper trail, and even buy life. All that was needed was cold hard cash to win the prize—a baby adopted illegally, and in Tina's case, against a mother's will.

Giana was missing, and only George had access to her. That was his royal flush. His guarantee. That was what made Tina so afraid that she'd tried to take her own life just to stop the fear.

George was right—I had no idea what I was getting into. But it had been too late to retract my offer to meet him, bringing along the balance of what Josef owed. I had offered to buy off Tina's freedom and the offer was accepted—no backing out now. I had emptied my entire savings account, accumulated from seven years of working overtime and frugal living, barely enough to afford his price, but a girl's freedom was worth it. Tina, on the other hand, wouldn't agree. She would tell me I was playing with fire with my behind-the-scenes wheeling and dealing.

Her daughter's life was George's golden ticket to keeping Tina under his thumb. I understood that. But we couldn't just let the sonofabitch get away with it. Especially since I had a wild card they didn't know about.

Tristan. My unofficial boyfriend cop.

I knew he would help me. And I knew he'd keep it our little secret.

"Do you think it will work?" I asked him over coffee and pancakes at IHOP. We managed to pick the rare hour in the morning when the wait was less than an hour long. North Carolinians sure loved their pancakes.

"With two days to plan this? His record is clean, I have nothing on him. And you're telling me I can't set up the kind of protection I would usually prepare for in this scenario. I'm putting you at a huge risk. If you'd just let me get the department in on this, we could handle it—"

"Out of the question, Tristan!" I barked. It wasn't an option—not with Tina and Giana's lives at stake ... again. Cops didn't care who they got killed, as long as they were in control. I wasn't about to let them eff up my only chance at helping Tina and saving her life. Wasn't Josef's death and Tina's attack clear enough proof that George wasn't bluffing? "One man was killed and his daughter stabbed because of this guy." *And an innocent baby's life could be next.* "George told me no cops. That means no cops. You're lucky I even came to you for help."

"Fine, Ari, I get it. I'm going against my gut here and obliging you. But I still think you're being a 'tard."

"Aw, how sweet of you to say." I grinned at the coarse way he worried about me ... he genuinely cared. It was nice in a warm-sunlight-on-a-cool-day kind of way. But it wasn't going to stop me from doing what I needed to do.

He frowned at me.

"Oh, relax. You're being a pansy. I'm just handing over a pile of money to a perv who preys on kids. I could probably kick his ass with my hands tied behind my back."

"First of all, it's not that simple. He could be carrying a gun or a knife. If he gets spooked he could hurt you—or worse. But no biggie, right?"

"You're being dramatic." This was a guy who stole little kids, who snuck up on Tina while she was sleeping—he couldn't even face her awake when he attacked her. He was a sniveling, whimpering coward.

"No matter what I say, there's no stopping you, is there?" His eyes pleaded with me, so I turned away. I couldn't deny those eyes.

"Nope. The ball is rolling downhill fast. Probably at warp speed by now, so there's no slowing it down."

Tristan shook his head with a what-are-you-getting-yourself-into smirk. "You know what else rolls downhill? Shit. And that's just what you're getting into. Deep. It's more than just handing cash over. Right now we have no case against him. We need to build a firm one. If he cleared out all the girls in his house and has no computer records linking us to his trafficking, we have nothing. Plus we have no testimonies other than Tina's. His defense could say she fabricated this and clear him. We have nothing showing any tie between them other than his word against hers ... and one voice message from a burner phone that may or may not sound like him."

It was sounding more hopeless by the minute. "So he's going to walk."

"No, not necessarily. Your exchange will go as planned, but I will have eyes on you the entire time. I'll put a wire on you, and you'll need to get him to agree that the money is in exchange for Tina's freedom, free and clear. Then once I catch him accepting the money, I'll step in. His confession on tape plus accepting the cash should be enough to put him behind bars, along with Tina's testimony, that is. She *is* willing to testify, right?"

I hoped so. I hadn't mentioned Giana to Tristan after being sworn to secrecy, but catching George was the only way to track down Tina's daughter.

"I will make sure she testifies." Even if I had to bind and drag her skinny ass to the courthouse.

We stopped by the Durham Police Department on the way home so that Tristan could sign out a wire for me to wear. I nervously chattered the whole way there, drilling him with true or false questions about what real police work was like compared to what I'd seen on television. Most of my questions he laughed off, but the more he shared, the more interested I became. Damned if I wasn't ironically drawn to the thing I hated most.

I sat across from him as he puttered around with some paperwork at his desk. Here before me was unlimited access to all kinds of databases and files and confidential information. I wondered just how much Tristan would let me tap into.

At what point in a relationship was it okay to ask for favors?

"Any chance you can look up something for me?" I asked coyly. Maybe I could flirt my way into access. Certainly there had to be perks to dating a cop.

"Depends. What are you looking for?"

"A name."

"Don't you already have one of those?"

I chuckled at his lameness.

"What kind of name?"

"The name of someone who might own a certain type of car."

"Oh, like a guy driving a Porsche? You looking to trade up, huh?"

"Always. Though I'm thinking something a little more lavish, like a late-1970s orange Ford Pinto." I had already spent hours searching online through pictures of orange hatchbacks from the 1970s, and surprisingly there were a lot to choose from. Who knew hatchbacks were so popular—and hideous—once upon a time? Thank God they fell out of fashion.

Benny had mentioned a Chevy Vega or Ford Festiva, and while they matched the body style I was looking for, only the Pinto had the yawning rear window I vividly recalled in my session with Dr. Weaver. I was 99 percent sure that was the vehicle I was looking for. Lucky for me, they weren't a popular vehicle in 2002.

"A guy with a Pinto? Sounds like the cream of the crop. You sure know how to pick 'em. I'm guessing this has something to do with your sister?"

"You're a smart one, you."

"That I am."

His fingers clacked along the keyboard as he entered the DMV registry, pulling up all records of orange Ford Pintos and their VINs.

"Looks like you're in luck. There are only a handful of Pintos in Durham, and only one orange one. I'm guessing that's our VIN, assuming the car is still in North Carolina. But the title is with a junkyard. I'll trace back the owners to see who owned it in 2002."

Biting on his lower lip, he concentrated in the most adorable way. Damn, I wanted to take a nibble myself. He made no attempt to push me away as I draped myself over his shoulder. A minute later he had a half-page list of names with corresponding dates of title transfer. Then he narrowed it to the year 2002. The list was knocked down to one name.

"You can ooh and aaah now," he said proudly, swiveling his chair around to face me. "Debra Littleton. I'm guessing she is a relative of the guy you're looking for. Maybe his wife. Well, assuming the driver was male. But don't you go getting any ideas, Ari," he said with a warning in his tone. "I will handle this. I'll contact her and see what I can find out. Got it?"

I glanced to the side, avoiding eye contact. Me—getting uninvolved? That was like asking a crackhead to give up his next fix. Not gonna happen.

"I need to talk to her myself," I pleaded.

"You don't know this person. She could be skittish about what happened back then—defensive. And it could get dangerous."

"Ha. I laugh in the face of danger. Besides, how dangerous can someone named *Debra* be?"

"Clearly you haven't met the kind of Debras I have. Someone's gotta look out for you, Ari."

I wanted to tell him that yes, I had met my fair share of mcth-addled, knife-toting ex-con Debras, no thanks to my family for putting me in that position. I wanted to tell him that I wasn't some damn sugarcoated innocent baby doll who needed doors opened for her and flowers delivered to her doorstep. I wanted to tell him that I was no dainty Southern belle giggling behind her church fan and looking to be set on a pedestal. I'd been taking care of myself, looking out for myself, and fending for myself my entire damn life. I didn't need him or anyone else telling me what I could or couldn't do.

But instead of saying those things, I tucked them away. I folded them into orderly thoughts, slid them into my back pocket, and breathed. He was trying to help, and getting agitated would get me nowhere.

216

"Look, having a cop show up will feel like an interrogation. Having a nice chitchat with another woman might be a better tactic. Please?"

He rolled his eyes in surrender. "Fine, but I'm not letting you go by yourself."

My smile did a victory lap. I was only one detour away from catching Carli's killer. Like Tristan really had a say in the matter. What he didn't know wouldn't hurt him.

Chapter 33
Rosalita

San Luis, Mexico
2000

A newborn baby cooed from a cardboard box in the corner as Rosalita, Mercedes, and Josef held their shot glasses high, clinking them together in their fourth toast of the evening. The alcohol was flowing freely tonight, even if it did cost them nearly two weeks' worth of meals. Despite Rosalita's protests, it was day to celebrate. And celebrate they did.

"A toast to Killian, my new son!" Josef cheered, his voice thick with liquor.

"*Salud!*" Mercedes cried in muddled merriment.

They had emptied half the bottle of Jose Cuervo Clasico Silver upon the arrival of mother and son from the hospital, and now hours later they were all feeling it. The potent tequila coursed through their veins, warmed their stomachs, and loosened the noose of the day.

Mercedes had birthed a boy! It was something to commemorate, Josef declared. Four hours ago she had arrived home carrying the bundle of brown flesh and ribbon of black curls, showing him off to neighbors as family after family dropped by with enough food to last a week and gifts rising halfway up Sophia's bedroom wall. The two-year-old had wanted to unwrap them all herself, but tuckered out about halfway through when she fell asleep on the sofa playing with a partially unwrapped knitted doll.

Now tucked away in bed, Sophia slept soundly while her parents and grandmother toasted to a new life of prosperity, a perfect family now complete, and general good health. By the fourth toast they were running out of blessings, and Rosalita was running out of patience.

She was certainly happy for the young couple and their beautiful boy. But with Josef out of work and another mouth to feed, her sewing income couldn't support a family of five. Especially since Mercedes refused to give up her comfortable lifestyle at home in order to pick up some odd housekeeping jobs to help out. As much as he tried, Josef's job prospects grew scarcer by the month. Too many laborers and not enough labor.

Despite Josef's promise that things would get better, from where Rosalita sat, their future was hidden behind dark, brooding clouds.

Poverty.

Hunger.

Weariness.

Death.

These were the heartbreaking conditions they had become accustomed to. Sophia still squeezed into her twelve-month clothes, if she wore clothes at all. The food they were blessed with today would have to be rationed to last as long as possible if they were going to get through the next month. And the gifts! While Mercedes and Sophia *oohed* and *ahhed* over each unwrapped gift, Rosalita mentally calculated how much she could sell them for to cover their monthly expenses.

It was a cycle of despair that gathered them up like a tornado and spit them out battered and weary.

Her reminders of their reality only infuriated Josef and Mercedes. Rosalita had become the dreaded mother-in-law, always nagging. But tonight she wouldn't harp about such things. She would savor this one small joy. Tomorrow the hardship would resume, as it always did.

"So, you're a proud *abuela*, *sí*?" Mercedes turned to Rosalita, her eyes mere slivers of almonds as the alcohol swept through her.

"Of course." Rosalita's words held the obligatory accord Mercedes sought.

Today Rosalita knew better than to speak her mind to any of her family, lest her meager joy in life—mainly Sophia—unravel like balled yarn. They didn't know about her darkest hour—the death she caused, the anguish that flooded the family—for if they ever found out, her life wouldn't be worth living when they filched her time with her grandkids.

"I gave you a grandson ... now you *owe* me, don't you?" Mercedes laughed haughtily, leaving her mother-in-law puzzled.

If anything, Rosalita felt the brunt of the family burden. Hadn't she done everything for these two ungrateful children? For that is what they were. Spoiled brats. Unwilling to grow up. Josef lazily sleeping in day after day while Mercedes squandered their money away on extravagances. Who watched Sophia day in and day out, taking her to school and helping her with her homework? Rosalita. Who prepared meals and worked her fingers to the bone paying for their bills and buying groceries? Rosalita. And who, dear God, who was going to take care of yet another baby, an unwanted result of this lie of a marriage? Who else but Rosalita.

The weight of debt was heavily in her favor.

"Owe you, dear? What ever for?"

"Oh, you know what for. I married your good-for-nothing son, gave up everything for your family, first Sophia and now him"—she pointed a wobbly finger at the napping baby in the corner—"so I think some gratitude is owed."

"Good-for-nothing son?" Josef shot back. "You shouldn't be so prideful, *puta*. Your looks are fading fast, now that you've squeezed out two melons. No one will want you now."

"I don't see you turning down my sweet *chocho* in the bedroom, you piece of trash," Mercedes shot back.

The drunken tension was simmering, about to explode into a boil. Rosalita had seen these two go at it too many times before, making her and Sophia their casualties of war, and the last thing she wanted was them waking a sleeping newborn with this nonsense.

Slap some sense into them—that's what she wanted to do. But she knew one step was one step too far. If she struck out, she'd never stop, like an attack dog gritting its teeth on its mark. There were moments when the killer instinct she spent a lifetime cramming into the heart-shaped hole in her soul would flare up wildly, ready to do damage. And every time she stuffed the rage back down, praying the thoughts could be overcome with sheer self-will and *Dios'* help.

So far she was barely hanging on to her sanity.

Rosalita longed for the nights when her dreams carried her to a land without Mercedes and Josef, to an imaginary shelter where she doted on her grandchildren and lived without the chronic sinister regret. That perfect place—that heaven—soon became an obsession, an obsession that with a dismal acceptance she knew was far beyond her reach. Too many sins held her soul captive to eternal hell. No prayer could save her soul now.

A whimper from the corner of the room rose amid the persistent bickering.

"Let's not fight," Rosalita urged. "It's a time to celebrate the food, the gifts, the *bebé* ..." She raised her shot glass one more time, urging the couple to do the same. "To always protecting our loved ones, no matter the cost."

Meeting Josef and Mercedes's eyes in turn, she saw their drunken accord and the tide shift.

"Salud!"

Chapter 34

Ari

Two days until dead

If you go poking around in shadows, you'll find darkness.

Shirley Road was not the kind of street a lone girl should have been traipsing down after dark. Police sirens screamed from a block away, waking a fussy infant in the house a driveway's width from where I stood knocking on Debra Littleton's front door.

An open window a couple doors down unleashed a dog's bark, a deep reverberating sound from something large and presumably with sharp, pointy teeth, like a Rottweiler. Amid the procession of decrepit homes, fancy cars dotted the streets, a stark incongruity. A shiny Lexus across the street, windows tinted impenetrable black. A custom-painted sparkly blue Hummer a few doors down, just waiting to be stolen. A red Corvette snugly nestled in the driveway that I had just parked in—presumably Debra's.

I had never understood the mentality: house poor, car rich. It was a common paradox on the proverbial wrong side of the tracks. The blight of poverty had such baffling patterns.

Others turned a blind eye to the slums, joking that a good carpet bombing was the best kind of urban renewal. And yet I felt oddly at home here.

Maybe because I was unwanted, just like the ghetto.

It wasn't the broken concrete footpaths or sea of trash in the yards that quickened a visitor's pace from their car to their front porch while Latin hip-hop blared from the stereo of a passing vehicle. It wasn't the decrepit pawnshops, run-down liquor stores, or multitudinous check-cashing storefronts. It wasn't even the boarded up windows graffitied with cryptic gang messages and Spanish profanities that scared most people away from places like this. It was the way the shadows moved, shifting menacingly. It was the huddle of bodies shrouded in hoodies, milling about on corners and sidewalks, moving without purpose. Streets barren during the day became a sea teeming with life at night.

Idle hands are the devil's tools.

In ghost towns old men observed passersby with watchful purpose from their creaky rocking chair perches, their eagle eyes like spotlights. It felt safe with them as the keepers. There was an eerie serenity about ghost towns. But here, in the slums, people felt the stark contrast as hidden watchers laid in wait with no other purpose than to intimidate, like a predator stalking prey.

I knew this because once upon a time I was the predator.

I had grown up as one of these kids. To the rest of the world I was the outsider, the hoodlum, the threat, but in the slums I belonged.

It was my home.

But today I was a visitor.

My knuckles rapped a little more feverishly on the door this time. If Tristan found out I had come without him, I knew he'd really pitch a fit. But he'd never know. It was my little secret ... to add to the heaping stash of other ones I'd been hiding.

"What d'ya want?" The snarl from the other side of the

door sounded like a former soprano leadened from decades of cigarettes.

"I'm looking for Debra Littleton." I was talking to a peeling strip of paint flaking off at my eye level.

"Who's asking?"

"Did you used to own an orange Ford Pinto?"

No response. Then a slivery gap opened between us. A haggish old woman with thread-thin lips peeked out at me.

"Why the hell are you lookin' for a car I owned years ago?"

"Because whoever was driving it killed my sister."

A pebble wedged itself in the back of my throat, resting contentedly where my voice box should have been. I coughed, hoping to dislodge the words I wanted to speak but instead tasted only the salty residue of unshed tears. There was no explaining the way I felt, sitting across from Debra Littleton, lonely widow and doting mother. What do you say to the mother of your sister's murderer? What words are enough? What words can heal a wound so cauterized that even I couldn't differentiate the scab from the rest of my broken heart?

Thanks for raising a killer.

How could you let him hide this for over a decade?

Why didn't you turn your son in?

Life clearly hadn't treated Debra kindly. Her hair looked like a giant wad of frayed steel wool with rusty patches that indicated her hair might once have been auburn. She had no eyebrows at all; dunes of fat surrounded her eyes, rheumy dots full of suspicion and judgment. She had wings that hung like fleshy hammocks under her arms, but the legs sticking out of her Wal-Mart shorts were slender, almost girlish. From head to toe her skin was sallow and crêpey. Her jack-o'-lantern mouth was overcrowded with nicotine-stained teeth poking this way and that, with occasional gaps where her tongue slipped through when she spoke. Her voice sounded raspy and strained, as if each word was a huge burden.

I glanced at the crushed pack of Winstons on the coffee table and wondered how many cancer sticks Debra had smoked in her lifetime. Obviously not enough to kill her yet, but she was trying. She waved the lit Winston around in her hand like a little baton when she wasn't sucking it into the hellish maw that was her mouth. I did my best to inhale as little as possible of the pollution she spewed into the room.

Perhaps I didn't understand the normality behind a mother protecting her child at all costs. It wasn't something I was ever exposed to. Mine tossed me aside at the first sign of hardship, but the depths and breadths of the innate mama bear instinct wasn't just a myth. The evidence was sitting cattycorner from me on a sofa smelling of cat piss and coffee.

"I figured one of these days you'd show up here," she said, the sentence rattling in her mouth behind those teeth. Those brown teeth that I felt the urge to scrape with my fingernail to see how much of it was rotting enamel and how much was calcified tarter. "Either you or the cops. I knew someone eventually would figure out my Richie was behind the wheel. Secrets don't stay buried forever, y'know."

Anger and confusion swirled within me, like a reckless tornado picking up momentum. I choked back a few choice cuss words, then more calmly said, "I don't understand what happened." I just needed an explanation. Anything to give context to the nightmares, the horrors I had lived through.

"Nothin' much to tell. Richard was coming home from a friend's house and was going too fast. Hit the brakes a moment too late. Got scared and took the hell off. By the time he got home he was afraid that he'd be in trouble for leavin' the scene, so he kept it a secret. I didn't find out until about a year later, when he was havin' regular panic attacks. The whole thing really messed him up. By that point it was too late to confess. No point in ruining two lives over a mistake he couldn't fix. That's all there is to tell."

It didn't make sense. None of it. What about the angle of the car? And why did he hide it so long from his mother? What was he *really* fleeing?

"Do you remember what friend he was visiting—where they lived?"

She gave vent to an explosive smoker's cough that just about rattled the windows. I involuntarily covered my mouth. "I don't know, honey. That was so long ago. I didn't ask for details. I just wanted him to move on. When he done told me what he did, I begged him to come clean to the cops, but he couldn't bear to think—well, you know what they do to sensitive boys in those jails. Richie'd never survive the night."

"But *you* could have given my family closure. Why didn't you?"

"I'm his mama, darlin'. You don't have kids of your own yet, I guess, but when you do, you'll understand. A mama does anything—*anything*—to protect her young."

There was a buried warning there, the low hum of a threat that this was as far as this would go. A dead girl wasn't her problem. Her son's freedom was all she cared about. Period.

"Can I talk to Richard?"

"I don't think so, darlin'. He's not home and I don't know when he'll be back."

"I just want to ask him a couple things to get ... peace ... about it. Certainly you can understand that."

For a moment I thought she was contemplating my request, maybe even empathizing with my trauma. Until she shook her head, the double chin jiggling like a bowl of Jell-O. "Best you just let it go, honey. I shouldn'ta told you anything to begin with, but that there's your peace. He didn't mean to, and it's time to move on. And if you dare say something to the cops"—a thick, stained fingertip poked my chest—"I'll deny this conversation ever happened."

A minute later I found myself shuffled out of her house and standing aimlessly on her front porch, wondering what the hell I was going to do now. I had a scattering of hollow answers, but they were only a deluded mother's version of watered-down events.

People die, memories fade, and facts can become distorted by the passage of time or shaded by personal grudges and agendas. I had waited long enough to sweep aside those lies we've told ourselves to sleep sounder at night.

I wanted the truth. And I didn't care what it cost me or anyone else.

Chapter 35

I had wasted a precious opportunity emancipating Tina first. I cursed myself for going off-track, nearly losing my momentum. *Nearly*.

As impulsive as teenagers are, they are also stubbornly predictable. The trained eye can read telltale patterns in their seemingly scattershot days and nights. Certain friends they see, girls they call, places they eat.

Killian Alvarez always stopped by his lady friend's house after her husband left for work. Always. At 8:35 the rich hubby left wearing his traditional gray suit and red tie—a power combo—and zoomed off in his Lexus. By 9:00 Killian pulled up in his Honda beater and did what young lovers do. New love was so passionate, wasn't it?

My sights had never been set on the innocent, though. I didn't want to go through the cougar to get to the cub. So I needed a diversion. Hence, I created one.

It took some extra planning I hadn't anticipated, considering the target. A disguise that wouldn't give me away—a bit more complex than a fuzzy nose and glasses. A Durham Bulls baseball cap helped to hide my face a bit, plus a cakey layer of costume makeup to contour my features. Aviator sunglasses topped it off. At least 90 percent of my face was hidden. I just hoped it was enough.

I sat at the intersection where I knew he'd be traveling, my foot resting on the brake. I had parked far enough from the stop sign so that any other drivers would naturally veer around me, but close enough that I could see his car crest the hill in my rearview mirror. I had picked a spot free from the prying eyes of a neighborhood watch, shrouded in a copse of trees. It was a street less traveled by white-collar husbands heading into the office or minivan moms taking their kids to soccer practice.

I heard it before I saw it—the grumble of an old muffler and rattle of loose engine parts. I hit the gas, hard.

He never saw me coming.

Never noticed my vehicle until it collided into the rear of his. Perhaps *collided* is a bit harsh. More like tapped his bumper.

Nothing serious enough to warrant the curiosity of neighbors. My intention wasn't to send him to the hospital. I intended to send him to the morgue.

Naturally, the rest was an unfolding drama that would organically take its course.

"I am so sorry." I hopped out of my car and rushed to his door. "This was all my fault. I didn't see you and my foot slipped ..."

He exited the clunker and inspected the damage. "Hey, hey, it's okay. As you can see, my car needs work anyways. Your dent matches the others."

We both chuckled nervously—him over the shock of the accident, me with relief that he hadn't recognized me.

"I really appreciate you not flipping out on me." My rehearsed accent was coming easier with each word. "This is my first fender-bender."

"Well, obviously I'm experienced." He gestured at the countless scratches and dings from bumper to bumper. "Hey, uh, if it's the same to you, I don't have insurance, so I'd prefer to just brush this under the rug. No harm, no foul."

"Oh, wow, that's really nice of you. You sure you don't want me to pay for the damage?"

"Absolutely. As long as you're okay, we can be on our

way."

"I think so. Though you look like you have a scratch on your forehead."

His fingers pattered across his skin, searching for the wetness of blood.

"Here, let me help." I moved closer, feeling his breath and smelling his minty aftershave, and I allowed myself to relish this last moment with him.

But I couldn't relish long. It was time.

While my approaching hand blocked his vision, my other deftly yanked out the concealed knife from my belt sheath under my coat, and jabbed it into his stomach. His eyes widened with horror, then he flinched and groaned, grabbing as if to collect the lifeblood seeping out of him. Distracted by the blood, he simply stood there without a fight.

The knife wedged into his abdominal tissue up to the hilt, dividing muscles and shredding skin. He swatted at me weakly, a pathetic attempt to push me away. Every moment I savored ... the wheezing breaths as Death stared back at me through his eyes. Death ripped at him, dropping him to his knees. He fell prostrate, cracking his head against the pavement. Blood gushing from his open wounds stained the cement in a widening pool.

Its simplicity had been poetic. The rhythm of his slowing breaths, the lullaby of his gurgled words caught in a mouthful of blood, the serenity of his drifting eyes, the vibrant contrast of sharp red against melancholy gray. The purest form of art—purging bleakness and embracing eternal youth in one swift blow.

I heard a distant engine rumble closer. By now minutes had passed. I'd spent too much time already.

I couldn't let them connect this to Josef or Tina. After slipping on a glove I'd brought with me, I leaned over, fished in the back pocket of his jeans, emptied his wallet of credit cards and cash, then tossed the leather billfold beside his body. Robbery gone wrong, they'd conclude.

Rushing toward my car, I pulled myself away from the delicious indulgence of watching Death envelop him, whisking him to a better place. I had never wanted him to be alone for those final breaths—the longest, loneliest goodbye—but a car could pass at any moment, a stay-at-home mom could happen by while walking the dog or pushing a stroller.

As I watched him shrink in my rearview mirror, I felt nostalgic relief. He had turned out to be such a nice boy, despite his irreparable brokenness. I felt confident there was a special place in heaven for him.

Though, a sad lingering thought toyed with me, taunting me as I left him behind. He had no idea who I was, what I was capable of. And I'd never get the chance to show him.

Chapter 36

Ari

One day until dead

My newly adopted bulldog cop routine didn't mesh too well with the protective boyfriend gig that Tristan and I were experimenting with. In fifteen minutes I was supposed to outwit George Battan into confessing his crimes before handing a bag of cash over, but no matter how many times we'd rehearsed it, debated it, and settled on it, Tristan couldn't jump on board with my involvement.

Hell, even I couldn't fully jump on board with it.

I could feel a migraine coming, no thanks to drama at every turn.

Back at my apartment, Tina nursed a broken heart after her cell phone rang with a call from the hospital explaining that her brother was in the ER in critical condition after having been robbed at knifepoint. He couldn't accept visitors yet and was comatose from a head injury after falling—*this is normal,* the nurse assured Tina, *after a brain injury like this. A few days of rest and he'll probably come out of it.* But her medical opinion was little consolation to a sister who had rebuffed her brother time and again, only to find him on the brink of death. The dark patches of skin under her eyes that morning were a telltale sign of guilt eating at her.

I hated leaving her home alone to brood over her

sisterly failings, but I had no choice.

"I ran out of vacation days at work," I had lied to her over cold coffee and stale bagels. I couldn't tell her the truth. Not until it was over.

So here I sat in Tristan's unmarked car, decked in scanners and police-issue tech stuff, rehearsing a plan that could get me killed.

What the hell was wrong with me?

"A cop should be doing this, not you, a civilian," he muttered while we waited in the parking lot where I was supposed to meet George. "Especially since you're a girl I care about."

The slate sky hung low with morning drizzle, adding a gray chill that worked its way through my sweater. Dense clouds stretched across the expanse, slathering a drowsy sleep upon the damp earth below.

I felt Tristan observing me, like the hundred-eyed Argus watching from his heavenly abode. My life had become a tragedy—or a comedy—depending on who was watching. A girl desperately searching for answers to a question that wouldn't fix anything. Like a mouse burrowing in the ground toward its escape, only to hit the plastic confines of its cage. Nothing would free me from what happened, but I'd be damned if I didn't try to make sense of it all.

I wondered what Tristan felt for me now. Pity, I imagined.

"You care about me?" I cooed.

"Of course I care about you. Why else would I be letting you do this if I didn't? I could get in big trouble for doing this on my own. But I know you want the satisfaction of bringing him down. I respect that."

"That, and I'm the only one he'll meet with."

He deflected my comment with a shrug. "I just want to get it over with. You remember what you need him to admit to?"

"Yep, let's not go over it again, please. You're making me nervous."

"You should be nervous. This is a big deal. Try to breathe, and don't forget I'll have eyes on you."

Tristan—my all-seeing eye.

"Oh, I got you a gift." Tristan handed me a small box wrapped in colorful happy birthday paper. "Sorry—it was the only wrapping paper I could find."

"Aw shucks," I said with a smirk. "I didn't get you anything to commemorate our first date."

Shaking it, I attempted to figure out if it rattled or chimed or rolled or clinked. Nothing gave it away.

"Just open it."

"Pushy much?" Carefully untaping each edge, I unwrapped the package, discovering a can of mace. I looked at him, eyebrows raised in a question. "How romantic."

"In case you need it. That stuff is highly effective in an emergency, and it attaches to your keychain."

He lifted my keys out of my hand and attached the bottle.

"Thanks ... for caring." My smile was genuine, even if mace was the last thing I would have put on my gift list.

With my mace swinging from my pocket, I stepped out of the car and headed to the bench where we had agreed to meet. The sticky tack of tape tugged at my skin, and I fought the urge to adjust the tiny microphone clipped to my bra, abrasively chafing my breast. I had only been standing a few minutes—I was too fidgety to sit—when a black Volvo parked in front of me and a slightly built man of less than average height got out.

With his neatly trimmed mustache and old-school Jeffrey Dahmer-parted haircut, he sure looked like a George. The wire-rimmed glasses reminded me of Dwight

Shrute's from *The Office*. The ideal sociopath's eyewear. He blinked a lot, his eyes huge and owlish behind the thick lenses. His fishy pallor suggested a subhuman creature not unaccustomed to coming out in the light, which is exactly what the bastard was. Bookish and altogether unimpressive. I wasn't afraid of him.

Standing next to me, eyes darting to and fro warily, he kept his jaw trained forward, but I saw the nerves twitch beneath his poker face. The sweat beading on his forehead. The habitual poking of his outsize square-ish glasses up his slippery nose. The way he fingered the gold bracelet of his Rolex.

His leg jitterbugged, as if shaking off nerves that wouldn't let go. For a man of his reputation, it was disconcerting that he was more nervous than I was. I guess he had a lot more to lose and a lot worse to gain—like a jail sentence.

I admit, I was surprised to see him show. I was almost certain he would have sent a minion to meet with me. He was ballsy.

"Anxious?" I asked, flicking my gaze over him.

"Ms. Wilburn, you assured me there would be no cops. I assume you kept your word? Because if I don't make it safely home, Tina will never find her daughter."

It was hard to match his words to his threat when I recognized the smooth, eerie girlishness of his voice. I couldn't tell if he was insinuating he knew Tristan was listening in, but I'd play blond-girl dumb.

"No cops—as promised." I hoped I buried the timidity of my lie under enough conviction to persuade him. "I'm guessing you're here for this." I patted the handbag swung securely across my shoulders.

"Is it the amount we agreed on?"

"You can count it if you want."

"I trust you wouldn't want more problems for you or

Tina—or Giana."

"So this means Tina is done, right?"

"Right."

He reached for the bag, but I pulled it toward me. I knew this wasn't enough to put him behind bars. I needed more.

"No, you said you would look me in the eyes and say it. Assure me that you'll leave her alone. No more sex trafficking, no more threats, no more debts." I pivoted, facing him, daring him to meet my stare.

Pushing his glasses up, he fixed his owlish eyes on me and said, "Tina's balance is paid in full. Consider our business done." With an outstretched arm, he flipped his hand at the money, urging me to pass it over.

Was it enough? I had only this one shot at catching him where I needed him, and since Tristan wasn't running toward us with his handcuffs ready, I could only assume I needed more.

"What about her baby? Can she get her baby back?"

George turned on me, his fish face now a shade of pink. "That was not part of the agreement. And no, I can't get back the baby. The baby has been sold. Nonrefundable. Now if there's nothing else, I must go."

Gotcha.

I lifted the strap off and handed him the bag, my fingertips still holding on. But there was one more thing … one nagging question.

"Wait." I gripped the strap tighter. "I want to know why you trashed my apartment. That was you, wasn't it? You made a mess of my place. What the hell were you looking for?"

His face screwed into a probing question mark, and his lips curled in disgust. "You think I have nothing better to do than to break into your apartment to toss it? Sorry, darling, but you have the wrong man. Clearly you have bigger problems to worry about if you have people searching your apartment. I guess I'm not the only one with secrets."

After unzipping the nylon bag and peeking inside, he rifled through the wads of bills and then lifted it from my loose hands as he headed to his car.

"It was a pleasure doing business with you," I called after him.

The chirp of a car alarm unlocking his door, then tires on wet concrete screaming to a stop behind his Volvo, then the clatter of brisk footfalls ... A blur of chaotic activity, and suddenly the dull slam of a body ... on top of mine.

I heard a scream I didn't recognize.

My own.

As my back smacked against the concrete, George circled around me, dragging me against him by my neck. A pinch bit into my jugular as he pulled me to my feet from behind, screaming, "Stay back or I slice her throat!"

Spittle sprayed my ear and the knife twitched against me, cutting a thin line.

It hurt like a paper cut, until the drip of blood slid down my throat under my collar.

He was crazy and panicked enough to really kill me!

In front of us stood Tristan, gun aimed ... right at us.

"George, you need to calm down." Tristan's voice was distant and calm. "Just let Ari go and we can talk about this."

"I'm done talking!" As George yelled the knife trembled against my flesh.

"George," Tristan soothed as if beckoning a child, "don't add murder to your list of charges."

But George was growing more frantic. I could feel it as the blade sank deeper.

My fingers blindly fumbled for the mace, but George's

face was pressed so close to mine that I was sure I'd end up spraying myself.

Suddenly I remembered a little Self-Defense 101 lesson from back in juvie. Forgoing the mace, I grabbed my car key, stuck it out through my fist, and jammed it backward right into George's eyeball.

Shoving me forward, he shrieked and clutched his eye socket, moaning in agony as his body drooped to the ground.

I ran toward Tristan, and the next few moments passed in frenzied action like pages in a flipbook.

The rush of activity was exhilarating as Tristan hoisted George upright and cuffed his hands behind his back, despite the obvious eyeball pain he was in. I missed the flurry of words from where I stood, catching only bits and pieces that sounded like Miranda rights while Tristan shoved him into the backseat of his car without guiding his head, which got slammed against the roof of the car.

I crept closer to watch with fascination, and as George shrunk into the seat not more than an arm's length from me, our eyes—or should I say *eye*—locked for a brief moment. I could feel the heat of his stare, I was breathing it all in, letting the relief wash over me like a cool shower on a hot day.

"An eye for an eye, you bastard," I seethed.

As Tristan moved to close to door, something popped into my head. It was just a tiny thought at first, a word here and there, scuttling about in my brain. But then they bloomed into a much bigger picture. A frightening image that siphoned all my strength. Puzzle pieces were scrambling together in my mind's eye, tying everything together in an appalling package.

"Wait!" I called out. I glanced at George, who looked up at me through the open backseat door, unsmiling, his jaw quivering.

"Burt Wilburn—my father—did you kill my sister to send him a message, you sick bastard?" Could it be that this man was the business associate Dad referred to?

But George's face remained unmoving, except for a slight upturn of his lips. Then his good eye narrowed and his lips lifted in a serpentine smile.

My father. George Battan. Carli. Tina. Josef. They were all connected in some twisted crime circle. That made my own father a suspect—of what, I wasn't yet sure. Murder?

Please, God, no. He's messing with me.

"Keep your family secrets close, Ari Wilburn, before they take you all down with them."

I waded in early afternoon sunlight that had broken through the blanket of overcast gray by the time I left the police station, dropping off my recorded conversation and written police statement that I hoped would put George Battan behind bars for a long time—at least as long as Tina's forced prostitution. As for all the other victims over the years, that would take time to build a case, Tristan woefully explained. But at least he'd be in jail, unable to do more damage for the time being.

Then there was my dad. George's smug smile foreshadowed that I would be unearthing quite a few hideous family secrets. Murder couldn't be one of them. Never. I speculated that it only regarded money—maybe Dad handled George's finances and was trying to get out, and that's why George came after Carli. My dad wearing the mask of a killer—preposterous.

At least Tina's drama was over, even if the taste of my first success as an undercover dick was bittersweet.

As I arrived home, I couldn't wait to tell her that we could start looking for her daughter, hopefully ending our silent feud. But when I opened the front door to find a tidy, empty living room, her bedding folded and neatly stacked aside, and her purse hanging crookedly from the dining room chair, my first thought was that she had taken a walk, probably still fuming at me for insinuating her brother was a killer while he lay in a hospital bed near death.

She'd forgive me once I filled her in on George's capture ... I hoped.

I rang her cell phone, but it went straight to voicemail. I left a message asking her to call me as soon as she got this, then wandered into the kitchen to see what scraps I could throw together for lunch. Something was odd, but I couldn't quite place what. Two dirty glasses sat in the sink, which in any other context wouldn't have been alarming, but why would Tina have used two different glasses? Perhaps I was overthinking it, searching for clues to a shadowy intrigue where there were none, but the unsettled feeling persisted.

After rummaging in the fridge, I piled ham and cheese between two slices of whole wheat—which Tina insisted was healthier, albeit too grainy for my taste—then tossed the empty baggie in the garbage. I took a bite, chewing thoughtfully. I wondered if she had left any clue as to her whereabouts. With no trace of a note anywhere, I pulled the lid off the garbage, just in case she had accidentally thrown it away. Nothing but the baggie I had just pitched and an empty liquor bottle.

We hadn't drunk together recently, so it was a curious thing to find in the garbage, particularly at this hour. Had she been drinking this morning? And with who?

I lifted the bottle out and set it on the counter.

Jose Cuervo Clasico Silver.

Something about it felt so familiar. So close to home. But what?

I couldn't imagine Tina having a sudden impulse for tequila. And disappearing like this? It wasn't like her. Something was wrong, my mind screamed. But I had no proof. She was an adult, able to make her own decisions, and she'd only been gone a couple hours. I figured I'd wait it out until evening before contacting Tristan. The last thing I wanted to do was paint myself as the panicky roommate putting together a search party for a girl who merely went shopping—but without her purse?

Ambling through the apartment with my mind still buzzing from the morning, I headed to the bathroom to wash my face. That's when I saw it. I hadn't noticed it before when we were cleaning up after the break-in, but there it was. Nestled along the baseboard in the shadow of a lamp table next to the bathroom door.

Chap-Stick.

Not my Burt Bees brand. And not Tina's Blistex. Yes, we had gotten close enough to know the brands of lip balm we each used—and even shared them.

It was an obscure detail to remember, but one that weaseled its way into my memory bank.

Killian. I remembered him lathering it on when I walked in the Waffle House.

If this wasn't Tina's, and I knew it wasn't mine, that meant he had been here. But now he was in a coma in the hospital and utterly useless for getting information.

Dread pulsed through me. An ill feeling nagged at me.

The front door hadn't been broken into. I checked the back patio sliding door—securely closed and locked.

She must have left through the front door. I wondered if anyone had seen anything, but in apartments like this people rarely did. We all hid behind the solitude of our walls, hoping to avoid human contact at all costs and calling it privacy.

I stepped onto the concrete pad where a plastic chair

and table collected mildew. From the earlier rain the yard was soggy. With squishy steps I crept along the side of the building but saw nothing unusual. No sign of anyone sitting outside who might have seen anything. And if they had, what would be remarkable about a tenant coming and going?

Nothing seemed out of place.

And yet everything felt so ... wrong.

An image flashed in my head. Josef. Blood spatter. Rivulets of crimson flowing along the table, coursing around the clutter on his table.

That's when it hit me. The familiar sight—the bottle. It was the same brand of tequila at Josef's crime scene. And suddenly I had an idea of where Tina might be.

With the only person who knew everything.

With the only person connected to them all.

With the only person who managed to survive.

Rosalita.

Chapter 37

I remembered.

I remembered her as a palm-sized pound of pink squiggling flesh. Arms reaching, fingers squeezing, toes flexing, mouth yawning.

I remembered, and then a sob choked me.

My little Sophia, once upon a time a beautiful stained-glass window of brightness and light, but now a mound of jagged shards. Her heart had become corroded, like a rusted nail that once held together something of value but lost its purpose as the oxidization steadily chipped it away into flakes of dust.

Sophia lay asleep in the chair, my tequila concoction forcing her into deep dreams while the breathy sounds of slumber rose and fell like feathery slips of air. Her eyelids twitched as if entranced in a dream. I wondered briefly what she was seeing, living in her distant dreamscape, before I was brought back to the moment by the task at hand. I stepped beside her, cupping her limp hand in mine. It felt lifelessly cool to the touch, clammy.

After what I'd done to Killian, I hadn't expected her to embrace me when I showed up at the apartment. I hadn't anticipated the warm welcome and laughter and tears. It was a succor to my aching heart. And it made her capture that much easier—a simple invitation for a drive.

So easy. So willing. So trusting.

Now that I held her tight, I yearned to tell her a tall tale, like back in the old days. Back when she would climb into my lap, her chubby arms circling my neck, her pouty lips kissing my cheek as I spoke into her ear so that she would know that it was true. Spittle would tickle my earlobe as she exchanged my stories for her deepest thoughts—the musings of a toddler. Her adventures with her baby doll, the party they planned, the leggy bug she'd discovered crawling along her bedroom floor.

She was my love at first sight, and I knew if she awakened she'd be scared to be near me seeing me like this, her body bound, but I hoped my words would penetrate her thoughts in an intimate prelude before our final moments together. Sophia's eyes had always been so dark, warm, and innocent, as though without a worry or care in this world. All faith and adoration. Until Josef's betrayal. It often haunted me. I imagined her tiny palms pressed against the glass, tears wet against her cheeks, as she was driven away from the only life she knew.

It was time to free her. To play our last game together.

I heard her breath quicken and I leaned down into her view. Her eyelids fluttered into open slits, but they were unfocused and hazy. I wondered if she recognized where we were, if she knew about the game. The more guileless the game, the more potential I saw filling up those pools with hope of a better future. Her face was framed in bleached curls like a Raphaelian portrait as sunlight streaked through highlights of red. High afternoon sun poured over us together in a final embrace, but it would only set on one of us tonight. One of us would die with the evening, while the other lived another day of agony until the restitution was complete.

I imagined her tendrils plastered back with crimson syrup. Her wet lips were a vow of a secret unspoken between us, until it burst like a jet of blood from her silky throat. There would be no more secrets. No more

245

lies. No more betrayals.

Her muscles tensed into taut strips, and her eyelids drooped open and closed. I felt an unseen hand on my back, prodding me forward. I could feel invisible fingers strangling my neck, a warning that I must finish what I started. But I felt fear. I was afraid of yet again failing.

I had failed too often already.

My little butterfly would flap her wings for the last time. Or maybe for the first time. If only I could keep her tucked away safely behind glass, I could protect her. But I knew the damage I'd caused. My fingertips smeared her colorful wings, and only my tears could repaint them in the black of death. She was no longer a butterfly but a ragged moth, wingtips chewed so she could no longer fly. Her metamorphosis would be a violent one, but from it she would emerge flying free.

Chapter 38

Ari

One day until dead

The motel was nameless and faceless, a generic haven for the perverts and drifters that frequented it under the dark wings of night. As I pulled into the dusty lot of cracked parking spots, I wondered what went on behind the one-story row of splintering green doors and closed blinds. I had remembered Rosalita mentioning she was staying somewhere on 98, and the pickings were slim.

After calling Tristan to let him know Tina was missing, he told me what I had expected to hear, what I wanted to hear. She probably went out for lunch. Or she might be visiting her brother at the hospital. Maybe she stopped in at work. Didn't he think I would double-check all those scenarios? Of course I had. And I turned up empty-handed, as expected. Killian was still in a coma and hadn't had any visitors when I finally got through to the nurse's station claiming to be his sister, and Tina's work hadn't heard from her since before her suicide attempt. Just as I suspected.

So here I was, the only place I could think of where she might be.

The only safe place. Unless it wasn't safe anymore. Unless Rosalita wasn't who I thought she was. Or perhaps she was exactly who I thought she was.

I couldn't imagine this sprawling line of grimy walls

and crooked doors and smudged glass seeing better days, considering it sat next to a rundown nudie bar where the women looked like grandmas who'd spent decades too long sunbathing, judging from the crones with cotton candy hair loitering outside on their ciggie breaks.

The front desk accepted a twenty-dollar-bill in exchange for the room number for Rosalita Alvarez, a bargain by my book. I trotted briskly to room number 5, hoping to pop in on them having tea together. But after the news about Killian, friendly visits seemed like an anomaly lately.

I rapped on the door, hearing a muffled response on the other side. The door clattered open, and Rosalita looked at me with a question in her eyes.

"Ari, right?"

"Yeah, is Tina here?" I inched closer, trying to look past her plump bosom blocking the open gap.

"No, why? What's going on?"

A fizz of panic crackled. Tina wasn't with Rosalita. She hadn't left a note. Her phone was turned off. But her intact purse was a stark message that she hadn't taken a leisurely trip to the store. And there was nothing but an empty bottle of alcohol leading me to her abductor. With George Battan as good as jailed right now, and Killian comatose, who was left that would want to hurt her? Were there enemies Tina hadn't told me about?

There were so many secrets, so many lies to unravel ...

Precious seconds were ticking down. Life-saving seconds.

I didn't care what the police would remind me—that it was too soon. She hadn't been gone long enough. No, it was time to report her missing. To send out search parties. To investigate, damn it! Too much had happened to let another hour pass, another minute where her life could be in danger.

I needed to think, but my brain was skipping all over on autopilot.

"Can I come in?"

"Of course." Rosalita moved aside and guided me to a single chair pressed against the wall. I fell into the stiff cushion like a dropped weight, hard and fast.

"She's gone. I think someone abducted her. I came home and she wasn't there. I don't know what to do." My words were rushed and furious, scattered and uncertain.

"Calm down. Breathe. First, how long has she been gone?"

"A couple hours, I guess. I was out all morning, but I came home and she wasn't there. Her phone's gone, and when I tried to call it was turned off—or her battery's dead. No note or anything. But she cleaned up before she left. It doesn't seem like she left in a hurry. I don't know what to think, what to do."

"Her abductors—I bet it's them. They've tried to get to her before."

I shook my head. "I don't think so. The guy who's been after her for the money, George Battan, he's in police custody right now. There's no way his people, or crew, or whatever they're called, would have had time to take her—or risked it right now. They probably don't even know about George yet. Besides, if they had, there would have been a sign of a struggle. Stuff knocked over. But it's too neat and tidy. It looks like she just up and left."

"Did you call the cops?"

"That's the first thing I did. They said it's too soon to do anything. They want me to wait to see if she calls or shows up. I just don't feel right. I need to do something."

"I don't know, dear. I don't know." Rosalita looked sadly at her hands folded in her lap.

"Do you know if Tina had any other secrets—anything else hidden in her past? Anyone in particular that might come for her? Someone she might have trusted enough to leave with?"

Rosalita looked up at me with alarm. "Secrets? Like what?"

"Like ... like her baby."

"A baby? There was a baby?" Rosalita's voice shattered just then, as if the words were delicate pieces of glass slicing along her throat.

I couldn't hide the lies for Tina anymore. Not from Rosalita, not now.

The secrets tumbled out like a fuse crackling wildly, about to explode.

"Giana. But she was taken from her at birth."

"No!" Rosalita looked nostalgic. And something else. Wounded? "Giana. It's a beautiful name. She must be devastated."

"She hasn't really talked to me about it. I found out accidentally. But it's just one of many lies she told me—or didn't tell me. I don't know what to think anymore."

"We have a lot of secrets in our family. It's a generational curse."

"What do you mean?"

Rosalita sighed, as if exhaling the weight of the world in one breath. "It all started with me. I doomed my family to pain when I was a child. I had a sister—a baby sister. My *hermanita*. I was watching over her one evening while my parents were out. They frequently left me in charge, even at such a young age. Back then children weren't really children. We grew up so quickly in those days."

I understood this intimately.

"I was bathing the baby when I heard my parents fighting outside. They fought a lot, mostly over money. We were so poor. Everything was such a struggle for us. I only left her a few minutes in the tub, but when I came back she was face up just below the water's surface. Unmoving.

250

Her eyes were open, glassy, unblinking. In a panic I picked her up, but she was already dead. Her body just hung, like a limp cloth in my arms."

Rosalita hugged her arms around her chest, as if clutching the memory of her sister in her arms.

"I didn't know what to do. I was terrified. So I hurriedly dried her off and bundled her in some fresh clothes and placed her in her crib, dead and cold, and let my parents find her that way. I never told anyone the truth before. And I've paid the price for my lies ever since."

I rose and sat beside her on the bed, the mattress sinking as it nudged our thighs together. Her body was racked with sobbing as I circled my arm around her narrow shoulders. I knew this pain personally. Neither of us had deserved the years of self-punishment, and yet we both fell beneath the weight of responsibility at so tender an age.

"I know how you feel. I lost a sister too ... and carried the blame alone."

"It's a burden no child should bear. But it's haunted me all this time, harboring the truth of what happened. I appreciate being able to share this with another person. I worry that it's this sin that has followed my family, cursed us—caused my only son Josef to grow up a monster and marry a horrible woman, and then my granddaughter was doomed to be a perpetual victim. I can't stop the cycle of devastation."

"No, don't say that. They have nothing to do with what happened to you, Rosalita. It's not your fault."

"But God casts the sins of the parents on the children, doesn't he? My deceit messed me up"—she tapped her index finger against her temple—"up here. And I passed it on to Josef. Even as a baby he was evil. I could just tell. In his eyes. As a result, he sold Sophia into slavery. It started with me, so it ends with me, doesn't it?"

Was it really that simple? One horrible mistake and your future would be fatally flawed? Was suffering so cut-and-dry, so black-and-white? I had always lived in the gray. In the gray I could escape the blame. In the gray I wasn't at fault. Richard Littleton was. But if Rosalita was correct, I would never escape punishment. My future children would get sucked into the cycle, forever damaged.

No, I couldn't accept that.

Her trauma was clearly buried so deep in her psyche that she was becoming self-destructive, her thinking debilitated. And then I thought of my own self-loathing. Friendless, until Tina. Alone, until Tristan. Aimless, until now. Was I looking into a mirror, seeing a distorted reflection of myself? Was my mind crumbling beneath the weight of my own past?

"It's not too late for forgiveness, Rosalita. We can't save Josef, but Killian and Tina still have a chance. Your family can be saved. But you have to forgive yourself first."

Rosalita sat quietly for a long moment, then turned to me.

"Speaking of forgiveness, I must ask for yours."

"For what?"

"I did something I sincerely regret."

"Okaaay," I said, wondering what she could have possibly done.

"I asked Killian to break into your apartment."

"Wha—why?"

"I feared for Tina's life, and I thought maybe staging the break-in would scare her into going to the police about her traffickers. I just wanted her to get protection and put that evil man behind bars. My intentions were good, I swear, but perhaps I only caused unnecessary fear."

Fear had become an art form. Manipulated to propel action, nurtured to instill obedience.

"It's okay. I'm glad you told me. In the end we'll all get

252

our wish—George behind bars."

Our visit was concluded with a hug and a promise to call if we heard anything.

"Tina's tough as nails," Rosalita reassured me. "She probably just needs some alone time to sort things out."

Perhaps she was right. We had fought. Her brother was near death. Maybe I was the last person she wanted to see.

I was worrying about nothing. I'd get home and there she'd be, and I'd apologize and pop some popcorn and throw in a movie. By tonight we'd be joking around again.

But why no note? A slip of the mind—after everything she'd been through? After her suicide attempt. Certainly she would have known how panicked I would be at her disappearing act. I'd tell her as much when I got home.

As clueless about Tina's whereabouts as when I arrived, I headed to my car feeling lost, like a child wandering a dark wood. With my head in a fog, I hadn't noticed the car slowly trailing behind me. It wasn't until I heard a grumbling engine revving when I looked up and saw it.

The vibrant red.

The sleek body.

The slick tires ... peeling across the pavement straight for me.

Chapter 39

Ari

One day until dead

"Y ou lied to me!" Tristan's ire hung on the phone line like a shirt angrily whipping in a harsh wind. "You said you wouldn't see Debra Littleton without me, and you did anyways. How can I trust you when you aren't honest with me?"

The instant the words had passed my lips, I regretted telling him about my detour to Debra's house, and then about nearly getting creamed by the exact same car I saw at her place.

"You mean like you were honest with me about your occupation?" I retorted.

"You put your life in danger. I was trying to keep you safe, Ari."

"Ignorance isn't safe, *Tristan*." I spat his name like it tasted sour.

I had apologized a hundred times over, and it still wasn't enough. It would never be enough for breaking his trust. And for nearly getting run over by a red Corvette. Richard Littleton's Corvette.

The little prick had tailed me to Rosalita's and tried to run over me, but he'd lost his nerve and swerved at the last possible moment. Or more probably he was just trying to scare me. Either way, the Corvette hauled ass out of the motel parking lot, and the last thing I saw was Richard flipping me off in his rearview. The punk had balls, all right, but he had no idea who he was messing with. I wasn't some flighty blonde who shrieked at a spider scurrying toward her. I was the type of girl who smashed the guts out of bugs who crossed my path, and continued to stomp them into the pavement until there was nothing discernable left. I'd do it to him too, if he wasn't careful.

I had recognized the Corvette from when I had blocked it in at Debra's house. It only made sense that her son still lived at home. Slackers usually did. And the car—too rich for their blood. Unless Richard had been paid off to kill my sister. That's what I suspected, and I wasn't going to let go until I got my answers. My only mistake was telling Tristan about it on my way to confronting Richard.

"Look, I don't want to fight with you over this, Ari." Tristan's tone softened as he spoke. "It's just that right now I'm working a case that involves a potential serial killer—one that's too close to home. Like, close as in possibly in our suicide support group."

"What?" I yelled.

"That's why I'm there undercover, to see what I can find out. So you putting yourself in any kind of danger freaks me out. I'm not trying to control you. I just want you safe."

"And I'll stay safe," I assured him. "But Richard isn't a serial killer. He's a punk trying to scare me off from turning him in. I've been through more shit than you can imagine. I'm not some wimpy chick who needs a man to rescue her. I can handle this. You couldn't understand unless you've lived my life, saw your sister die. But I have to do this."

"Then do it with me beside you."

I considered the offer. Maybe if he waited in his car out of sight ... I just couldn't afford him scaring Richard off.

"Fine. Meet me one block away from Richard Littleton's

house. I'll see you there."

As I pulled the phone from my ear to hang up, I heard Tristan's fiery curses about me being irrational, but hey, at least we both got my way.

✬✬

Twenty minutes later I left Tristan a couple doors down as I headed up Richard's front porch. I promised to stay outside, in sight, in case anything went awry.

I banged my fist on the door, yelling at Richard to come out. I knew he was home because the Corvette was parked in the driveway, the engine still warm. The coward must have run inside to his mommy for protection.

"Richard, I'm going to break this damn door down if you don't get your ass out here!" I yelled.

Hell hath no fury like a woman scorned. The devil had nothing on me today.

When no one answered, I threw my leg up and kicked, rocking the door violently against its hinges.

"You better hurry before this door comes down!" I screamed.

As I lifted my leg for another kick, I heard a pleading voice on the other side and waited. Finally he was going to listen to reason.

The door rattled open, the worse for wear, and a guy— not a *real* man by the looks of him—stood there looking at me as if he hadn't a clue who this crazy woman banging down his door was. He couldn't have been much older than me, maybe thirty. His glassy eyes, set in dark hollows, had a haunted aspect, like someone whose depression or remorse had for years robbed him of a good night's sleep. His body jutted out in angular elbows and knobby knees, a walking pile of skin clinging to bones. A ratty goatee rounded his mouth in a patchwork of brown

256

hair. I cringed at the thought of kissing him, but I didn't know why the thought even surfaced.

"You know who I am and why I'm here," I stated. "Talk. Now."

"Wanna come inside?" he asked. "As long as you can keep your voice down?" His voice quivered and his neck craned inside the house. "Don't wanna wake Mama."

I wondered if he was more scared of his mother finding us together or me kicking his ass.

"No, let's talk on the porch. But if you think you can run, think again."

He only glanced warily at me, then nodded toward the metal folding chairs in the corner of the enclosure.

"For starters, why did you follow me and then try to run me over?" I demanded.

"I knew you came by. I wanted to send you a warning to back off."

I laughed. "You—warning me? Now it's the other way around, *Richie*. You shouldn't have missed."

"I wasn't trying to hurt you. Just scare you into leaving me alone."

"Well, that's sure as hell not gonna happen now. Start talking. I know you killed my sister. And I know it wasn't an accident."

His blue eyes widened in horror. "How do you know that?"

"Because I *know*, Richie. You swerved up on the curve, didn't you? You aimed at my sister, didn't you? That's how you afforded your Corvette, right—you got paid, you sonofabitch! Am I right?" When he sat there dumbly, I decided to soften my blows. I knew I was scaring him into silence. "Look, I just want answers. I want to know why my sister had to die. You know why. Please tell me. I can't stand to wonder anymore. Please."

The tears came unbidden. I hadn't wanted to cry,

hadn't thought I was even capable of peeling off the calloused layers in front of this murdering stranger, but I slipped out of my safe place and wept.

Sometimes a woman exposing her soul is enough to make even the hardest hearts crumble.

"I was only sixteen. I didn't know what I was getting into. I'm sorry."

He stopped, and I wondered if he would continue, or if he couldn't face the truth either.

Then he spoke again, his words rambling and hasty, like he was on speed. "A friend of mine knew a guy who paid cash for jobs here and there—random things, like roughing up someone who owed money, things like that. I wanted in. I needed a new car, I didn't want to get involved in dealing drugs 'cause I'd known too many kids getting pinched. This one job would pay a fortune, and it sounded easy enough. Your dad—Burt—it was supposed to be a message for him. Just scare his kid and that was it. It wasn't supposed to kill her. Hurt her a little, but not kill her. I didn't mean to hit her head-on like that. The steering wheel slipped—like, jolted in my hand. I must have been going too fast, I dunno. I was so nervous. So scared. And then next thing I know I'm just trying to get out of there. I didn't know she died until I read about it in the papers the next day. I'm so sorry."

"I guess a Corvette is a whole lot easier to handle than a piece of shit Pinto, else I'd be roadkill too. Huh, *Richie*?" My voice dripped with sarcasm.

"Look, I said I was sorry, didn't I? What do you want from me? Your dad's the bad guy in this piece, not me. I was just the scapegoat."

"Wrong, asshole! You got off—I was the scapegoat."

I had to take a moment to process all this. My bones had known my father was involved ... but to what extent? And why? All this time it had been his fault. All this time I shouldered the blame when my father was responsible. The message was for him. Carli's life—her death—was a message to *him*.

"Who hired you? And what was the message about?" Asking my father would lead to tight lips and a swift boot out the front door. I needed more meat, something bigger to bring to him—indisputable facts that would finally make my father talk.

"I wish I could tell you. All I know is that my friend Jay Boyd hooked it up. He kicked your father's ass the night before, and my job was to make sure he knew the threat was real. But the guy who hired me and Jay, I never met him. Jay handled the payout and everything."

If I could speak to Jay, maybe I'd get what I needed. "Do you know where Jay is now?"

"You can find his ashes on his mama's mantel. He died back in '08 from a robbery gone wrong. Got shot trying to flee."

It wasn't everything I wanted, but at least I had enough to shake my dad for more. Jay Boyd—that was who showed up the night before Carli's death. One name mentioned to Dad and I bet I could get him to talk.

"There's nothing else you can tell me about Jay's connection? Didn't Jay use a name when he referred to his boss? Think, Richie, please."

He closed his eyes, as if concentration mustered every ounce of his strength, and then popped them open like he'd flushed out a memory. But he shook his head instead. "Your dad would know for sure. The guy musta been real gangsta, though, because Jay was scared to cross him."

There was only one way to find out who was behind the hit-and-run—and my dad held the key. Maybe Tristan could shake the truth out of him. I'd pass this along to him and cross my fingers.

Richie prattled on, pulling me back to him. "The dude paid Jay a lot of money to do stuff for him—mostly picking up young girls and collecting money—but after what happened with your sister I never went back. I couldn't handle it after that. I'm so sorry."

Another meaningless apology that couldn't change the past. He shook his head, shame washing over him as his eyes turned runny. After all this time I almost felt sorry for him. Almost.

"Would you be willing to turn yourself in? Help the police figure out who hired you and why?"

His nod was slow, solemn. "Anything to get rid of the guilt."

It wouldn't fix everything, but maybe it would give Carli justice. Maybe it would end one small circle of crime that revolved in my town. Maybe it would scare whoever was responsible into coming forward.

One voice—that was sometimes all it took to cut open the seeping wound to clean out the deeper infection.

I needed to expose and eliminate the infection—starting with my own father.

Chapter 40

Tina awoke with a cold thud of panic. I could see the fear spread across her face, like a starburst sprouting in her eyes, then working its way across her features in a silent scream. The hush gasped around us, then her eyes, like flares, darted across the room.

I sensed her relax at the familiar surroundings, finding the calm in my smile, then she struggled violently against the bindings on her arms and legs. I had doubted the wisdom in bringing her here—was it too soon? There was a chance we could be easily found. But I had run out of time ... and options. With Killian still alive, according the news report, it was only a matter of days before he'd wake from his coma, put two and two together, and my name and a police sketch of my face would be plastered all over the media. With the speed information is spread, I needed to move faster.

I had used up nearly an entire roll of duct tape attaching her to the chair, immobilizing her for this moment. This glorious moment of homecoming. Perhaps realization was dawning on her now. Perhaps she understood why I had brought her here. Not as a long overdue reunion, but as a final good-bye.

The past few hours had grown heavy as I found myself unable to work, paralyzed by a sense of duty to protect her. And yet I was protecting her, wasn't I? I was rescuing her from this life. I was delivering her into heaven where everything would be better.

And yet here I stood, frozen, entombed in my own mind.

My voice stuck in my throat, and then wriggled free.

"Sophia. You're awake."

I must have startled her, or it was a delayed reaction, but she shrieked like a banshee wailing about an impending doom. "Help!"

It hurt to hear her cry. I would tend to her—didn't she know that? I wasn't too worried about the neighbors overhearing, but I grabbed a dusty rag and shoved it in her gaping mouth regardless.

"Shush, dear. No need to alarm the whole neighborhood."

She muttered against the fabric, attempting to spit it free.

"I'll take this out if you promise not to scream. Can you act calm?"

She nodded rapidly, her eyes wide and staring with horror. It hurt me to see such terror toward me, her savior. I needed to smooth things over.

I removed the rag, and she coughed and sputtered.

"Would you like some water?" A peace offering. I hoped to quell her nerves. There was no reason for there to be hostility between us. Not now, not at this most pivotal turning point in our relationship.

"Yes, thank you."

Glad that she accepted, I brought her a glass and tipped the edge up for her to sip.

When she finished, she looked at me, sad but hopeful. "Why are you doing this to me?"

Her voice was like a worm wiggling and burrowing into my heart. Didn't she understand this was a mercy I was gifting her?

"My beautiful girl, I'm rescuing you. I've watched you suffer for too long. It's time to be free, and I'm going to free you."

"Free me? Killing me isn't freeing me."

"Then why did you attempt to take your own life not more than a few days ago? You apparently thought death was freedom back then."

"I was wrong. I don't want to die. If you love me at all, please let me go."

Didn't she realize what was happening? Her birth was an exclamation point—a beautiful, wondrous event. But after her father exchanged her for a handful of coins, her life dwindled down into nothing more than an asterisk in someone else's perverted story. She could depart with dignity. I was giving her that. I was handing her a chance at immortality. Couldn't she see?

"I can't do that. It's too late. I'll not have you live the rest of your life in mediocrity. You were meant to be great. I'm here to ensure that with your last breath."

Chapter 41

Ari

D-Day

According to Tristan, George Battan wasn't talking. The clues weren't talking. Nothing was talking about where Tina could possibly be.

The hours had crawled by. It was now the following afternoon and no sign of her. Tristan had agreed to put pressure on the Durham Police Department to put out an APB on her, but he couldn't guarantee any recourse until evening. By tomorrow they'd take me seriously.

Only, I had a feeling that tomorrow would be too late.

I paced my apartment, feeling enclosed and trapped within my brain. The past two weeks had felt endlessly long, convoluted, chaotic. I traced the jagged edges of what I'd unearthed, painting in rough strokes the bigger picture of what happened with Carli.

Benny's witnessing my dad getting beat up by Jay. Richie getting hired to emphasize a message. Yet the finer details of my father's involvement remained shrouded in mystery. They had as good as pointed a finger at my dad being the root of it all, but the dots weren't fully connected yet. What the hell did my father do to piss someone off enough to kill my sister?

And then there was George Battan—Tina's abductor and possibly the man who killed Josef.

George, George, George.

All the evidence kept pointing back to that name. But he was in police custody—untouchable to me—and yet Tina was now missing. If I removed George from the equation, who was left? Not comatose Killian. Not mourning Rosalita. Possibly my father, but it wasn't likely. There was an x variable I hadn't accounted for. But who?

Why couldn't I figure out where she had gone? Like grains of sand, the answer slipped through my fingertips. It was right there in my grasp, but too slippery to hold on to.

I needed to move. Do something.

I stood at the sink, sudsing the two glasses and plate left there earlier. As I wiped and washed, I noticed the glasses for the first time—really noticed them.

Tina's familiar scarlet lipstick stained one edge—a vibrant color she once forced upon me and I had just as quickly wiped off—and the other glass had a vague spidery imprint of a pale shade of pink. Two colors, two different lip prints.

Had I just scrubbed away the only DNA evidence that might have linked to who was here earlier?

Shit shit shit.

Other than me and Rosalita, what other female friends did Tina have? Who else was in her life that she had mentioned ... or hadn't mentioned? Was it one of her fellow sex-trafficking victims playing the Grim Reaper?

The glasses—and the tequila—were my only clue. There had to be more to it. Initially they led me to Rosalita, because I remembered the tequila at Josef's crime scene. The whole murder had felt familial, intimate. Sitting down to a shot or two together before the kill. Then framed as a suicide. It only made sense that it was someone with a personal vendetta. Rosalita had been my prime suspect, but she had proven her innocence. If not her, then who?

It had to be a woman, someone from Tina's past. Someone who would want Josef and Killian and Tina dead.

Someone with ties to all three.

And suddenly the answer congealed—I knew who she was with and where to find her.

Grabbing my keys and cell phone, I ran out the door hoping I wasn't too late.

Chapter 42

Ari

D-Day

The deed had been the answer all along. Such a minor detail, and yet so significant. I should have known that only a woman would have cleaned up so meticulously, vacuuming and sprucing up behind her killing spree.

Only a woman would toast for nostalgia's sake before her kill.

I arrived at 813 Gregson Road and the first thing I noticed was the living room light dimly peeking through the closed curtains. The gray of early evening shrouded the surrounding woods, creeping eerily toward the house as night settled in, enhancing the glow from the window.

Someone was home. Maybe sitting on the bloodstained sofa. Maybe creating another crime scene.

Pulling my cell phone from my back pocket, I pressed the button to dial Tristan but it was dead. Damn. I had forgotten to charge it last night. Just my luck. I was an hour and a half away from the only person I trusted with no cell phone to call for help. I considered my options. Go straight to the Dunn police station, or check things out first on my own. I really didn't know what was going on inside. It could be perfectly harmless. Tina could simply be cleaning up the mess, finally going through her father's belongings in a wistful moment.

I peered into the dusty garage door window and saw a beat-up SUV inside. I hadn't checked the garage the last time I was here, so I had no clue if the vehicle was a permanent resident here or not. As I stepped out of the shadow hanging over the home, a splintering crack slammed across the back of my skull. A flash of white blinded me.

Then nothing.

My pulsing head jerked me awake. The rhythm of my blood pooling and swirling and vibrating behind my eyes created a wave of nausea that I struggled to choke back. *Don't throw up. Don't throw up.*

A migraine was brewing.

The sting of tears in my eyes turned my surroundings into a watery mirage I couldn't quite make out. A bright orb blinded me from one corner of the room. I stretched my fingers out along the carpet beneath me, its texture coarse. I slowly, steadily lifted myself upright, groaning and pushing through the razors ramming into my eye sockets until I was propped up against a wall behind me. I couldn't remember where I was or how I got here. A burrowing, throbbing torture—the only sensation that felt familiar.

I allowed myself a momentary reprieve to let the agony abate, like a gently lapping wave slinking back into Mother Ocean. Opening my eyes again, the scene was crisp. I hunched against Josef's living room wall, mere feet from where his dead body had pooled his lifeblood into the sofa a handful of days ago. The stench of stale death and copper hung in the air, magnifying my queasiness.

Muffled voices reached me from down the hallway where I remembered Josef's bedroom had been. With wobbly steps, I stood up and inched along the wall, resting one hand along the cracked drywall for support. When I got to the open bedroom door, a frail Hispanic woman spun to look at me. I saw Tina sitting strapped to a chair behind her, wet mascara streaking down her cheeks, ruby lipstick smeared across her chin, eyes rimmed in seeping black eyeliner.

In one hand the captor clutched a knife and reflexively jerked the jagged blade toward Tina's neck as I startled her with a step forward.

"Back up!" she yelled.

I retreated half a step.

"Ari!" Tina cried.

"You must be Mercedes." I fixed my stare on hers. "Nice to meet you," I said in a monotone.

Eyes still on me, Mercedes steadied the quivering blade firmly against Tina's flesh, indenting the splotchy pink skin of her neck. With how jumpy Mercedes was, one wrong move could slice right through Tina. I needed to get her to drop her defenses and lower her arm before her impulses took over.

"And you must be Ari, the *savior*." She sputtered the word like it tasted of venom.

"Just a friend checking in on her." I shifted a foot forward.

"Glad to see you've woken up. I hope I didn't cause any brain damage." Her voice was calm and even—too much so for the circumstances.

"So you're the one behind Josef's death, Killian's attack, Tina's abduction, huh? Can I ask why?" I stepped forward as I talked, closing the distance between us.

"I'm saving my family. Simple as that."

"Saving them? How do you figure?" Another step, the gap closing.

"You wouldn't understand," she said, turning away

from me to stroke Tina's hair.

"Try me."

"You want to know so badly? Fine. My family is cursed. Josef sold our daughter into sex slavery. My only son was turning into his father, which I couldn't let happen. And Sophia, well, Sophia will forever be tarnished by what she went through. Heaven is the only home for her now—where she can be blameless and pure again. Where we can all be together, but happy this time."

"You know I can't let you kill her, don't you? It's not up to you to fix her. It should be up to her what happens." The serenity of my tone belied the panic bubbling beneath. Now an arm's reach away, my brain was spinning, my thoughts frantic and hasty. Lowering my hand cautiously to my hip, my fingertips grazed what they were searching for. A bulge Mercedes hadn't noticed when she knocked me out and dragged me in here.

There was only one way out of this situation—the messy way.

"I'm her mother! And who are you to her? Don't you dare tell me what Sophia needs or doesn't need."

Tina yelped as the knife nicked her, leaving an inch-long sliver of blood. The trail dribbled down, absorbing into the bra that peeked out from her tank top.

Bile rose in my mouth and I gagged back the acidic taste.

Mercedes was losing control, and in a moment I was about to lose my lunch. The headache was too much. Grisly scenarios played out on a mental screen. Tina's throat spurting blood. A knife plunging into my gut. The pair of us dying together. But that was all the dying I had time for. I needed to get myself together and stop this psycho.

With a staggering lunge, I leapt forward, pulling the mace out from my pocket and spraying Mercedes directly in the eyes. She screamed and covered her face with her free hand, frantically rubbing at the mace with her fists. But what I hadn't expected her to do was fight back. The thrust of metal into my abdomen caught me off guard as I wrestled with her over the knife—her still covering her eyes while swinging blindly at me, me doggedly dodging her while cupping the hole in my stomach. I started to feel woozy from the blood loss—or the head trauma, God knows which—but a burst of enraged adrenalin kicked in, giving me the edge I needed to knock Mercedes off balance.

As we tumbled to the floor, I wrenched the knife from her grip as we landed, but the weapon disappeared in a heap of clothing and bodies. Hot wetness oozed over my hands, through my fingers, and as I glanced down, it bloomed over the front of my shirt. Too much blood. I was soaked. I knew in a few minutes I was as good as dead. I hadn't even gotten a chance to tell Tristan goodbye ... or how much I wanted to jump his bones.

And then I blacked out.

Chapter 43
Mercedes

2005

Mercedes Alavarez had endured much. As far as she was concerned, too much. Married too young. A no-good drunk for a husband. A nosy mother-in-law who lingered like a bad virus. And now children doomed to misery—the only child she had left, that is.

It was already ten o'clock and Josef still hadn't arrived home. Some nights he'd spend at the bar until dawn, leaving her restless as the hours passed, then furiously exhausted come morning when she had to deal with a temperamental son and hung-over husband ... and a drained bank account.

But not anymore.

Her bag was packed.

The secret stash of money she'd socked away month after month tucked in her purse.

The escape arranged.

The end of suffering finally near.

Sophia had been sold not even a year ago, and every day since was a hell she couldn't bear. Her firstborn. Her sweet little girl. And yet Josef went about as if nothing had changed. How nice for him to be so unaffected as he doted on Killian, bonding with his son over *futbol* in the yard. Only Mercedes, despite her flaws, felt her world crack a little deeper as the sun rose and set on her pain.

THE ART OF FEAR

Her only daughter, gone. And for what? Financial freedom? They still spent too much on booze and food. But food was only good for nourishing the body. What about the soul? What reprieve could she find to bandage a soul sold to the devil himself?

The agony of her own part in Sophia's fate haunted her fiercely this morning. If only she hadn't complained to Josef about the new heels Bernada wore that Mercedes couldn't afford. Or the stunning couture dress Isabel wore to the grocery store—yes, the grocery store! Who wore designer clothes to shop for produce? Her own green monster was the reason Josef first contacted George Battan. By her own hand she pushed Josef into action, not realizing the repercussions of greed.

Unlike his chatty sister, Killian had become a taciturn five-year-old ever since his sister's disappearance. His small voice could barely be heard over the arguments in Mercedes's head anyways. The endless loop of condemnation clung to her gray matter, breaking her psyche little by little. They had never explained to Killian where Sophia had gone each time he asked, only stating that his sister was taking a long trip and would be back soon. Yet his nightly weeping into his pillow told a different story about how much he understood.

She had traded her daughter in exchange for misery. It was not something she could overcome. No matter how much Killian attempted to wrest her from the sadness with hugs and cuddles and kisses. She simply turned him away, refusing to be comforted. She didn't deserve consolation. She didn't deserve Killian's unconditional adoration. She earned a death sentence.

Death—the freedom it promised grew more enticing by the day.

Death—life's ultimate journey, a final destination.

Death—what she wished she could offer Sophia to stop

her suffering.

In Catholic tradition, Mercedes believed in heaven, where death was only the beginning. She hoped that this selfless sojourn to rescue Sophia would be enough to please the saints into letting her through those pearly gates.

The minutes ticked by and the night grew dimmer, and Mercedes knew the time was ripe. She couldn't risk running into Josef, or the neighbors, who now held their children a little tighter to their chests when Mercedes walked by. All their whispered suspicions about what exactly happened to Sophia only intensified the sense of isolation she felt. No good mother would want their child near her, which of course ruined Killian's social life as well.

Killian's stifled whimper slithered down the hall as she hoisted her belongings onto her smooth, bony shoulders. With one last peek into her son's room, she blew him an unseen kiss and uttered her undying love for him. Maybe one day she would return to him, after she found Sophia and rescued her. But what if she couldn't find her daughter? She only knew that George was from the States, but nothing else. It could take a lifetime to find her. But she would. She swore to herself it was the only way to make amends. Either that, or killing herself.

The latter was a last resort.

As her footfalls removed her from the house she'd known for six years, the yard her children once played together in, and then the street that she walked daily, she wondered how her disappearance would impact Killian. Would he be okay with Josef? What would Josef even tell the boy, his young mind too innocent to truly understand the complexities of life?

Sophia was never coming back.

Mommy left us.

She heaved a sorrowful sigh, knowing Killian would never fully recover. But her mind wasn't right. It would never be right until she saved her daughter. She could fix everything else later, once Sophia was safe in her arms again. And if the damage was too much, if her daughter's life was stripped down to nothing but ash?

Well, there was always the fresh breath of death.

Chapter 44
Ari

D-Day, Hours After

S o this is what dead feels like.

It feels like nothing at all.

Pure oblivion.

I didn't walk toward any white light.

My life didn't flash before my eyes.

It was simple, black nothingness ... a deep, restful, dreamless slumber.

Damn, it felt good.

And then my senses awakened as warmth permeated my body, the smell of antiseptic cleaner invaded my nose, and the abrasive rub of rough fabric clung to my skin. Something beyond my eyelids brightened in a canopy of orange-red, and the Grim Reaper scuttled away just like that.

I had been dead for approximately two minutes, the nurse later told me. It was a miracle, really. I shouldn't be alive, but I was a tough little bitch.

When I came to, the first thing in view was Tristan gazing down at me, stark white heavenly lights illuminating a halo around him like an angel. When I realized it wasn't heaven but the hospital, and felt the sore row of stitches running along my side tingle like thousands of ants crawling across my skin, I almost wished I *had* died. But his smile welcomed me back to

Earth where I suddenly felt warm and safe ... and the ants suddenly didn't feel so bad.

The past few hours were a blur of events I couldn't quite piece together.

"What happened?" I asked, my tongue sticky and dry.

He handed me a ginger ale, which I greedily sipped from the straw poking out of the can.

A sense of dread engulfed me as he coughed lightly, clearing his throat. It was bad news. I remembered falling beneath Mercedes, and then nothing. Mercedes must have gotten to Tina after I passed out.

"You sure you're ready to talk about it?" His voice was irritatingly gentle.

"Please just tell me."

"You saved Tina, that's what."

"What? She's okay?" I couldn't believe it! How had she survived? How had *I* survived?

"Yep, when you tackled Mercedes, the knife ... she landed on it. Tina was able to get free and call for help once Mercedes passed out. I guess you lost consciousness before you knew you incapacitated Mercedes."

"Is she—?" I couldn't say it. I couldn't push the words out: *Is she dead?*

He nodded his head yes. Nothing else needed to be explained.

"Is Tina okay?" Discovering her mother had been behind the murders—I wondered how she was taking it.

"She's alright. Hanging in there. Thanks to you and your mad linebacker skills. You should try out for the Pittsburgh Steelers. I bet you'd make the team with tackling like that."

"I don't think they'd let me use mace on the field."

"Yeah, probably not."

I smiled appreciatively at his levity when I needed it most. Laughter truly was the best medicine—until the fact that the gash in my belly was laced up like a football reminded me that I needed to laugh a little easier.

"Don't make me laugh, dammit," I pleaded with a grimace. "Don't want to tear my stitches."

Cupping my hand where an IV stuck into my vein, Tristan lifted it tenderly to his lips and kissed my fingers. His eyes turned watery.

"Don't get sentimental on me," I joked, but something was wrong when he didn't crack a smile. Something he wasn't telling me. "Are you okay?"

"You almost died, Ari. Actually, you did die. Your heart stopped and they had to revive you. I almost lost you." By the quaver in his words, I could tell he was barely holding it together. "It's lucky Tina was able to get free and call an ambulance." By now he wasn't even trying to check his emotions. "I can't lose you. You've changed me, you know."

He wept against my shoulder, stifling the sobs in my hospital gown. "Doing what I do—catching criminals—made me lose a part of myself that values life, that values flawed people. But then you came along, with your magnetism for those broken souls, Ari. My broken soul. You made me believe in humanity again, my own humanity." He wiped at his runny nose. "Attractive, huh? I guess even tough guys like me have pansy moments."

I adored his pansy moment.

"Hey, it's okay. And I'm okay. I can't say the same for my gown, though."

He lifted his face to mine, his mouth a breath away. "I really like you, Ari. I don't think you realize how much."

"Oh, I have an idea," I whispered.

He leaned forward and kissed me, sweeping me into an eddy of desire and passion. I wouldn't have admitted it to him before this kiss, but I really liked him too.

Epilogue

The lake was placid, occasionally ruffled by a gusty breeze. Maidenhair fern lined one edge of the lake where the soil ended in a subtle cliff of exposed roots and rocks. I shifted my weight when one leg went numb, crunching the crushed shingle underfoot. The beach was empty, save for our humble group of friends. Tristan held my hand as I stood next to Tina, the sun sinking into the burnt orange and purpled horizon. It was the perfect setting for a funeral, a last goodbye.

Everyone from the suicide support group was kind enough to show, me in clean jeans and a button-down black blouse, everyone else wearing more appropriate attire. Blame my unrefined funeral etiquette on my lack of upbringing. Standing in a semi-circle in the balm of evening, we allowed Tina and Killian to meditate in silence, to remember what they wanted to remember and forget what they wanted to forget. Even Rosalita made an appearance, though her jaw remained clenched as she lingered in the background.

No one spoke. There were no priests or caskets or flowers or door-sized pictures of Josef or Mercedes smiling. Just two urns of his-and-her ashes, a husband and wife, a father and mother. That's how we would honor them.

Carli's was the only other funeral I had attended, so I wasn't sure what was appropriate to say or do or feel. So I did nothing. I simply held Tina's hand when she needed it,

279

and let it go when she stepped a pace toward the lake and gazed stoically. No tears for her.

I wasn't sure if that was good or bad.

First Tina emptied the ashes of their mother over the beach, then Killian emptied their father's, allowing the wind to whisk them away into the water where the dust settled on the glass until clusters of fish picked at them. I lost sight of where the ripples eventually carried them.

It was a pristine moment, one I was glad Tina suggested after her adamancy against a funeral that first day I met her eons ago. Well, at least it felt like eons.

"I'm thinking of having a memorial for my parents after all," she had suggested a week ago. "Just to say goodbye. Whatd'ya think?"

"I think it's perfect," I had agreed.

And it was.

No grand finale. Just two siblings bidding adieu to their lousy parents. We'd decided against a formal wake but instead offered up a potluck dinner back at my place. It was about time I started opening my front door—and life—to people.

"So that went well," I commented to Tristan and Tina as we scattered back to our cars. We piled into his sedan, shutting out the warm breeze edging in on the deepening evening.

"Yeah, I feel like I at least got some closure." Tina's voice was softer than usual, as if her loss had chipped away her rough edges. "You know, losing my parents has got me thinking. I want to find Giana, my baby. Do you think you could help me, Ari?"

"Me?" It was flattering, yes, but what did I know? I stumbled upon a murder or two and suddenly I was an expert in solving cases? But what the hell. It was something to do. "I don't know anything about investigative stuff, but sure, I'll try my best. Thankfully, I think I have an in with the police department. What was Undertaker's name again? Buchanan? Do you think he's single?"

"Oh shut up!" Tristan laughed. "And what the hell kind of name is *Undertaker?*"

"You've never watched wrestling?" I huffed. "Well, I guess that explains the bracelets."

"I'm never gonna live that down, am I?"

"Nope." But I sweetened it with a quick smirk.

"Private Investigator Ari Wilburn," Tristan said. "It's got a nice ring to it, doesn't it?"

It actually did. In fact, I really liked the sound of it.

"You think so?" I asked. Tristan joked so much it was hard to tell when he was serious or sarcastic.

"Absolutely. Bitch by day, PI by night. Fits you perfectly."

But I didn't want the jokes. I needed it straight. Did I have a chance at doing something I loved ... and succeeding? I didn't succeed at anything in life up to this point. So why now? When would this house of cards topple into a pile of discarded dreams? I couldn't bear to taste something sweet, only to find out it was poison. I'd lost too much already. Hope was all I had left.

"No, seriously, Tristan, do you think I can do it?"

"Why not? You got your sister's killer to confess after over a decade, you put a major child trafficker behind bars, and you solved a murder. I think you earned the credentials. Just take some criminal justice classes to learn the ropes, buy some useful Internet and database software, and I'll even get you one of those detective badges from the Dollar Tree."

"You just had to end that with being an ass, huh?"

"Always, babe. You can always count on me for ass."

I rolled my eyes and turned to face Tina in the backseat. "Excuse the little boy up here. Some kids never grow up."

Tina chuckled, then said, "You know, I believe in you too, Ari. So what's your first job as a PI gonna be?"

Find out what nefarious business my dad was involved in that cost my sister's life? Find Tina's baby? Save the whales? Achieve world peace? Take your pick.

"Reuniting you with your baby, of course. Duh. And finding out whose dog keeps shitting right outside my back porch, then kicking the owner's ass for not cleaning it up."

Tristan started the car and pulled out of the parking lot.

"You're so professional," Tina adulated.

"I know." I winked back at her. "So, anything you can think of that I can start with—like do you remember the day Giana was taken from you? Details like who was there, when it happened?"

Even though I had turned my attention to the road to avoid getting carsick, I could picture the tears stinging her eyes as her voice cracked with each word, teetering on the brink of sobs. "I'll never forget it. George of course was there, and Giana was a month old. I guess he was biding his time for the highest bidder. But a guy shows up at the house with a black duffel bag of money—cash, but I don't know how much—and I'm sitting on the sofa watching TV when he walks in the baby's room.

Tina's voice quickened, intensified, heated as the words tumbled out.

"I immediately jump up and start clawing at him, pleading with him to leave her alone, but George comes up behind me, restrains me, and the guy takes her out of her crib and walks out, just like that. Not a glance back at me. Nothing. Wouldn't even let me say goodbye to her. It was awful. Losing Giana was worse than everything those men had ever done to me."

She was quiet for a moment, except for the random gasp of a stifled sob, then her words rolled out forcefully. "But it wasn't just me. There were others that he tortured."

I heard the zipper of Tina's purse *whoosh* open, then a crackle of paper.

"Here, read this." She handed me a folded piece of paper yellowed with age—a carefully clipped news article.

MISSING GIRL FOUND DEAD IN ENO RIVER PARK

June 12, 2015
Durham, NC
The body of Marla Rivers, a 10-year-old Durham County girl who has been missing since December of 2013, was found in Eno River Park on Monday when a pair of hikers wandered off their trail. The hikers noticed a large area of disturbed dirt where an animal had unearthed part of Rivers' skeletal remains, buried in a shallow pit and covered with organic debris.

After accessing recent missing persons reports and using dental records, investigators concluded that it was Marla Rivers. At this time the cause of death has not been determined.

Rivers first went missing after school on Friday, December 6, after taking the bus home from school. The bus driver, Anna Burke, remembered dropping her off at her usual stop at the corner of Heckley Road and Bridgestone Drive. But an hour later, when Marla never arrived home, her parents Bill and Justine called Durham Police, requesting a search be conducted for their daughter.

With no substantial leads, Marla's disappearance eventually became a cold case.

Police are currently searching for forensics evidence that will identify the killer. No suspects have been named for

Rivers' murder.

Marla is survived by her parents and younger brother, Tyler. The details of her funeral will be made public once they're available.

Police are asking that if anyone has any information that might lead to Marla's killer, please come forward and contact the Durham Police Department.

I saw the writing on the wall. The scrawl of a killer. "Did George do this?"

"I can't say for sure, but Marla was with me right before I left. I wanted to go back and help her, but I was scared for Giana. I didn't know what to do. So I did nothing—and she ended up dead."

"It's not your fault, Tina, that he did what he did. He was holding your daughter's life over you to coerce you to obey. You didn't have a choice. He killed her, not you. But you can testify against him, you can make sure he never gets out of jail. You can give Marla's family peace and closure now about what happened to their little girl."

I knew from life experience that closure was for doors, not for the murder of a loved one. But knowing justice was carried out made healing a little easier.

"But he's the only one who knows where Giana is. If I testify against him, he'll never tell me how to find her. Plus what if he can still get to her—you know, through his contacts? What if he hurts her to get back at me?"

I saw Tristan's eyes dart to the rearview mirror, pass over Tina's face, then return back to the road. Unreadable. But he was silently absorbing every detail.

"Tristan, you can't say anything ... not yet. We need to figure out how to protect Giana first."

"Maybe we can work out some kind of plea bargain to get Giana back in exchange for reduced charges. We'll figure it out, I promise."

I trusted Tristan. For the first time in years I actually trusted someone.

"Please don't make me regret telling you," Tina pleaded.

"We'll find her." My oath felt awfully empty. I didn't know the first thing about tracking down a stolen child. But there had to be enough clues to work with. Certainly George couldn't be the only person who knew of Giana's whereabouts. He wasn't singlehandedly selling babies. There had to be other hands in the pot. I just needed to follow the trail to sniff them out.

Tina witnessed every bleeding moment. Someone else was there. Someone else took Giana.

"What about the man who actually took her? Did you get a good look at him?"

"If you can describe him to our sketch artist," Tristan added, "we could look him up in our criminal database and see if we get some hits. Guys like that usually have some kind of criminal history, even if it's minor."

"Do you remember his features, Tina?" I probed. It was a long shot, having been about three years ago, but some faces you never forget. Especially the face of the man who stole your baby.

"I'll never forget," she whispered. A trancelike silence fell upon the three of us while I let her stew in her memories. She sat for a long moment, then gasped.

"What?" I asked.

"Oh my God, Ari. I know who took her."

"You know a name?" How could this only *now* be coming up?

"Well, I didn't before, but now I do. He changed a little since then—he lost the mustache. But remember how I thought your dad looked familiar?"

Mother. Effing. No. Way.

Was that the dark secret my father had been

harboring? He was selling babies on the side?

"It was him—Burt, your dad. I can still see his face, it was definitely him. I remember him looking so dejected, like he was truly sorry, until he walked away with my baby and never came back ..."

We were lucky I wasn't driving, because I would have definitely run off the road and headed straight into a tree, oncoming traffic, a house. This wasn't what I had expected to learn about my own father. It couldn't be true. My father was a bank manager. A typical everyday workingman who came home every night for dinner, pushed his daughters on the swings, laughed along to episodes of *Home Improvement,* and barbequed on weekends. He couldn't possibly be involved in a major criminal network ... could he?

Then I thought of Carli. Richie's hired hit-and-run. Jay's attack on Dad the night before. The business associate named *George.* All the lies. All the cloak-and-dagger shit. The many countless secrets. What did I really know about him, other than that my family pushed me away, holding their lies closer than their own daughter?

I realized that this was my moment. Everyone gets one, but most people spoil them. That moment when they can change the course of their lives with a single decision. This was that decision—to uproot myself from my tiny, comfortable, ill-fitting life and do something big with myself. I vowed to uncover my family's skeletons, I would find Giana and bring her home, and I would be the best damn PI this side of the Mississippi.

Private Investigator Ari Wilburn—I had died and been reborn with purpose. And it felt damn good.

Continue The Little Things That Kill Series with *The Death of Life,* and discover if Ari's able to find Tina's long-lost baby and uncover her parents' dark secrets.

Author's Note

As a mother of four young children, ever since that first moment I held my oldest in my arms I've dedicated my life to them. Everything I do is for them. Even my darkest fears revolve around their safety. Once upon a time I put myself first; those days are long gone.

With parenthood comes a lingering fear of something horrible happening to one of my kids. As news stories pop up more and more often of children being abducted from grocery stores, I began to research child trafficking. As destiny would have it, I ended up meeting a woman who was a victim of child trafficking, and thus this story was born.

Child trafficking is a real horror that exists in our world. It's a perverted underground lifestyle that many children are subjected to, and it's growing at an alarming rate. But it's not a hopeless situation. Being a friend to your neighbors and getting to know the kids you meet can go a long way in detecting child abuse and sex trafficking, because unfortunately, it *is* that close to home.

The Art of Fear, inspired by my friend's personal experiences in the sex-trafficking industry, shares a small glimpse of what it was like for her. Her own neighbors had no idea they were living next to a child predator. But she was a lucky one. She broke free. And there are many more happy endings out there when we open our eyes to the needs and struggles of those around us.

THE ART OF FEAR

I hope you enjoyed the tale and will stick around for the next book as Ari, Tina, and Tristan set out to find Tina's missing baby ... and find themselves in the midst of a murder spree.

Acknowledgements

The people who have supported me along the way are too numerous to name. But I'll try, regardless.

Not a single word is typed without the support of my husband, Craig. It's the kid-free time he provides that allows me to escape to my writing world, and without him I wouldn't be living the dream. So to him I owe it all.

Then there's you, my dear readers. When you buy a book, you are supporting a family of six, allowing me to give my special needs son the focus he needs at home, donating to a horse rescue farm (and a rescue of countless other animals that cross our path), supporting autism awareness, and hopefully enjoying the book along the way. I write for you—to tell the tales of people I've met in my life who have inspired me or intrigued me.

Of course there's my family and friends—my beta readers, my editors, my support group, and my thin grip on sanity. They keep me from going bald from the stress of late-night work hours, they talk me off the ledge after a dozen diaper changes in a day, and they remind me of the many reasons life is worth living to the fullest.

To my editor Kevin Cook and the team at Proofed to Perfection who strive to bring out the beauty and power of my words—you guys are the best.

Lastly, to my children: Talia, Kainen, Kiara, and Ariana. You drive me nuts, but I wouldn't want it any other way. I live for you, I love for you, and I write for you, my darlings.

A Final Word...

If you enjoyed *The Art of Fear,* follow the next book in The Little Things That Kill Series called *The Death of Life,* as Private Investigator Ari Wilburn uncovers the truth about her family's scandal and searches for Tina's long-lost baby. And you might meet a serial killer targeting the suicide group ... but can Ari and Tristan catch the killer before one of them becomes the next victim?

Find an error in one of my books? I'd love to fix it, since even the best editors miss things (they're only human). Please email me at pamela@pamelacrane.com.

Want to support me as an author? I'd be honored if you'd review the book. If you're kind enough to write a review, email me at pamela@pamelacrane.com and I'll thank you personally with a free gift!

If you'd like to be notified of my upcoming releases or enter my giveaways, join my mailing list at www.pamelacrane.com for chances to win free prizes and pre-release offers.

PAMELA CRANE is a USA TODAY best-selling author and professional juggler. Not the type of juggler who can toss flaming torches in the air, but a juggler of four kids, a writing addiction, and a horse rescuer. She lives on the edge (her Arabian horse can tell you all about their wild adventures while trying to train him!) and she writes on the edge...where her sanity resides. Her thrillers unravel flawed women who aren't always pretty. In fact, her characters are rarely pretty, which makes them interesting...and perfect for doing crazy things worth writing about. When she's not cleaning horse stalls or changing diapers, she's psychoanalyzing others.

Discover more of Pamela Crane's

books at

www.pamelacrane.com

Made in the USA
Middletown, DE
03 December 2022

16850025R00182